Ted Lew... ... 1940. After ... ... Art School, he worked in London, first in advertising, then as an animation specialist in television and films (among them the Beatles' *Yellow Submarine*). The author of nine books, the first of which was published in 1965, he died in 1982.

By the same author

ALL THE WAY HOME AND ALL THE NIGHT THROUGH (1965)

PLENDER (1971)

BILLY RAGS (1973)

JACK CARTER'S LAW (1974)

THE RABBIT (1975)

BOLDT (1976)

JACK CARTER AND THE MAFIA PIGEON (1977)

G.B.H. (1980)

TED LEWIS

Jack Carter and the Mafia Pigeon

a&b

This edition
first published in Great Britain in 1994 by
Allison & Busby
an imprint of Wilson & Day Ltd
5 The Lodge
Richmond Way
London W12 8LW

First published in Great Britain by
Michael Joseph Ltd, in 1977

Copyright © 1977 by the Estate of Ted Lewis

The moral right of the author is asserted

This book is sold subject to the condition that it shall not,
by way of trade or otherwise, be lent, resold, hired out or
otherwise circulated without the publisher's prior written consent
in any form of binding or cover other than that in which it is
published and without a similar condition including this condition
being imposed upon the subsequent purchaser.

A catalogue record for this book is available from the British Library

ISBN 0 74900 177 1

Printed and bound in Great Britain by
Cox & Wyman Ltd, Reading, Berkshire

Chapter One

The rain slides down my bedroom window.

"You've got to be joking," I say to Audrey. "You and me! I mean, do me a favour."

She rolls over on top of me and puts her mouth next to mine and our lips brush together briefly and she says: "I'm just about to."

"No," I tell her. "Be serious. Just for a bleeding minute."

"For a lot longer than that," she says. "For quite some time, in fact. Unless something's happened to you since last week, that is."

She tries to find my mouth again but I twist my head to one side and grab hold of her wrists and heave her off and over, reversing our positions. .

"You know," she says, "considering you feel about that suit the way some people feel about their racing pigeons, you're not exactly looking after it proper at the moment. Let me put it on a hanger for you."

"When you stop being so fucking stupid, yes," I tell her. "And just as a matter of interest, what time was it when you had your first livener this morning?"

"I'll tell you," she says, smiling a particular kind of smile. "If you really want me to."

I look at her without any expression at all.

"Then I'll begin," she says. "Now what time was it? Oh yes. About quarter to six – "

"Quarter to six?"

"Could have been ten to. The curtains were drawn and you know how small the luminous figures are on my watch and how I always forget to wind it up."

"You wind me up something chronic," I tell her.

"Do I really?" she says, all mildness and moderate surprise, so I shake my head and let her get on with it.

"Anyhow, it was about that time or thereabouts, when what should happen then but a strange man opens the door and walks into my bedroom, and as you know there's no one stranger than my old man, and stranger still for him to be coming home at that time of the morning. Normally he never comes home at all, excepting weekends we're at the house in Surrey."

I open my mouth in order to tell her to leave out the domestic arrangements when she raises her head and sticks her tongue into my open mouth and draws back quick and goes on:

"So I'm asleep, aren't I? I mean, I know something's up by the way he slings his jacket across the room at the chaise longue and it doesn't hit right but this morning he doesn't go over and pick it up, and he's a bit like you about his gear so there's got to be something hasn't there?"

"All right, all right," I tell her. "When do we get to the bit about the three bears?"

"Just one bear in this story, sweetheart," she says. "So anyway, he starts taking off the rest of his clothes like he's trying to make the Guinness Book of Records and while he's doing that he says to me, 'You awake, Aud?' And I lie there as though they're about to sink the screws in me lid and Gerald says: 'Don't fucking con me, you slag, I know when you're awake and when you're not, so let's be having you.' Which of course is precisely what he wants, to be having me. Although I don't know that yet. So I prop myself up on my elbow and switch on the lamp and ask him what the bleeding idea is waking me up at this time of the night, what's the matter, has Terri's burned down. While I'm asking him this he's standing at the bed end, slipping out of his Austin Reed knickers and I can see he's stoking himself up a hard-on and then of course I get the idea and I say to him: oh no, no chance, you don't think you're coming back here after getting fuck-all elsewhere and waking up the old lady to get rid of your inhibitions. No fucking chance at all. Go and run some blues and have one off the wrist. Then he hardens up in more ways than one and drags all the sheets off the bed and gets on and starts crawling up the bed and I try to roll off it but he grabs hold of my ankle so I'm hanging half off the bed and he crawls up a little bit more and hauls me back on the bed, but I'm still struggling, see, which I shouldn't be doing because I should know better, I'm likely to get one in the mouth any minute, and I do mean a punch. But I'm so pissed off with it, common sense doesn't enter in to it, so in the end Gerald gets astride me and pushes my nightie above my head so that my arms aren't free any more and he takes hold of the hem and knots it round one of the brass rails at the bed-head. You remember those brass rails, Jack, don't you, that one time you were there?"

"I remember," I tell her. "I remember thinking at the time, how appropriate, brass."

She tries to bring her knee up into my crutch but I'm ready for that one and I've already slid a little to one side but I'm still keeping a tight hold on the wrists above her head. She lies silent for a minute before carrying on and then she says:

"Bit like this it was, really. In fact a lot like this. Me with me arms above me head, immobile, arms and head all bundled up in the nightie, like I've got a sack over me head. In fact I remember saying words to that effect to Gerald at the time, about he needs to sack me before he can poke me, but I don't think he really heard, the words being a bit muffled, like, and in any case, he's already started going to work, and saying a few things himself. I mean, you can imagine the kind of thing Gerald chants while he's pumping, being the kind of bloke he is, you know, you cunt, you bitch, you whore, you cock sucker, etcetera etcetera. I expect you can imagine."

"What I can't imagine, you're going to tell me anyway."

"Go on," she says. "I bet you're imagining already. Let go of my wrists and let me see if I'm right."

"No way," I tell her.

She smiles.

"I am right, aren't I?" she says. "Anyway, like I say, Gerald goes to work, and do you know, it's funny, I begin to start liking it, all trussed up like that, unable to do anything about anything. I mean it's quite a new experience, being raped by your old man. Sort of adds a new dimension, know what I mean?"

She rolls her eyes a little bit, indicating the grip I have on her wrists. I know what she's getting at, but there's no way she's getting it, not yet.

"I think Gerald quite enjoyed it, too," she says, "because afterwards, he didn't leave me there like a drawn turkey and he didn't roll off and start snoring right away. He lay on his back and lit a fag and got quite expansive. Started talking about you, how you'd been taking a lot of weight on your shoulders on the firm's behalf recently. How it was about time you had a bit of a holiday."

I look at her.

"It just doesn't occur to you, does it?" I say to her. "You're so fucking sure of yourself, it just doesn't occur to you. You ever hear of free association, and I don't mean what they do in Sweden. It never fucking occurred to you that Gerald has you, straight after that he starts thinking about me, straight after that he starts talking about me going away and that. Bleeding stroll on. You barmy or something?"

Audrey's expression changes to one I've seen often enough but not very often when we're just on our own.

"If I was barmy those two chancers wouldn't care because we'd be in bits and pieces in Epping Forest."

"Maybe they're just barmier than we are."

"You know what they are and I know what they are. We're the firm, not them."

I shake my head.

"And it'll just be down to them if we do what you're suggesting."

She shrugs again. There is a silence. Then I say to her: "What else did he say?"

"He didn't say anything else. That's all he said." She pauses. "Except a minute or two later he bursts out laughing."

I look at her. Then she bursts out laughing.

"You bitch," I tell her. "You bleeding cow."

"Well you should never have asked me when I had my first livener, should you? I mean there's liveners and liveners, isn't there?"

"Right," I tell her, and start giving her the treatment she's been asking for all along, and outside the rain keeps coming down as though it's never going to stop.

Chapter Two

And an hour or so later it's still beating against the glass of the Penthouse as I find out Audrey hadn't been joking at all. Gerald and Les are sitting on the low white leather settees with the backs placed where the split level breaks down into the sunken square in the room's centre. They're sitting opposite each other in poses that perfectly describe their different personalities. Though they're both relaxed, leaning back in the plump leather, holding their glasses, Les is not relaxed enough for his pose to create any more wrinkles in his mohair than are absolutely necessary. He's resting his glass on a neatly crossed knee, one hand on the glass, the other holding his cigarette close to his shoulder, delicately, almost effeminately, and not a speck of ash on his mohair, whereas Gerald, of course, looks as though he's been letting Les use his suit as an ashtray and there are so many wrinkles in the material that you'd never guess the suit was one of a half dozen he'd had sent round from Sammy three weeks ago. He's sunk down in the leather with his legs wide open and his shirt half out and the drink in his glass about to slop out onto his left shoulder.

"Jack," he says, twisting round, giving the final impetus to his drink. "Jack, my old darlin', we just been talking about you, haven't we, Les; ain't that so?"

Gerald looks at Les as if he's asking to be backed up in a barefaced lie and Les answers as if he couldn't give a fuck about anything at all.

"Yeah," he says. "We were just talking about you."

Gerald gets up, beaming, expansive, vindicated.

"You see?" he says.

"Yeah, I see," I tell him. "All depends what the fuck you've been saying, doesn't it."

Now it's time for the hurt look.

"As if we'd ever say anything nasty about our number one son," Gerald says. "As if we would, Les, eh?"

I walk over to the drinks cabinet.

"That's right," says Les. "Make yourself at home."

One of these days, the years of cool I've maintained with Les is going to unfreeze and he's going to go sailing out through the plate glass into the darkness of W.I.

But not today. Today, I'd rather just pour myself a drink.

"I thought as number one son I'd be entitled," I say to Les, dropping a slice of lemon in my glass.

"Les," says Gerald, "you know what your trouble is? You're petty. You've always been petty. Even as a kid, when mother broke her leg that time and couldn't get out the buildings for a month. Any errand she wanted doing you always tried to get a tip out of it. *Before* you went."

"I never bleeding got one, though, did I?" Les says.

"Listen," Gerald says to him. "One of these days you'll learn the value of public relations. You'll learn how to show people how much you value what they do for you instead of crapping all over them."

"It's all right," I say to Gerald. "Don't macaroni. I don't give a fuck the way he is. I'm satisfied with what I get in this firm. I don't need bonuses from that wanker."

I take my drink and sit down on an armless easy chair in the floor level part of the room.

"Now see what you've fucking well done," Gerald says to Les.

"Piss off."

"And this was going to be a nice friendly chat when we showed Jack some appreciation for all he's done for us this year."

"It's all right, Gerald," I tell him. "Take it that I appreciate your appreciation."

Gerald looks at Les. There is a long silence. Then Gerald says:

"Look, let's forget it. Jack, have another drink." He walks up the few steps from the centre of the room and takes my glass from me and back to where the drinks are. "No," he says making the fresh drink. "What we were talking about, what we've been thinking of — we'd been saying, what a good year we'd had, mainly due to the way you'd looked after your side of the business." Not to mention every other fucking side of the business, I think to myself.

Gerald comes back with my drink.

"So, how can we show our appreciation." He stands there, palms appellant. "Money? Jack don't need no money. Birds? Jack takes care of that himself. A gift? What can we give him his money can't buy? And that's what made us think of it, What can't money buy?"

Gerald waits for me to ask him what money can't buy and when I've done that he says:

"Time."

I look at him.

"What, you going to shop me, are you?" I say to him.

Gerald blinks then bursts out laughing. "Great," he says. "Fucking great. Isn't that great, Les."

"Favourite," Les says.

Gerald laughs so hard he nearly bursts a gut. That goes on for another two or three minutes and then when he's finished Gerald says:

"No, but seriously. When did you last have a holiday?"

"Skegness, fifty-three." Les says.

I look at Les.

"Something like that," I say.

"Shut up," Gerald tells Les, without looking at him.

Then he goes on. "Jack, you should take a holiday."

"Fine," I tell him. "I'd like that. Can I start now?"

"No, I mean a real holiday," Gerald says. "A proper one. Not lying on your back in your flat all day, not in this country, in this weather. No, you should go abroad. The sun. Get some sunshine down you. A fortnight's worth."

I look at him but I don't say anything.

"So what we thought was," Gerald says, "why don't Jack use the villa for a fortnight?"

I still don't say anything.

"The villa," Gerald says. "In Majorca." He looks at me with the expression of a conjuror who's just done a trick. When the applause doesn't materialize he goes on:

"It's great, you know it is. You've seen the slides. Way up in the hills. Miles from anywhere. The pool. The sunshine. What more could you want?"

I look at him. Gerald closes his eyes then smacks the side of his head with the palm of his hand.

"The birds," he says. "Of course, the cunt." He opens his eyes again. "Listen Wally Lomas'll fix all that up for you. He knows the form out there. No need to take nothing with you. Like taking coals to Newcastle with old Wally fixing for you."

"Wally Lomas? That old slag?"

"Yeah, well, I know he's past it, but we gave him the job on account of what his old lady asked us on her deathbed that time Wally was given a compassionate and was on his way to see her. Only he got there too late, didn't he? She asked us to see if we could do something about keeping Wally out of nick on account of their baby daughter, Tina, because she didn't want Wally's mother getting her hands on the offspring. So we promised her we'd see what we could do and with that she expired. Five minutes later Wally arrived. What a scene.

Anyhow, next time that Wally gets out, we put it to him like this: There's this villa we've just had converted and we need somebody to look after it and see to us and our guests whenever we're out there which, as you know, is often. Course, Wally needs some persuading because he sees himself as an embryo Charlie Richardson but we tell him he's already done more time than Charlie'll ever do, including Charlie's present stretch, and in any case, Wally should have stuck to the restaurant business like his old dad, because Wally's almost as good as his old dad was. You should taste his meat balls in sauce. Anyway, in the end, we finally get through to him, and he's been out there ever since. Never regretted a minute of it, he hasn't."

"Have you?" I ask Gerald.

Gerald smiles.

"Listen, don't be stupid. Whose name's on the contract? Who do you think it says owns the villa?"

I don't say anything.

"Right," Gerald says. "Wally's finally made it. At last he's got his castle in Spain. In a manner of speaking. So it works out fine for all of us. He's a big wheel and we've got a front."

I shake my head.

"Besides," Gerald says, "Wally was so chuffed the way we attended to his old lady's arrangements, he felt he was doing us a favour, not the other way around."

I light a cigarette.

"Lovely," I say to him. "A fairy tale of old Soho. Warms the cockles, it really does. Wolf Mankowicz should write it." I click out the lighter flame and inhale. Then I say: "What was it Wally's old lady went out with?"

There's a small silence before Gerald says:

"Now look – "

"Cervical cancer, wasn't it?" I say.

"Now look – "

"Fine looking woman, Harry's old lady was. Pity she was took from us so soon. A great loss."

"Now look – "

"You see?" Les says to Gerald. "See how your fucking policies divvy up?"

Gerald turns his back on me and looks up at the ceiling. "Jesus Christ," he says. "Jesus fucking Christ. You start doing some cunt a favour and then you digress a little bit how you do some other cunt a favour and suddenly it's all snide innuendo and that. Jesus fucking Christ."

"I tell you," Les says, "that's what you get if you try and treat the workers as equals. They bite at your balls."

I smile and look at Les.

"In that case I don't know what you're so stand-offish for," I tell him. "Seeing as how you've got no balls to lose."

Les stands up and Gerald snaps out of his supplicant pose and shifts his body between Les and me although Les doesn't move an inch in my direction once he's got up. There's a lot of eyeball stuff between the two of them and eventually Les sits down the way he was always going to do. Then he gets up again and goes over to the drinks and makes himself another one and sits down where he was before and then he lights a fresh cigarette. Gerald doesn't move, he just stands there with his back still to me.

The silence goes on for a bit longer and I'm just about to finish my drink and get up and go when the door opens and who should come in but Audrey looking for all the world as though she's spent the afternoon relaxing at the hairdresser's instead of humping away in bed with me. Everybody looks towards the door when it opens and Audrey stands there taking in the atmosphere before she closes the door behind her. Then she says:

"What happened? Did the Arsenal lose the replay?"

Les clears his throat and would complete the job by spitting if it wasn't his own carpet. But Gerald behaves differently from usual: instead of going through the slagging routine with Audrey he walks over to her and puts his arm round her shoulders and shepherds her into the room like a protective host would a shy late arrival. Audrey looks at him in complete suspicion.

"What's all this in aid of?" she says.

"You know bleedin' well, darlin'," Gerald says. "Don't come the old one-eyed soldier with me."

Gerald and Audrey make their picturesque way over to the drink cabinet.

"Now then, sweetheart," Gerald says. "What would you like to drink?"

"Jesus Christ," says Les. "My stomach isn't this strong. What's the matter with you?"

"Leave it out, will you?" Gerald says. "We celebrated our wedding anniversary last night."

"What the fuck are you talking about?" Les says. "Your wedding anniversary isn't till April."

"So?" Gerald says. "What do you do on the night you get married?"

Les just looks at him.

"Right," Gerald says. "So we celebrated that, didn't we."

Audrey shrugs his arm off her and starts to make herself a drink.

"Bit of all right, wasn't it, darlin'?" Gerald says to her.

"I don't remember," Audrey says.

Gerald grins at Les and he puts his hand up the back of Audrey's skirt and feels her fanny from the rear at which Audrey knocks over the glass she's filling as she starts fetching round a swing which is intended to connect with the side of Gerald's head, but he's prepared for it and he grabs her wrist before she can connect. He laughs and says: "What's the matter? Frightened Jack might get a flash of your sweet little bum?"

Audrey doesn't answer, not verbally anyway. She just gives him the look.

"Well don't you worry about that. Jack's broadminded. He's seen plenty, haven't you, Jack?"

"I've seen some," I say to Gerald.

Audrey wrenches her hand away from Gerald's grip and turns back to the drinks and sets her glass straight and starts all over again. Gerald winks and walks away from her and says: "Giving the old lady a seeing to from time to time makes a nice little change. You forget that nobody does it like the old lady. But you single men don't know what I'm talking about, do you?"

Les ignores him and I stand up.

"Where are you going?" Gerald says.

"I've got some work to do. I'm one of the workers, remember?"

"Hang about, hang about," Gerald says. "Les didn't mean what he said. It's just his time of the month."

Les doesn't say anything.

"You didn't, did you Les." Gerald says, looking at him. Les shifts a bit on the crackling leather and looks out at the black plate glass and says:

"No, all right. I didn't mean it."

14

Both Audrey and me look at Les as though we're witnessing the second coming. Gerald beams at me and says: "You see? If Les says he didn't mean it, he didn't mean it."

"You mean he didn't mean it when he said he didn't mean it."

Gerald looks blank.

"Forget it," I tell him and start towards the door.

"What in Christ's name's going on?" Audrey says.

"Oh, nothing," Les says. "We're only offering him the holiday of a lifetime, two weeks of carefree sunshine at the resort of his choice."

Audrey looks at me and you've got to hand it to her, she's a great little performer.

"So what's wrong with that?" she says to me.

"I told them I'd prefer Skegness."

"The villa," Gerald says. "He can have the villa to himself for a whole bleeding fortnight."

"I might get lonely," I tell him.

"What's the matter?" Audrey says, her face absolutely straight. "You frightened of flying or something?"

I just look at her but not the way I'd like to.

"Here," Gerald says, and for once I'm glad he's missed the point. "Is that what it's all about? You scared of aeroplanes?"

I'm about to answer when Les cuts in.

"You ever been abroad before, Jack?"

I don't answer.

"That's it," Gerald says. "He's never been abroad before."

"As a matter of fact, no, I haven't," I say to him. "But that doesn't have fuck all to do with it."

Les slaps his thigh and comes as close as he'll ever come to laughing.

"Brave old Jack," he says. "Jack the fucking lad. He's nervous of leaving his patch."

"Listen," I say. "Leave it out."

"You're right," Audrey says. "He wouldn't know how to say 'Leave it out' in Spanish."

"Listen – "

"Fuck me, Jack," Gerald says. "You should have said. Now I understand what the routine was all about."

"The routine – "

"Come fly with me, come fly, let's fly away," Audrey starts off singing.

"Listen," I say. "I didn't say anything. If there was a routine, it came from that cunt over there, and that I can do without."

"So why are you cutting off your nose to spite your face?" Audrey says.

"I – "

"That's right," Gerald says. "Don't let Les put the mockers on it."

"That'll be the fucking day, when he puts the fucking mockers on anything I ever do."

"Right," Gerald says. "Then you'll go, then?"

"I – "

"What's to stop you?" Audrey says. "Obviously not the flying. Obviously not Les. And obviously, if you get my meaning, not the foreign parts."

I look at her. There is a silence. Then Gerald says. "Great."

And having said that, Gerald skirts the room's depression and goes over to the plain white Swedish desk over by the plate glass and picks up an envelope and walks back again and hands it to me.

"There you are, then," he says. "No sweat. Tickets, money, the lot. You leave four o'clock Thursday afternoon."

I look at the envelope. Audrey anticipates my saying anything by saying to Gerald:

"While we're on the subject, I'm going to Hamburg next week; I need a couple or three new birds downstairs. Those last ones are nine day wonders."

"Well you fucking fixed them up, didn't you?" Gerald says.

"As a matter of fact I didn't," Audrey says. "Sammy did. That's why I'm going myself this time."

"Well I don't give a fuck what you do," Gerald says. "Go wherever you like. Only I want those chancers out."

"They're already on their way."

"Well don't worry me about it, then," Gerald says. "I've got more important things on my mind."

Gerald turns back to me.

"All right then, sunshine?" he says. "All set? And by the way, if you want to know the Spanish for cunt, you just ask old Wally boy. He'll put you right."

Chapter Three

"You're fucking barmy," I tell her. "I mean."

Her fingernails trail slowly down my spine and she kisses the lobe of my ear.

"You'll get us both done before you're finished. I mean for a start, how are you going to get out of Hamburg?"

"By going."

She digs her nails in, just a little pressure.

"Oh yes?"

"I go, I spend half a day telling Monika what I want, then I fly down to Palma. Three days later I go back, approve or disapprove, then I fly back to London."

"Great idea," I tell her. "Only say something clever happened like Gerald's old mum darkening out and he wants you back quick and he tries to get in touch with you? That'd be fucking favourite, wouldn't it?"

"That old string bag's never going to go."

"Don't be thick on fucking purpose."

"Well," she says. "I won't be telling Gerald where I'm staying. I never do. And in the event of unforeseen circumstances he's hardly likely to send Interpol round looking for me."

"No, but he knows where Monika is, doesn't he?"

"So he knows where Monika is, but Monika doesn't know where I am, and if he gets in touch with her, I'm sussing out different sources, aren't I."

"And of course, Gerald wouldn't let anything like a bit of suspicion cross his mind."

"Look," she says. "Let me tell you about Gerald. Gerald thinks he's Mr. Wonderful. He's so convinced of that fact that even if he lived forever like his old mother, he wouldn't believe it, it wouldn't occur to him that I'd jeopardize my life with him by so much as even sharing a lift with a feller."

"And what about me? What about the times him and Les have been away and left us to look after the job ourselves. Nothing's crossed his tiny mind about those times, I suppose?"

"No," she says. "You're one of the workers, aren't you? And

Gerald's never read Lady Chatterley's Lover."

I give her the look and the pressure from her fingernails is renewed and she says:

"Oh, for Christ's sake. You're Gerald's blue-eyed boy and you fucking well know it. He knows how the business couldn't survive without you even though he may not think it. He makes out that the opposite is true, so that he can save his face; that all the time Les and him are doing you favours. So can't you see nothing ever'd cross Gerald's mind as far as you're concerned?"

I shake my head. "You've lost me," I tell her. "But what's the fucking difference? You're not coming, whatever you say."

"Too right I fucking am," she says, and the finger nails begin making fresh indentations.

Chapter Four

Of course, the manner of my going's typical of those two wankers. They only get me on a package in and out, because that way it's cheaper even though it includes the bill for the hotel I'm not going to use. So I have to join the un-legislative club of package creeps all the way from Euston to Luton to Palma, including, as the song says, all the stops along the way: hanging around with them at the air terminal, hanging around with them at Luton, hanging around with them at forty thousand feet, hanging around with them at Palma Airport waiting for the luggage to come spewing out onto the bit of fun-fair.

But it's in the air they get on my tits most, and the group that gets on them more than any other is a family I haven't been able to get away from since the air terminal. There are nine of the bastards: a couple of kids, fathered by two mid-thirty Dagenham workers, real-life brothers; they are swaggering would-be hardcases using the fashionable manufactured folk-dialogue of the East End, hairstyles courtesy whichever North London footballer's salon happens to be nearest, decked out in expensive machine-made holiday clobber but wear their eiderdown-like windcheaters with the Ford emblem on the breast-zip pockets and the ceremonial racing stripes rippling down each of the arms. They look for all the world like T.U.C. 1975 equivalents of the Few, the major difference being the swift skinniness of their eyes, darting this way and that with the tense paranoia of those that observe others, eyeballs with a view to discover who's for and who's against. Their wives are anonymous but noisy late beneficiaries of their husbands' collective hundred-pound--a-week wills, all crimplene, hairstyles ten years behind those of their husbands'. Enlarging the group were the brothers' parents, the woman past the age of caring, desperately rowdy, her husband trying to stretch himself back to be a brother to his sons by wearing the same kind of clobber and all that does for him is to accentuate the impression he gives of regretting that the present difference hadn't started to spiral about nineteen-thirty-five. And topping off this familial layer-cake is the inevitable and definitive Old Dad. Hogarth and Leonardo couldn't have cross-hatched a better model.

From the nose back everything about his face recedes and sinks into the depression of his hand-stitched mouth only to sweep out again to the bone of Punch-like chin. But the support his mouth lacks tooth-wise doesn't stop his endless jaw-bone solo. Not that any of the other generations of his family are paying much attention, they're too busy leading off in their own directions. And it's just my bleeding luck to get surrounded by the whole lot of them. My seat number places me next to a porthole and in the middle seat there's one of the brats and the aisle seat is taken by one of the sons of Daghenam. Across the aisle is number two son, number two brat, and the middle-aged father. Behind me is mum and the two wives, and in front of me old dad has been sent to Coventry by the numbering of the seats. One of the three is empty but the wall seat's been taken by a young girl of around fourteen, airline logic having placed her parents about ten rows down. The old dad starts by saying to the young girl:

"Do you mind if I sit down next to you, young lady?" The dirty old bugger's question is quite irrelevant because she's got no choice. She shakes her head and number one son who's stacking the old dad's coat while the old dad creaks down next to the girl, his eyes venal and his tongue peeping through the recession in his lips. "Watch his left hand, darlin," the number one Dagenham son says to the young girl who takes no notice of him or the old dad. He looks at me and gives me a swift deadpan wink and I give him a slow deadpan turning away of the head and I hear him sniff as I look out onto the wet tarmac and as he sits down there is an echo of his disdain in the crackle of his windcheater as he settles himself in.

The old dad starts up a routine with the young girl. "You ever been to Majorca before, young lady?" he asks her.

"No."

"Ah," he says. "We been coming five years now. Five years ago it was when I first come. Course, took me seventy-five years to actually get round to having a continental holiday. Not like you youngsters nowadays. We had it different in my day. I was brought up down Wapping Steps. But you can say what you like, there was a strong sense of community feeling down there, them days."

Behind, number one son cracks a laugh. "And he should know, the old sod. Did all the feeling, he did."

"My Uncle Ernie used to live down there," the girl says flatly. "He said it was dead nasty."

The old dad changes tack, his attitude and voice betraying a lifetime of compromise.

"Oh, yes," he says. "Of course we moved out in the end, that's why we moved out. Went to live in Vauxhall, we did. Very nice, it is."

The way he says Vauxhall, it sounds like a bronchitic's expiring breath.

"I wouldn't know," the young girl says. "I've never been to Vauxhall."

So the young girl successfully ends the conversation and then Dagenham son number one smacks his hands together and says towards the stewardess who in no way can hear him:

"Come on then, darling's. Let's be having you. The above have arrived. Get cracking. Start wheeling out the duty frees."

He turns round in his seat and looks towards the back of the plane.

"They're not a patch on last year's, Benny," he says to his brother across the way. "Remember that little spade? What a little cracker that was. Remember? I always fancied a bit of black for that."

"I'll give you a bit of black if you don't leave off," his wife says from behind.

"The day you give me anything'll be a day to remember. Here, Benny, last year she gave it up for Lent and you know how she never could count, I never had the heart to tell her Lent's over and done with. I never looked back since."

Benny bellows his appreciation. Number one son's wife says: "You just bleeding watch it or I'll tell them stewardesses all about your operation. That'll slow you down a bit." There's a trio of screeches from behind. Number one son puts his hands on the back of his seat and raises himself up slightly and gives his old lady a freezer. "You're asking for one in the mouth, you are," he says.

"Ooh, yes please," his wife says. "Only not yours, eh?" Three more shrieks.

"Here, Barry, can you arrange one for me," the other wife says. Three more shrieks.

A stewardess pauses in sweeping by and says to Barry: "Would you mind fastening your seat belt, sir."

Barry swivels round in his seat and says: "I was hoping you'd fasten it for me, darlin'."

The hostess smiles and keeps going so as to prevent herself spitting at him. Then she goes into pantomiming the oxygen drill, every action exaggerated, eyes fixed on a point somewhere slightly above the heads of her audience, like a bored stripper waiting for her disc to end, the voice of the unseen stewardess like a send-up of a fashion house commentary. When the visible stewardess has finished her act the Dagenham sons give a round of applause. The stewardess walks back and is very good at totally ignoring the sons while seeming to smile very sweetly at everybody before her. Barry gives a crooked arm and a clenched fist as she deports herself by. The old dad turns to his left but the aisle seat is still vacant and it strikes me how none of his family's bothered about sitting next to him, nor do I fucking well blame them. Of course part of the thought occurs to him too.

"Ere, ain't none of you lot going to keep me company, then?" he asks.

"Can't be done, can it, my old son?" Barry says. "It's down to the numbering of the seats, innit?"

"Yers, well, how come I'm the one as is on me own? Why can't one of the nippers change places?"

"I was afraid he'd think of that," Barry says under his breath. He speaks to the old dad: "Look you're all right where you are. Besides, we don't want to put the mockers on a budding romance, do we?"

"I'll change places with Grandad," the brat next to me says.

Oh Christ, I think to myself. Vauxhall here we come.

"You stay where you bleeding well are," Barry says. The kid does as it's told and I breathe at least one small sigh of relief.

But the relief is only temporary. Because ever since we left the terminal, I've been as tense as a minder who's having to wait a minute longer than he ought to. Not that I ever felt that kind of tenseness myself. But I've seen it in others. And that is what I'm feeling now. Those clever sods up in the Penthouse had sussed it. I'd never flown before.

Of course, I've often thought about it. And after having thought about, I've always sworn nothing would ever get me in the inside of an aeroplane. I mean, the things you read. Those reports in the papers. (Reports I always read, not missing a detail; I'm drawn to them; if there's one on the front page I always lap it up, even before I've turned to see how Spurs have gone on.) Bodies strewn over a ten mile radius. Tape recordings of the last minutes in the flight deck. Pictures of the stewardesses, smiling. And on T.V., it's even more favourite with my stomach muscles. The smoking wreckage. The anonymous sheets on moving stretchers. Zooming in on a chiffon scarf hanging from a tree branch, a briefcase, a kid's spouted drinking cup lying on its side in the drizzle. I mean, it's not that I'm frightened of going. If it was that, I'd have taken up flower arranging years ago. When you're gone, you're gone, no argument, seeing as how that's the one thing there's no answer to. No, it's just that I like the idea of having some say in the matter of my going. Not to mention the matter of when.

I'm all for self-determination. I like having odds. Somebody's coming at you with a knife, you've got chances. Somebody's got a pump action massaging your vertebrae, you can always make a decision. A motor coming at you down the wrong side of the M.6, you can still take evasive action. There's a chance. And, besides, experience is a great teacher. You know what happens with a knife, a pump-action, a steering column. If you're going to go they all have one thing in common: the swiftness of progression from cause to effect. Whereas it's always struck me that in a plane, there's fuck all the individual can do about anything. No room for any determinism there; no chance for the individual with the quickest reactions to take evasive action. You just go with the rest, and never having been a lover of crowds, the close proximity of other people – that descent of a minute or a minute and a half, surrounded by the wailing and the screaming of the assembled throng – would seem as long as the eternity we were all about to enter. Another thing: when I used to organize tickles, there were never any wankers on a team of mine. If I asked a specialist his opinion of a particular facet of his part in the job, I'd expect a straight answer; no flannel just so he could row himself on something for the sake of possible readies. Whereas a mate of mine, Jimmy Fish – he once told me he was in this plane coming in to land one time. It was mucky weather, the plane was circling, and the tannoy came on when it shouldn't and the whole fucking planeload heard the captain saying to his co-pilot: "Well we can't stay up here all night going round and round; let's go down and have a crack at it."

Unbelievable. That kind of thing gives me the fucking creeps.

So eventually the plane begins to trundle out onto the runway, and out of my porthole I can see the wing shuddering, the unsettling crudity of the bolts holding the individual metallic sheets together, the simplicity of the wing flaps. I turn away and re-read the William Hickey column, concentrating on the given reasons for the display of today's ear to ear smile. Then when the plane is (presumably) pointing in the right direction for take off, there is a small pause. The jets reach screaming pitch, the plane begins to move, accelerating along the runway like an arrow from a bow, only I hope this particular arrow isn't going to emulate the one in the nursery rhyme. Then the runway slants away and we're up and streaming through the clouds and, although I'm still concentrating on the words in that boxed caption, the statistics going through my mind are of a different variety, the statistics for the incidence of major disasters during the first few minutes of take-off. Of course, the Dagenham Boys have their own method of passing the time by joking loudly about all the various forms disaster could take, just to prove they'd been through it all before.

"Hope the rubber bands are new," the one called Barry says.

"I hear Charlie White give them a price on a job lot of tyres," Benny says. "Should make for happy landings." They both bellow with laughter and it's a toss-up whether the nearest one gets a knuckle or I keep my clenched fist clutching the newsprint.

The plane veers and suddenly we're above the clouds and the quilted whiteness that stretches to the horizon is reassuring enough to counter-act the Mike and Bernie Winter cross talk on my left. Then the illuminated lettering goes opaque and I shuffle my Players and my lighter out of the mohair and light up and inhale gratefully, and after I've done that I try and get myself into a position that will cause as little stress and strain on the mohair as possible; I don't want to be seen getting off the plane looking like Gerald.

Then, at last, they wheel out the trolleys, and after the Dagenham lot have performed I order a handful of Vodkas and some cans of tonic and settle down to get quietly and methodically pissed.

Chapter Five

Of course, they'd said, Wally'll be there to meet you. Don't you worry about that. Wally'll be there and waiting while you're still up in the wild blue yonder. So don't you worry about that. Once you've landed you're on velvet.

When the plane lands and the doors are opened I stand as upright as is possible between my own seat and the back of the seat in front and wear the Dagenham family's commotion while they get themselves sorted, holding up the flow behind them as they play pass the parcel with their Adidas bags. Finally, Christ knows how, they manage to get themselves in the aisle and the queue starts to move and eventually I'm let in and I get to the door and the stewardess smiles and hopes I've enjoyed my flight, and I nearly tell her, but I don't.

Outside the sunshine's like a multibarred electric fire. The dry heat tingles through my mohair and I can feel the warmth of the runway through the soles of my shoes. I adjust my sunglasses and the bunch of us weave our way towards the airport buildings, and inside we mix in with a crowd off an earlier flight, gathered round the oval conveyor belt, gazing at its monotonous emptiness. Of course, the Dagenham crowd have to show everybody they've been through it all before by making a production of settling themselves down to wait on some of the airport furniture. While they're doing that I go to the sunlight end of the lounge and look out into the brightness and see if there are any signs of Wally. There's a line of coaches and beyond the coaches a line of hoardings black against the sun, but no Wally, at any rate, not in my line of vision. I turn away and look round to see if there's a bar or anything but there's nothing and I begin to wish I'd brought some of the duty free stuff on the plane, to pass the time by keeping myself stoked up. And there's some time to pass because the luggage from the first flight doesn't spill out for over half an hour. The travellers pick out their luggage and move like moths towards the light at the end of the lounge and when they're outside I watch them flutter some more as they sort out the relevant coaches. Inside, the lounge is relatively quiet again. Outside, a coach begins to move off, then another – revealing nothing, I look at my watch. I swear to myself and light another cigarette. I'm fucked if I'm going to have another look for Wally. Another twenty minutes goes by before the luggage from my flight begins to flop onto the conveyor belt. A new crowd collects and I join it and of course my case is among the last to appear. I grab it off the belt and walk across the lounge and out into the still sunshine. I put my case down and scan the forecourt. Nothing, except the stacking of the cases on the remaining coaches and the push and shove of the customers. Then they all get settled and the motor of the final coach starts up and somebody gets off the coach and starts walking towards me. She's dressed in some green drag and there's a badge on her lapel with her name on it. She gives me a thoroughly routine smile.

"Hello," she says, "I'm Barbara, your Funbreak representative. Which hotel are you going to?"

"I'm not," I tell her.

A slight frown.

"I'm sorry – "

"I'm not going to a hotel."

She looks down her check list.

"You're – "

"Carter. Jack Carter."

She brightens again.

"That's right," she says. "Las Arenas. I thought we'd lost you."

"I'm not going to a hotel."

"But you must be. You're on the list."

"I know I'm on the list, darling," I tell her. "But I'm not going to the hotel."

She looks at me as though I've just told her the earth's flat.

"I'm sorry, I don't understand," she says.

"It's paid for, isn't it?"

"Well, yes – "

"So why worry?"

"Well I – "

"Tell you what," I tell her. "You've got an empty room for a fortnight, right? But it's paid for. Now I'm entitled to that room whenever I like, right?"

"Yes, but – "

"Well I tell you what you do; you nip in there every night, warm up the sheets, all right? Part of the job, yes? Only, one night you're warming it up, I might pop in to test the mattress, right? One of the

26

perks of the job, O.K?"

When it sinks in her face becomes a blank and then I get the total ignoration and she walks off back to the coach. "Hasta la vista," I call after her, then I sit down on my case and light another cigarette. The buses rev up and move off in dusty convoy and when they're gone all I'm left with is nothing apart from a distant group of Spanish porters, hands in pockets, talking about whatever Spanish porters talk about. Well, at least it won't be Millwall, I think to myself.

The other thing I think to myself, while I'm staring unseeing at the blank hoarding, is stoicism. Why that word should drift back into my mind after all these years, I'll never know. I can see the situation where I first heard the word, a dusty June classroom, old Henry explaining why this particular character in this play we were going through, why he'd just accepted the fate that was about to be dished out to him. None of us could figure it out. Why, he was asked, why should the guy just accept it, why didn't he earhole the bastards that were out to get him, at least do down fighting? Henry'd smiled and agreed with the difficulty we'd had in accepting what the gut accepted. Only, he'd said, maybe twenty or thirty years from then, some of us might become stoics. No chance, the chorus'd been. Only, a couple of weeks later, I'd gone to the Star and seen this picture, *The Killers,* starring Burt Lancaster, and he'd been this guy, lying on a bed, and somebody'd come and warned him of two killers were coming up to see him off, and he'd just lay there relaxed on his bed, virtually saying, let them come. Let them do it. The rest of the picture had been in flashback, showing why he'd reached that stage, how Ava Gardner had helped him reach it.

I shake my head. Funny, I should think of that right now. I look at my watch and fuck Gerald and Les from Bow to Bromley.

It's only an hour, an hour and a quarter later, that something actually happens. And, as begins to seem usual round here, the happening is encased in a cloud of dust.

A car rounds the corner of the terminal building and draws up opposite me. The dust falls away like midges at sunset and a door opens and a Spaniard approaches. I remain seated. He smiles and stretches out his hand. He's dumpy without being fat, he's fortyish, and he's got a very nice haircut.

"Mr Carter?" he says.

I nod. The hand stays outstretched. I shake it. His grin widens. Then he goes into his act. I gather it's all about why he's here instead of Wally, why he's late, and what's wrong with the car. Only most of it's in Spanish, but I don't have to speak Spanish to gather there's got to be something wrong with the car. Faulty plugs sound the same in any language.

So I get up and he takes my case and carries on with his soliloquy while I get in the back of the car, making my first mistake: there's about enough knee room for one of Billy Smart's midgets. I begin to try and signify that I'd rather sit in the front but it's too late, the driver's scraped in gear and off, u-turning across the forecourt, and a minute or two later we're hammering along a stretch of motorway at thirty-five miles an hour. As I look around at the flanking scenery, I think to myself: they could have left Ealing Broadway out of it. Because that's the impression I get: the architecture's different, the climate's different, but there's the same anonymous scruffiness, the same feeling of characterless uniformity re-enforced by the office blocks that passed for hotels squeezing yards away on my right. But we're only on the motorway for about ten minutes and then the driver turns off.

It may be just the angle I'm sitting at, or the vague positioning of the driver's pointing arm, but I get the impression he's aiming his finger not at any of the lower reaches of the range, but at the highest peaks, the ones reflecting most brilliantly the disappearing sunlight, and, if I'm right, that the villa's as high as is possible. Knowing Gerald and Les it's probably balanced on a peak like something out of Road Runner, liable to tip over the edge if you flush the lavatory a bit fierce.

About ten minutes later we get to a small town, the main road going straight through the middle, and this place has a completely different atmosphere to the sprawl we left half-an-hour ago: a real Spanish village, as Spanish as an English market town is English. The only thing about this place, set out to catch the passing tourists, is a leather-work shop with a lot of hide skins tacked up on the outside wall. I tap the driver on the shoulder and manage to get over that I want him to stop, which he does, and gets out of the car and runs round the back and opens the door for me, beaming all over his face. I struggle out, and when I'm out I stretch and try and de-crease my clothes and while I'm doing that he's already half way across the road, making for the leather shop.

"Here," I call after him.

He stops and looks at me. I shake my head and point to a bar on my side of the road.

"There," I say to him.

His face falls a bit. No taxi-drop commission tonight. I walk across the broad pavement with the driver padding along behind me and we go into the bar.

The bar has a modern aluminium and glass frontage inset in the old shuttered structure of the building, a miniature version of the airport façade, and inside there are resonances of the airport, leatherette stools and booths, formica topping on the bar. Formica in Spain. I wonder how they pronounce it.

Some of the town's top guys are sitting on the stools screwed into the floor along the front of the bar, eating sea-food from dainty saucers and drinking beer from bottles that look like they should have Schweppes Ginger Beer inside. You can tell they're the town's top guys. There are four of them and at least two of them are obviously brothers, but that apart, they're all out of the same mould, short, portly, beautifully barbered greying hair, similar kinds of sportswear and slip-ons. Even the frames round their glasses seem to match. But the thing that tells you what they are is the atmosphere they have about them, an air of mild unease, dissatisfaction, only submerged when they are concentrating on their food. It's an attitude I recognise from my adolescence, among the small builders and the chemists and the haulage contractors who used to gather at the bar of the Con. Club in Scunthorpe; they all looked somehow disappointed by their success too.

"Vodka and tonic," I said to the fifteen-year-old behind the bar.

"Vodka-tonic," he says, already half filling a glass with crushed ice. I turn to the driver who's at my shoulder and I raise my eyebrows to let him know I'd like to know what he'd like. He beams and clears his throat and very carefully he says, "I would like a large gin and a tonic please."

I smile to myself. When it comes down to essentials, the barman can understand what I want, and the driver can make himself understood. But Christ alone knows what a large gin's like because the lad behind the bar's still pouring my vodka. No measures, nothing. I motion for him to stop, so's there's room for my tonic to go in and then I begin to tell him what the driver wants but he's already started to take care of that so I just stand there and watch. When he's finished he puts all the stuff on a tray and while the driver's taking the stuff to a table I give the lad behind the bar a five hundred peseta note and he rings it up and very carefully counts the change out into my hand. I gave him too much back as a tip and then I go and join the driver, who is splashing the tonic in both our drinks. I sit down and the driver raises his glass and downs half his drink as though he's drinking lemonade.

"Cheers," he says smiling broadly.

"Cheers," I say, and raise my own glass and take a long drink but not as long as his: it takes me all my time not to spit it out all over him because he's given me the wrong fucking drink. He's got the vodka and I've got the gin. And gin to me is like water to a Jock; it turns my stomach. The smell's enough to make me throw up. The driver catches my expression and spreads his hands and raises his eyebrows to ask why? I push the glass over to him and get up and order another vodka and tonic and the lad behind the bar puts a glass and bottle on another tray and so I take the second tray back to the table and sit down again and by that time the driver's finished his drink and started mine as if there's no difference between the two drinks. Then we both stare out of the plate glass windows at the dusky pink evening. A bus draws up outside the leather shop opposite and unloads a load of tourists so that they can play a part in supporting cottage industries. The taxi driver makes a gesture at them and grins and I think to myself, yes, and wouldn't you like the percentage.

The lad from behind the bar comes round to the juke-box which is about two feet away from my right ear and shoves in a coin and there is a whirring sound and then the bar is full of music, Spanish popular variety. I manage about two and a half sides of this Eurovision reject stuff before motioning to the driver it's time for us to go. He looks disappointed. I wonder if he's on commission from here too.

Outside it's a little bit cooler than before. The tourists are still in the leather shop and the bus driver is talking to a representative of the local filth who looks like something out of the Pirates of Penzance. No wonder they need shooters, with that clobber. Otherwise they'd die of embarrassment from all the verballing they got.

This time I get in the front seat and we're out of town inside three minutes and making for the mountains again. I try and get out of the driver how long it's going to take us to get to the villa but all he does is to keep looking at his watch and giving me the fucking time, so in the end I give up before he thinks I've gone round the twist.

We carry on in silence for a further twenty minutes until we reach the foothills and a place called Incas. On the outskirts there's a walled set-up that looks as though it could be the local nick. The driver catches me looking at it and says one word.

"Cemetery," he says.

I don't say anything. He points at the walls.

"People, in there," he says.

I look at him.

"See," he says, then starts another charade. First he closes his eyes for a second then looks at me and makes a cut-throat gesture. I nod, then he takes his hands off the wheel and mimes digging. I nod. He shakes his head and digs again, and shakes his head and says No. I nod. Then he points at the walls and looks at me. I nod. He takes his hands off the wheel again, mimes gripping something and pushing it away from him. This time I don't nod. He sighs and points groundwards and shakes his head. I nod mine. He nods his. He points at the walls, then makes the gripping gesture again. This time I get it. He's putting something in the walls. But although I am getting it I frown signifying my perplexity and now he beams and nods his head vigorously and goes through the gripping motions again and again points at the walls.

"People, in there," he says.

I light a cigarette and turn my gaze to other pieces of local colour.

It takes us about ten minutes to get through Incas and then the road begins to rise even more steeply and there's no choice but for the road to become a never-ending series of hairpin bends rising up and up into the dusk. At the first bend the driver indicates the nub of the corner and points upwards to the top of the mountains.

"One hundred twenty-four," he says. "One hundred twenty-four." Then he laughs and reaches down between his legs and comes up with half a bottle of Hine and shoves it in my direction. I look at him and remember the treble vodka and tonic and treble gin he'd knocked back and shake my head. He unscrews the top and takes a long pull and I don't give a fuck whether there are one hundred twenty-four fucking bends just so long as we negotiate all of the bastards safely.

It's like a location for a rotten movie. The road dog legs steeper and steeper and the drops get deeper and deeper and the brandy in the bottle gets lower and lower. I begin to look back to the hours spent on the plane almost with nostalgia as the car grinds round each new bend. At one point we meet a tourist coach head-on and so the taxi driver reverses back round one of the bends, faster than the speed he'd formerly gone round it. Then he pulls in against the slanting face and somehow manages to get a couple of wheels up on the

31

slope. The bus manoeuvres by and the strains of "O Sole Mio" sung in about six different accents drifts through the evening air and finally rattles away into the distance with the slip-stream of the bus, but not before the taxi driver's caught the melody and started sending his own version across the deepening purple of the canyons. Then, before he crashes back through the gears, he reaches for the bottle again but before he can start unscrewing the cap I take the bottle from him. He looks at me, surprised at first, then grins and gestures for me to take a drink but instead of doing that I take a couple of hundreds out of my wallet and press them into the driver's hand. It's time for him to look surprised again but not as surprised as when I roll my window down and hurl the bottle out into the spacious canyon. He begins to speak but I cut in on him.

"Incas?" I say to him.

He looks at me. I say it again.

"Incas?"

He frowns and nods.

"People in walls?"

Another frown, another nod.

I mime him drinking from the bottle and then I point to each of us.

"People in walls," I say to him.

This time he just frowns. Then he turns away and takes it out of the gearbox and we're off again. Faster than before. I shake my head and light another cigarette. You can't win away from home.

Chapter Six

Half an hour later the taxi stops and I half expect the driver to try and have the last laugh by attempting to leave me on the empty mountain road. Because that's where we are. Nothing by empty mountain road. No obvious features to justify stopping the car. Just silence. I look at the driver. He points at the roadside.

"Villa," he says.

I look at the roadside. All there is is a load of still foliage and beneath the foliage what must be a small inclined plateau and beyond that the usual sheer mountain sides.

"The villa," I say.

"Si, si," he says, pointing as if his hand is on an expander. "Villa."

I look closely at the undergrowth and eventually I manage to detect a darker patch in the uniform gloom of the foliage.

"There?" I say.

"Si, si," he says, then waves his arms, hands limp at the wrists, flapping away from him, to signify beyond and upwards past the gap in the foliage.

"Ah," I say and sit there for a moment thinking various thoughts. After I've thought them I get out of the car, and he gets out of the car and hauls my luggage out onto the road and stands there. He obviously has no intention of moving any further so I pick up my luggage and begin to move towards the gap. After I've taken a few steps I feel a hand on my arm.

"Excuse me," he says.

I put the luggage down and turn to face him.

"Fare," he says, "the fare."

You've got to hand it to him, he really is a little trier. I smile at him and take hold of his open neck shirt and lift him up and carry him a few steps back to the car. Then I sit him down on the bonnet and still keeping a grip on his shirt I take my wallet out and lay it down on the car's warm metal and flip it open and with my thumb and forefinger I slide out a couple of hundred peseta notes and stuff them in the pocket of his shirt. He knows that I know that he'll already have been squared up by Wally but even at this stage he feels obliged to give me a long *spiel* whether I understand it or not so I just carry on holding him on the bonnet until he's finished, until he realizes there's nothing he's going to say will make any difference, in any language.

When he's finished I give him two minutes' silence, just giving him the eyeball contact before I let go of his shirt. He slides his arse off the bonnet and plants his feet on the ground but other than that he doesn't make any other movement. I give him a pat on each cheek, backhand, forehand, then I turn away and pick up my luggage and make for the gap in the undergrowth. Behind me the driver clears his throat and there is the sound of spit hitting the road's dusty surface with some force but I don't bother to turn round. He's lost if he's got to spit. A minute later the car barks into life and tyres scratch the road's surface as the driver u-turns and begins to make it back down the mountain. The sound of the car dies and dies and so here I am, up in the fucking mountains, in the middle of a road as empty as Gerald's head. I turn round to look down the mountain at the dark plain stretching away to the flat curve of the sea. The only way I can tell the difference from land and water is by the endless strip of resort lights. But at least there are lights. Not as heartwarming as the one's I'm used to. But there are lights. Unlike behind me. I turn round again and look at the foliage and the darkness of the gap and of the mountains beyond. A few more words flow through my altitude-ventilated brain. Then I pick up my luggage and make for the gap. The gap's well over a car's width and now I'm up to it I can see that beyond it there's a track that over here is meant to pass for some kind of drive, a kind of approach road disappearing into the dusk. The fucking taxi driver probably knew about this approach, and fuck him. So I start off down the track. The ground is hard under the skimpy layer of dirt, the sound my feet make is subtle and resonant at the same time. I'm conscious of a slight rise as I progress along the track, and in front of me, although it never seems to get closer, there's a kind of phony back-lit horizon preceding the genuine silhouette the twilit mountains are making, indicating a small roll in the landscape, concealing a night-reflecting dip.

My Christ, I reflect, the track's going to be a roller coaster, a Gerald and Les switchback, designed for the tourist in search of the unusual, a mystery tour for those with a taste for the out of the ordinary, horizons unlimited, who knows, beyond one of the humps you might find a fucking villa.

I trudge on.

I have to admit, the night smells are not un-pleasant. They're not Gerrard Street, or Frith or Greek, there's no sourness, no close atmosphere of animal, vegetable and mineral decay, no rising around of spit-slick late Saturday night pavements, but they have a certain Spanish *je ne sais quoi*. Not that there's any way they're going to alter the thoughts that are lodged in my mind.

I reach the brow of the first hill. The first small horizon reveals the aspect of a second, further horizon. I look down into the depths of the intermediate depression. No villa. How you say: Fuck all Hacienda. Just quiet mountain gloom, lying undiscovered at the bottom of the depression. I put my luggage down and take my cigarettes out and light up and think about vodka and tonic, slices of lemon, cubes of ice. And eggs, two eggs; Gerald and Les by name. I finish my cigarette but I don't finish thinking about those two. I pick up my luggage and set off again.

The second horizon, another depression. More gloom at its base. But this time I can pick out an even deeper darkness crouching in the shadows. A slight rise, and from my viewpoint, on top of this rise, an oblong the scale of a cigarette packet. I concentrate hard and after a moment or so's concentration I come to the conclusion that this must be the villa. Unless of course it's a Spanish Public Karsi for nightwalkers that get caught short. But even a Public Karsi has lights. This place, no lights. Of course, it could be the wrong place. It needn't be Gerald and Les's at all. But that would be too easy. It's got to be theirs. It's got to be, because if it was anybody else's and I was staying there, it would be all lit up and there'd be a welcoming party and everything on ice, not to mention being met at the airport and dropped straight on the doorstep. Oh no. This belongs to Gerald and Les. Wally's probably in his pit snoring holes in the mosquito net. No fucking idea I'm ten minutes away from him. Likely he doesn't even know I'm meant to be coming. Well, he soon will. No danger. He'll be the one who'll get the surprise party when I interrupt his fucking snoring.

I start down the slope. The closer I get to the villa set-up the more details I can make out. The first thing I notice is the high surrounding wall and the thought occurs to me that it's lucky for Gerald and Les I've been around for the last five years or they'd have a bigger and better wall to look at when they're on their holidays. I can make out quite a few arched gateways, their vacuums filled with wrought iron – the kind of arrangements you find in Hendon or Bromley, separating the houses from the garages. But high as the wall is, one angle of the gradient enables me to see the villa. As far as I can make out it's set on a kind of man-made plateau and the building's got more split levels than a cracked mirror, a suitable reflection of the collective personalities of Gerald and Les, so many split levels it ought to be called the Villa Schizophrenia. But it's not called that, because when I get to what I imagine are the main gates, the name I've been led to expect is there on the wall, inlaid in a different stone. So at least I'm at the right place.

I put my luggage down and try the handles. Nothing. I don't really believe it. So I try them again. It's quite true, the bastards are locked. My first reaction is to scream Wally's name and give the gates a good kicking, but that would be stupid. That would spoil the kicking I'm going to surprise Wally with in a few minutes' time. I don't want anything to spoil that. So what I do is leave my luggage where it is, and do a tour of the walls and their assorted gates. When I get back to where I started from I have the knowledge that all the other gates are locked and shuttered just like the main one. That knowledge makes everything nice and neat and engenders all kinds of lovely thoughts in my mind. Saying Boo to Wally is being sweetened up by all these lovely thoughts I am having.

I climb up the main wrought iron and sit on top of the wall and look at the villa. Dim, night-reflecting light from the motionless swimming pool is mirrored in acres of plate glass splashed right across the front of the villa but beyond this pale phosphorescence there is still no internal illumination (illumination that is other than ephemeral). So I turn about and go down the other side of the wrought iron. The track I've walked from the mountain road continues this side of the wrought iron, a little better made up than the other side, curving away from the main bulk of the villa, ending up at what I take to be the garage, set much lower than the rest of the building, so that its flat roof is on a level with the footings of the villa itself. Rising up on my right to the level of the villa itself is a sort of scrubby shrub-cum-rock garden and winding their way up this slope are some irregular slabs of stone serving as steps that are meant to get you to the upper level, or to help you break an ankle, whichever. I negotiate these steps and now I'm faced with half an acre or so of flagstones surrounding the still swimming pool. I walk across the flagstones towards the villa. Occasionally the flagstones break to allow squares of soil to support bushes and small trees.

There's also landscape furniture, tables and chairs and benches over by the pool. When I get to the villa itself I can see that the cloistered arches are resting on a three foot high stone platform that runs the whole length of the front of the villa, mosaic and glowing from the reflected light in the plate glass. In the plate glass a figure moves but it's only the ghost of myself. I stare at the apparition and reflect on its presence. Then I reflect on the presence of Wally beyond the glass and I walk up the steps and inspect the shiny blackness for signs of a way in. In the darkness I work out that one of the plate glass panels is meant to glide open and give entrance to the villa's interior. I almost don't try to shift it; I don't want to do one other thing that will confirm the pattern, that will cause me to place myself head first through the plate glass. But I overcome my distaste at being proved right and give the slider a go, and on Mrs Fletcher's life, it moves. The fucker moves. It's open. There's a way in. No need for any over-emotional forehead work. It moves. There's a way in. I step forward.

I'm in a hall. Rectangular, echoing the face of the villa. But it's not as quiet as it was outside. There's the sound of running water, like someone pissing against porcelain but it's more constant than the noise of ten Saturday night drunks. I locate the noise and it's coming from an odd shaped lump in the centre of the hall, thrown into relief by the night-whiteness of the far wall. I walk over to the lump and discover it's a small fountain, the stone carved in the shape of some curlicued, non-existent fish. The water is spewing out from between the fish's thick lips and I wonder how long Gerald had to sit still so that the stone carver could make such an exact likeness.

I start to move slowly down the broad steps and when I'm three down the whole place is suddenly flooded out with light. I blink my eyes and when they're open again the first thing I focus on is an antique wooden straight-backed chair about half way across the room from me, just before another drop to another level that flows onwards to the panavision proportions of the windows opposite. The interesting thing about this chair, the reason it's much more interesting than all the other various items of furniture and objets whole length of the front of the villa, mosaic'd and glowing from the reflected light in the plate glass. In the plate glass a figure moves but it's only the ghost of myself. I stare at the apparition and reflect on its presence. Then I reflect on the presence of Wally beyond the

For Wally, his voice doesn't shake too much, his expression isn't too full of self doubt and anxiety mixed in with that natural expression of his apology for being alive. In other words, he looks as though his Grannie's just caught him giving a labrador a hand-job.

"Hello, Wally," I say to him, my words effectively jamming all the alternatives that are racing in my mind about the manner of our meeting, but in spite of that a part of my brain fixes on the fact that Wally is sweating somewhat in the class of Pancho Gonzales. "Warm for the time of year."

The entire lower part of Wally's face begins to move and I realise from all this muscular activity that Wally's trying to get his laughing tackle into training in order to say something to me. Finally he manages to make the tape.

"Jack," Wally says to me, "it ain't like what it appears to be. Know what I mean?"

I shake my head.

"Oh yes," I say to Wally. "Now I feel really at ease. What it appears to be, a shooter shaking in your sweaty little palm, that isn't what it really is at all. The million reasons for the shooter and your sweat, they're all beside the point. I can relax about them. I can leave all that out. Thanks a bunch for setting my mind at rest, Wally. Just allow me to thank you for your warm and wonderful welcome."

Wally does a bit more lip trembling and the shooter drops it's angle slightly in deference to Wally's embarrassment. I fold my arms.

"Well then," I say to Wally.

"Look," Wally begins to say, but I interrupt him and describe, in detail as graphic as I can muster, of what I think of it all so far, since I stepped onto the fucking aeroplane. Wally's shooter trembles at each new twist in my story, and when the shooter's twitching enough to shoot holes in himself let alone in myself, I say to him:

"All right, Wally. What is it? Are you piss-green about night-walkers or did Gerald and Les tell you that I might not be in too good a mood by the time I got here, seeing as there was nobody there to meet me at the airport. Or is there something else, some message Gerald and Les wanted you to deliver when I got here, some message they'd rather have you impart?"

"Jack – " Wally says to me.

I begin to walk towards him.

"Fuck the shooter," I say to him. "On you a shooter is just decoration. An embellishment. As dangerous as a bunch of flowers. You're not even a creep, Wally. A creep finds the ability from deep down inside him, in this kind of situation, to smile, he can galvanize his mouth even though his guts are somewhat less than iron. A creep has guts of a sort, Wally, but you have none. None whatsoever."

Wally moves his lips like a bad ventriloquist, shakes his head like a poorly-made ventriloquist's dummy.

I continue my advance.

"Tell me what you have to tell me, Wally," I say to him. "Before get to you."

But I don't get to him. Because a voice behind me says something and that causes me to stop walking.

"Well," the voice says, "it's Jack Carter, I guess."

The voice is American. I don't turn around to see what sort of American. I don't do anything. It's a situation in which you wait to be told what to do, and then it's up to you to decide whether or not you're going to do it.

"It's O.K.," the voice says. "You can relax. You can turn around if you want to. Only remember, your man there ain't the only guy in this room that's carrying."

I look at Wally a little bit longer until finally Wally averts his eyes and then I turn round and look at the man who's spoken to me. He's wearing a white oatmeal short-sleeved shirt, open at the neck, coat style, not tucked in to the waistband of his slacks, which are white and very sharply pressed. He is wearing canvas moccasins and it strikes me how sensible it is of him to be wearing dark glasses so that the lights wouldn't disorient him for what might have been a crucial second when he switched them on. But the most striking objects of his apparel are the two holsters he's wearing. One is a standard shoulder holster built to house an automatic. The other one is to carry a 38, and is fixed on the belt of his slacks, only partially visible because of the way his shirt's hanging. Only this holster has anything in it. The occupier of the shoulder holster is pointing straight at me, and it's not being held the way Wally's holding his companion piece.

The man isn't tall, isn't short. His muscular arms are black with hair, and what's left of the hair on the top of his head is extremely well barbered. His face is broad without running to fat, his shoulders are broad too, but the flow of his shirt doesn't quite conceal the slightest of paunches that blemishes his otherwise well cared for body. Twin lights dance in his dark glasses.

"Yeah," he says. "I guess this is Jack Carter."

"I bleeding told you it would be," Wally says.

There is a silence.

"Well," I say. "Now we know. I'm Jack Carter. I'm glad we've got that cleared up."

With his free hand the man takes off his dark glasses and allows himself a small quick smile, then his face is impassive again. His eyes flick up and down from my head to my feet, judging. Then he puts the automatic back in the holster and un-sticks himself from the wall and walks over to a low glass table. On this table there is an ice bucket with a bottle of champagne in it. Next to the bucket is a glass jug filled almost to the top with squeezed orange juice and slices of orange and lumps of ice. There are also some glasses on the table.

The American takes the champagne bottle out of the ice-bucket. "Wally, see to the drapes, will you?"

I hear Wally get up from the chair behind me and walk somewhere and press a button and there's a whirring sound as the curtains draw together, but I'm not interested in Wally's execution of this operation. All my attention is fixed on the man with the champagne bottle. He pours some of the champagne into a tall glass and then fills the other half of the glass with orange juice from the jug.

He looks at me.

"Want some?" he says.

I don't say anything. He pours another one anyway. Wally shifts past me and makes for the entrance hall. The American picks up one of the glasses and offers it towards me. I walk a few steps forward and take the glass. I notice the American doesn't pick up his own glass until I've taken hold of mine, and that he stays on his side of the table. There is some more whirring and swishing out in the hallway and Wally re-appears and begins to walk down the steps back to our level, but when he sees the look I'm giving him he stops in mid-step looking something like the character in the old joke who's walking in backwards pretending he's going out.

"Skol," the American says. "A votre santé. Cheers. All the rest of that crap."

I look at the American again. He's still watching me over the top of his glass.

I take a drink myself. It's a great drink. One of the best. A favourite of mine.

"Wally, less light, hey?" the American says.

Wally looks from him to me like a mongrel whose just shit and wondering who's going to give him the biggest hiding. He does a kind of bantam step and gets himself down onto our level and flits about doing whatever necessary to get rid of the main lights, doing his best to avoid any eyeball contact between me and the American. We, the other parts of the trio, we stand there holding our drinks, looking at each other, until such time as Wally has finished his chores and doesn't know what else to do with himself apart from to pretend he's not in the room, he's not in the villa, he's not even in Majorca, he's anywhere in the fucking world other than where he happens to be at this precise moment.

I finish my drink and take a couple of steps forward and put my glass down on the glass-topped table. Wally tries to ease himself out of my line of vision as if in some way that will make me forget he's there, but there's no chance of that because I say to him:

"Wally, I know what you're like. I know you're just a frightened little rat-bag. I know you're feeling like shovelled shit at this particular moment. And I know you're likely to get your dentures in a twist if you try to speak to me. But that's what you've got to do, Wally. Speak to me. Tell me all about it. You don't want me copping for you, but look at it this way: if you don't speak to me, I'll cop for you. If you do speak to me, I probably won't like what you've got to say, and I'll still cop for you. So you really can't lose, can you? It boils down to the same thing one way or another."

There is silence from Wally. The American takes another drink and continues to look at me and I continue to look at the American. Then Wally says:

"I don't know what you mean."

I take my eyes off the American and turn my gaze on Wally.

"I mean..." Wally says, taking his hands out of his pockets and not being able to find anything better to do with them, putting them back again.

"Wally," I say to him, not shouting, "just tell me what the fuck's going on."

Wally looks at the American but there's nothing for him there.

"Well, we had to be careful, didn't we? I mean, you know."

I shake my head.

"No, I don't know."

"Well, I mean. The situation."

"What situation?"

Wally looks at me as though I'm giving evidence for the prosecution.

"The situation," Wally says. "This."

"This being what?"

Wally begins to speak but the American cuts in on him and says to me:

"You're asking some pretty damn stupid questions."

"Oh, yes," I say. "Well, for a start, here's another one. Just who the fuck are you?"

Now it's the American's turn to give Wally the eyeball treatment.

"And here's another," I say to him. "I know it might sound, well, a bit niggling, a small point, I know. But the shooters. The pair of shooters front of and back of me, just when I'm starting off me holidays. I mean, I don't mean to carp."

The American's hand strays to his breast, not too far from the automatic's holster.

"You sure this is Jack Carter?" he says to Wally.

" 'Course I'm bleeding sure," Wally says. "Christ, I should know. I mean. Fucking stroll on."

Wally's uncharacteristic anger seems to reassure the American a little bit.

"So why," he says, turning back to me, "the games? The charades? Why the crack at the Oscar?"

I look at him and I look at Wally. After I've done that I pour some more from the jug into my glass and take it over to the chair Wally was sitting in when I made my entrance, and sit down. The only thing that breaks the silence of the room and the mountains surrounding the villa are the ice cubes in my glass.

The American concentrates on me for a while longer until he slowly turns and focuses his attention on Wally. Now Wally's beginning to regret his previously re-assuring anger. He doesn't actually move, but the impression he gives is of moving about five miles backwards from where the American is. Still, of course, with his hands in his pockets. It occurs to me that by now his ballocks should be red raw.

The American doesn't say anything. He doesn't say anything for so long that finally Wally has to say something himself. He draws on his great reserves of imagination and ingenuity and says to the American:

"What?"

Wally's response doesn't stop the American looking at him and it doesn't stop the American not saying anything to him. Wally eventually manages to swing his eyeballs in my direction and he looks at me as if I can get the hook out of his left gill, but from me he gets the same response as he got from the American. A clink of ice, a mask of face, and Wal, beside himself, farting in the wilderness.

But as in all situations, as in all of life, the point of no longer fucking about has to be reached, a situation has to be resolved, a decision has to be made. Things have to be answered and answered for. Likewise, this situation.

I always believe, in all situations, in being as direct as possible. Up to now, I think to myself, this is the way I've been, what more could I have said or done so far? Apparently not enough, so, being a little trier, I try again.

"Wally," I say, indicating the American. "Who is this?"

Wally goes blank again.

"You know who it is," Wally says.

I close my eyes, because if I left them open I'd have a lovely bead on Wally and I'd hurtle my glass across the room so that it smashed against the thickness of his forehead. "Wally," I say to him, eyes still closed, "he knows who I am, he knows who you are, you know who you are, I know who you are, and I know who I am." I stand up. "So for fuck's sake, who is he?"

My eyes snap open as my voice reaches shouting pitch. Wally shakes like Krakatoa.

"Well, he's the man, isn't he?" Wally says. "I mean, he's the geezer."

"What geezer would that be Wally?"

"Beg pardon?"

"Which man, Wally?"

Of all the silences thus far, the one that follows is the longest. Because during this silence things are beginning to dawn on Wally, and on the American. They're beginning to get my meaning, so to speak. They're beginning to realize that I'm not actually bananas, they're beginning to realize that I don't actually know what the fuck is going on. The silence is broken by Wally. It's his turn to close his eyes.

"Oh, Christ," Wally says.

"Yes," I say, agreeing.

"Now wait a minute — " the American begins, but I cut him off.

"No, you wait a minute. Let Wally speak. While he's still capable."

More silence.

"Wally?" I say.

Wally makes a decision and decides to handle the situation this way; he decides to talk to me as though I know what's happening really, as though I've had a temporary lapse, and it will all come flooding back to me as his discourse progresses and refreshes my memory.

"Well," Wally begins, all brightness and snap. "This is Joe, isn't it? Joe D'Antoni? The geezer? The friend of Gerald and Les's friends? The ones from over the water?"

I don't say anything. I just let him wait for the interruption he's hoping for until he can't wait any longer and he has no choice but to go on.

"The Americans," Wally says. He's like a club comic straining (sweating) for the first laugh.

"The Americans," I say. "Yes, I know about the Americans."

Wally's bowels almost open in relief and gratitude. At last, I've agreed with something he's said. He's no longer on the left hand of God. From now on it's downhill racing all the way.

"Yeah, that's right. You know, the Americans. What come over all the time. Their friend. This is their friend, Joe. You know. The geezer what's staying here. At the villa, like."

I nod my head and say:

"This is Joe, who's staying at the villa. The friend of the Americans."

"Yeah, just for the fortnight, like."

I nod my head again.

"Just for the fortnight."

Wally's smile seizes up owing to the fact that it's the American's turn to speak to him.

"What is this?" the American says.

Wally begins to spread his hands but before he can finish the action the American has taken hold of Wally by the throat and in that manner he guides Wally along until he's close enough to the wall to be able to slam Wally up against it.

"What is this?" the American asks again, which is pretty stupid of him because all the breath has been driven out of his lungs and even if there were any left it would have been impossible for Wally to force any of it past the grip the American has on his trachea. No, naturally, Wally doesn't answer. And naturally the American gets a little bit more mad and gives Wally a selection of back-handers across the chops, to which Wally can only respond by giving a fair

44

impression of a spectator watching a speeded-up tennis match. In the end the American gets tired of that and leaves it out and turns towards me. Sweat is black under his armpits.

"You didn't know?" he says.

Oh, I think to myself. Comes the dawn.

The American looks at me for a moment longer then he goes over to the table and pours himself another drink. He gargles half of it away then smashes the glass down causing the remains of his drink to fly out his glass and splash all over the knees of his crisp white slacks, but for the time being all he's interested in is describing in as many ways that he can think of his opinions of Gerald and Les. While he's doing that more sweat appears on his Samuel Fuller brow and his eyes glaze over and he looks like someone who's just thrown up after eight hours boozing. But even though the American is temporarily oblivious to the room and anything in it, Wally stays where he is, stuck to white wall like a gargoyle and approximately the same colour. So I take the opportunity of the American's absence of mind and walk over to Wally and talk to him a little bit.

"So apart from the geezer," I say to him, "what additional aspects of the situation am I supposed to know about?"

Wally darts a glance at the American and even Wally can see that the American's not with us so he says:

"Look, I don't know nothing, do I? I mean, I only know what Gerald and Les and the geezer tell me, don't I, and that ain't exactly choc-a-block with extraneous information, is it?"

"Just tell me what you do know, Wally."

Wally breathes out and seems to lose six inches in height.

"All I know is what I already said."

"Say it again."

"Look, I get a call, don't I? From Gerald and Les, right? Tell me this geezer's coming for a fortnight. Just passing through, so to speak. So I'm to turn over the villa all nice for his stay, like, as if I don't keep it like a bleedin' palace all the time. And they also mention that you'll be here for the same period, keeping a watching brief, so to speak."

"They say why?"

Wally shakes his head. I indicate the American.

"He say why?"

Wally shakes his head again.

"All he been saying since he got here last night is asking when you're going to be getting here. Been fair getting on my tits, he has. What with that and his fucking walking about. Jesus, he never stops. Kept me awake all last night, he did – "

"All right, Wally. All right. Where's the phone?"

Wally looks at me as if I've just asked him for the tenner I lent him that time in nineteen sixty-three.

"The phone?" he says.

I close my eyes. Wally doesn't want to chance it too far, so he says: "Oh, the phone. About that. See, we had a rainy week last week. You get the rains this time of the year. Comes down something shocking it does. A monsoon. Come down so hard last week it put the phone on the blink, didn't it? Been on to them no end, haven't I, but you know what it's like out here, bleedin' mañana and all that, ain't it? God knows when it'll be on again."

I give Wally a long look and then to his great relief I turn away from him and walk back to the drinks table and re-fill my glass. Here we all are, the American still chanting the words as if he's trying to summon up The Geezer at a black Sabbath, Wally sticking to the wall as though he's in a queens' bar and me, looking at the slices of lemon in my glass that remind me of the two lemons back home I know and love so well.

The American finally runs out of ideas and the room is silent again. Wally doesn't move. I sit down in a chair. The American turns round and looks at the drinks table. It seems to remind him of the real world because after a moment or two he wanders over to the table and pours himself another drink. He looks at his glass as if he's trying to evaluate its molecular structure. Then he takes a drink and turns to face me and looks at me for a long time.

"You don't know who I am," he says.

I look at him

"You are Joe D'Antoni and I claim the five pounds," I say to him

There's a short silence and then he says: "They didn't tell you I'd be here."

I don't answer him.

"They didn't tell you why I'd be here."

That's not worth answering either.

"They didn't tell you why *you'd* be here."

Neither is that. There's another silence. Then D'Antoni says: "So just, you know, why the Christ are you here? I mean, how would you kind of describe that?"

I take a sip of my drink and raise my glass and wave it in the air.

"On my holidays, aren't I? It's Wake's Week, Mediterranean Style. I come to see if the paella and chips is any better than what they do down the Elephant."

D'Antoni looks in Wally's direction but mere looking doesn't seem to give him any satisfaction whatsoever, so he moves across to within an inch of where Wally is and stops up the eyeball treatment.

"This is the guy, huh?" D'Antoni says. "The guy you been telling me about. The man. The guy the Fletchers picked out for the job. The guy who'll take care of things like you never seen."

At this point D'Antoni's voice rises to a screech.

"Christ, he don't even know I'll be here."

I could swear Wally's bottom lip begins to tremble a little bit.

"Leave it out," he whispers.

D'Antoni changes pitch again. Softly he says: "The phone. Get those mottors on the phone."

I begin to feel quite sorry for Wally, but not sorry enough to be unable to smile at his current expression.

"I was just saying to Mr Carter – " Wally begins, but D'Antoni doesn't let him finish.

"The phone," he says. "Get the phone."

Wally tries to look over D'Antoni's shoulder for some help from me but D'Antoni crowds him even more and Wally's eyeballs are resting approximately on D'Antoni's clavicles.

"The phone's off, D'Antoni." I tell him.

D'Antoni turns round very slowly but somehow his big gun has appeared in his hand, like as if it had been there all the time.

"The phone's off?"

"That's what I hear," I tell him

There is a long silence.

"How'd you get to hear that?" D'Antoni says.

"I listened," I tell him.

D'Antoni continues to look at me.

"While you were casting your mind through Webster's dictionary for the correct description of my bosses, Wally told me. See, seems like they have this rainy season. Hard rains. Affected the lines, hasn't it? Isn't that right, Wally?"

Wally looks really pleased I've invited him into the conversation.

"Seems it rained stronger than usual last few days," I say. "Interfered with the service; well, I mean, it would, wouldn't it?"

The American turns back to Wally and Wally says, "Look, honest, leave it out; oh, I mean, I wouldn't take the phone out, now would I, I mean to say, do I look as if I would?" but none of this vocally: it's all expressed totally through the eyes. D'Antoni's gaze does nothing to reassure Wally that his silent monologue is getting through. The silence continues until Wally speaks, as if he's been speaking all the time.

"Honest," Wally says.

D'Antoni looks at him a little longer and then he says: "You got it made here, don't you?"

Wally nearly nods his fucking head off, glad at last to be able to agree instead of deny.

"It's a great set-up," D'Antoni says.

More neck-work from Wally. D'Antoni continues.

"I mean, a layout like this. The climate. No worries. No hassle. A fairy tale. A guy like you, you must keep pinching yourself."

If Wally nods any harder he's going to beat a hole through the plaster.

"But then," D'Antoni says, "I don't know. Maybe there's a flaw. Maybe it's so great. You get the need to own something like it yourself, instead of just being the janitor. What do you say, Wally? Maybe you'd like the kind of loot'd buy you a set-up like this of your own."

"Eh?" Wally says, too shit scared to grasp D'Antoni's meaning.

"Maybe somebody offered you the kind of loot you could use for a place like this, if you did them maybe a couple of favours."

This time it sinks in. Wally says: "Leave it out. I mean to say. Gerald and Les'd have my guts for garters. They'd have a face like Jack here tell me I'd taken a dead bleedin' liberty and I wouldn't relish that, I can tell you. Stroll on."

D'Antoni's look remains hard but Wally seems to have convinced him because he says nothing else on the matter although I could have provided him with my own theory, that being that it's likely that my bosses, the eggs that go by the name of the Fletcher brothers, have had Wally interfere with the telephone so that I can't communicate to them my views on the situation with which they have presented me, and also, should I refuse to accept what that situation appears to present, my refusal won't fall on their ears. Typical of the brave bastards. They probably agreed to the set-up in Terri Palin's knocking shop, drunk with Dom Perignon and gym-slips. No wonder the cunts were so keen to see me on that plane. The whole fucking issue is an object lesson on how those two eggs behave. But as eggs go, I reflect, they're not as big as I am; I'm working for them, not them fo me. But I'm the one that got on the aeroplane.

The room is full of silence again and it's my turn to have D'Antoni gaze at me.

"So you know nothing," D'Antoni says.

I light a cigarette.

"That's right," I tell him. "And that's as much as I want to know, my old son."

D'Antoni frowns but I answer him before he can say the question. Standing up I say: "In fact, I'm not even guessing. Fuck all is all right with me. I'm knackered. All I want right now is my pit and I'll work out what I can't guess on the flight tomorrow morning. You got clean sheets laid out for me, Wally?"

Wally's given up. His dentures are about to slip out onto the floor and chatter away across the parquet.

"What are you doing?" D'Antoni asks me.

"Nothing is what I'm doing," I tell him. "Nothing except finding my bedroom and staying in it until I wake up."

D'Antoni stares at me.

"Where's the bedroom?" I say to Wally and now Wally's caught between the devil and the deep blue sea because D'Antoni says to me:

"You're not going anywhere, friend."

I pass my hand across my eyes.

"Yes I am," I say to him. "And I'll tell you why I am. Because you're not going to stop me. Because the only way you could stop me is by using your shooter, and you're not going to do that. I mean, it stands to reason, doesn't it, when you think about it?"

D'Antoni stares at me some more.

"The bags, Wally," I say.

Wally stays where he is. So I walk over to Wally and grasp him by the back of his scrawny neck and walk him over to where the bags are parked.

"The bags," I tell him again, exerting the pressure on the back of his neck so that he has to bend forward, his arms dangling like Tarzan's best friend. I let go and it's almost a reflex action when he picks up my stuff. It certainly isn't a conscious decision on his part, seeing as how he doesn't want to provoke a hiding by a mere thought process. He straightens up and his legs manage to start moving and he begins to walk towards the broad steps that lead down into the room from the hall.

"Hold it," D'Antoni says.

Wally snaps up as if he's on a parade ground.

"You," he says to me. "You're right. You're not expendable. The same does not go for him, or for his kneecaps."

"Jack – " Wally says.

"Wally," I say to him, "just keep walking, will you? Nothing's going to happen."

"That's right," D'Antoni says. "If he keeps walking, nothing's ever going to happen to him ever again."

I turn to face D'Antoni and start walking in his direction and while I'm walking towards him I say:

"Have you ever been tired? I mean, really tired? So tired that you don't give a fuck about anything, so that anything can happen to you, just so long as you get your head down?"

D'Antoni fixes me with his look but I don't stop walking and I don't stop walking and although I can't see him I know Wally is standing in exactly the same position. D'Antoni's gun is just as rigid as Wally's pose, but I don't give a fuck about that. I'm pissed off to the gills with the whole fucking situation. I keep going and D'Antoni starts backing off but still holding the shooter level with my chest.

"Back off," D'Antoni says.

"I'll leave that to you," I tell him.

"You got a job to do."

I shake my head.

"You came here to protect me," he says.

"From what? The midges."

"The midges? Who are the midges?"

"The fucking mosquitoes, you cunt."

D'Antoni now stands his ground but his gun hand isn't as steady as it was before.

"No, come on," he says. "These midges. Who are they?"

There's nothing for it; I have to laugh. I sink down in a nearby chair so I can do it in comfort. It's a weak, soundless laugh, the vocal equivalent of the after-effects being worked over by a good masseur. In my amusement I forget about Wally but I'm reminded of his presence by the unison sound of a snort and a fart; I look towards him and he's still facing the same way, still holding my luggage, still holding the same pose, but in spite of his macaroni state the humour of the situation has got through to him and the snort and the fart are as a result of him trying to prevent himself from laughing, like a hysterically frightened kid at his first Grammar School Assembly. But even after he's cleared his throat he doesn't alter his stance, doesn't even put the luggage down. "I'd suggest you open the window to let the warm air out, Wally," I say to him. "But on the other hand Mr D'Antoni might be afraid that you'd let the midges in."

Wally convulses again but this time all his pipes stay silent.

"Listen," D'Antoni says, "I had enough. I was guaranteed. Instead I get the Smothers Brothers. I may as well take you two out right now for all the use you'll be."

"Oh, yes?" I say to him. "And how much ravioli and chips does it take to get as hard as you?"

"Listen, you cockney craphouse, we saved your asses in the last war and we'll do it next time around, you bet we will."

Whether to slap his teeth out for his allusion to the last war or for his calling me a cockney, that is the question. I begin to rise while I'm deciding which motive will give me most satisfaction and while I'm getting up I say to him:

"I was born in Lincolnshire, friend, not London, and in Lincolnshire there's an airfield called Scampton which you'll never have heard of, the reason being that many of your B-29 flying heroes could never keep their guts inside their flying jackets after they'd flown their first mission from there; which of course is why you'd never have heard of it."

D'Antoni says: "No, and I suppose you never heard of a place called Dunkirk, either, did you?"

I'm all ready to connect but the sound of my luggage being dropped on the floor stops me from moving.

"Now look here," Wally says, "you're nothing but a fucking mouthy yank and you know fuck all about anything like that. It's about time one or two of you was set straight. My Uncle Henry was in on that Dunkirk business and I'd just like you to know if there'd have been any yanks there they wouldn't only have surrendered, they'd have been manning the guns for the other mob, I can tell you."

D'Antoni and I both stare at Wally, who is nothing but aggro, all directed towards D'Antoni. Then Wally's heat begins to evaporate and with each drop down the temperature gauge Wally's regret at the ferocity of his bravery begins to show in the lines on his face.

"Well, well," I say. "The Bulldog Breed is alive and well and living on a mountain in Majorca."

"Well," Wally says. "I mean to say."

"Shit," D'Antoni says.

After that there's another silence. D'Antoni breaks it.

"You know why you're here," he says to me.

"Sunshine," I tell him. "All I can do is guess. But I don't want to guess. All I want to do is to crawl into my pit."

"They must have told you."

"There is no must about Gerald and Les. If you're a friend of theirs you should know that."

"They fixed it. It's been fixed for months."

"Maybe. But I haven't. Thank you and goodnight."

I turn away, and walk over to Wally and my luggage and it's time to forget Wally so I just pick up my stuff and begin to make for the upstairs part. D'Antoni comes after me but I keep on going. I reach the stairs that lead to the gallery.

"Listen, you bastard," D'Antoni screeches. "You're my protection. You're here to protect me."

I whirl round on the stairs.

"Just one question," I say to him. "From what?"

D'Antoni looks at me and he's quieter when he answers.

"Nothing, maybe," he says. "Probably nothing at all. Just in case, is all."

"In case of what?"

D'Antoni shrugs.

"Nothing. Maybe it'll be a quiet two weeks."

I put my bags down on the steps.

"Jesus Christ," I say. "What you think I am, thick or something? You're twitching like a stripper's jock-strap and it's just because of probables? You think I'm going to hang about on the side of a fucking mountain for two weeks and finish up my holidays getting it in the neck just because it's probable? I mean, I can't imagine anybody bothering to go to all that trouble just on account of you, but stranger things have happened, and if it does, I'm not going to be here."

I pick up my luggage and turn round and start climbing the steps again.

"You're paid to do what you're told," D'Antoni says, following me up the steps.

"That's right," I say, "but the thing is you don't pay me and I haven't been told by those that do."

I reach the gallery and stop.

"Wally!" I shout.

Wally appears from the lounge, peering round the corner as though he's expecting to be shot at.

"Which room's mine, Wally?"

D'Antoni is half way up the steps deep in thought.

"They must have had a reason," D'Antoni says.

"The opposite side Mr Carter," Wally says. "Second door along."

I start making for the opposite side, second door along.

"I mean," D'Antoni says, "they must have had a reason."

"Course they had a fucking reason," I tell him. "If they'd told me, the eggs, they knew there was no chance I'd even have come here in the first place."

"But you work for them," D'Antoni says.

I put my luggage down again and grasp the balcony rail.

"Oh yes," I tell him, "I work for them all right. Just an employee, I am. I mean, all I do is sort the jobs for them, engineer the jobs, go out tooled up on the jobs to make sure they work in spite of the chancers around these days and then after the job's over I take the money home and put it on the desk in front of them so they can have the fun of divvying it all up and holding it and all that kind of nice fun, before the other kind of fun which is where they put on their mohairs and go out and spend it. I'm just a cog in the wheel, that's all. Like Dagenham. They don't need me at all. They especially don't need me when people in a similar line of business put it about that they might feel like slapping Gerald and Les's hands for them. That's the last time they need me. They'd be quite capable of sorting out a non-event like that, those brave fellows. They wouldn't need me, would they, Wally? I'm just one of the works. Isn't that right, Wally?"

Wally shuffles back a bit round the corner but not far enough to obscure my view of his usual expression, that is to say, looking down his nose from one slipper to the other. D'Antoni just stays where he is on the steps, looking up at me, silent. After a little while he begins to grin.

"What you laughing at," I say to him.

D'Antoni shakes his head.

"Maybe there's method in their madness," he says.

"What are you talking about?" I ask him.

D'Antoni slips the shooter back in the shoulder holster and folds his arms.

"The Fletchers," he says. "Maybe they knew what they were doing."

"Fuck off," I tell him. I pick up my luggage and walk towards the bedroom. The bedroom, predictably, is very big. There are a lot of carpets hanging on the walls. Nice, I think, if you wake up with a hangover. When you get out of bed you try and walk on the bleeding wall instead of the floor. In fact the amount of Spanish Wilton on the walls far outnumbers the stuff on the floor. Just a few rugs tastefully scattered on the shiny done-up stonework. In fact the whole bedroom is tastefully empty as possible. There's a bed, sure, and it's beautifully covered in some golden brown silk smutter, but next to it there's just a small square bedside cupboard made out of marble, would you believe — a cupboard made out of marble. And apart from the soft metallic glow of the single wall light and the plain thick gold-coloured curtains and the fitted wardrobes running the length of one wall, that's all there is to it. Very Gerald and Les, very Espence. I slide open one of the doors to the fitted wardrobes. Nothing, but half a dozen hangers, which mercifully are neither marble nor examples of local peasant handicrafts. But even so the wardrobe has a warmth, is a fucking sight cosier than the rest of the bedroom.

It occurs to me that I might just skin a passing mountain goat, make a sleeping bag, slide the doors behind me, and camp out in the wardrobe for the rest of the fornight. Some fucking hope.

I slide closed the wardrobe door. I traverse the horizontal masonry and make it to the drawn curtains that echo the colour of the stonework. I part the curtains and there's more sliding glasswork, opened to allow the perfumed mountain air in as far as the heavy material. Beyond the glasswork there's what appears to be a balcony, its confines stretching much farther than the usual kind of arrangement, floored with similar stonework to that in the bedroom. I walk out into the evening air and I have to admit it does me a lot of good, provides enough balm to give a brochure writer Wanker's Cramp.

Where the balcony ends, there's a low, white-painted, wrought iron fence. I wander over to this retaining structure and have a look over the edge and the impression I get is that it's like looking out of the aeroplane port-hole again; apart from a little bit of the patio-type area across which I made my approach that curves round beneath my gaze, there's nothing but mountainside, dropping away into the blackness beneath the blueness of the dusk. I look away and back towards the sliding glass of the bedroom and work out my bearings a little bit and I realize I'm standing on top of a jutting-out part of the split-level open-plan where D'Antoni first introduced himself to me. Then I raise my eyes a little and in the gloom I work out that part of the upper storey levels off to stop against some more mountain.

I light a cigarette and turn round to face the backdrop again and consider the solitude. But it occurs to me that the splendid silence of the surrounding mountains has nothing on the macaroni stillness that is wafting out of the windows from Wally and D'Antoni, so I smile to myself and cross the balcony and walk back into the bedroom and present myself at the marble bedside cupboard and pick up the piece of Local Cottage Industry and look at it for a moment. Then I go back out through the windows and walk back over to the wrought iron-work. I inhale some of my cigarette then I heave the objet d'art out into the abyss, gauging the arc so the piece splinters on the edge of the patio before shattering out into the canyon's darkness. Then I inhale some more and walk back into the bedroom and listen.

The shocked silence is still hanging in the well of the gallery. Then D'Antoni says:

"Wally?"

Wally weighs up the pros and cons and finally decides that his name is in fact Wally and that unfortunately D'Antoni knows that it is so he says, as non-committally as possible:

"What?"

D'Antoni doesn't reply immediately. There is a crackle of leather as the holster is cleared again.

"What do you mean, what?" D'Antoni says. "Don't give me any of that; you heard what I heard."

"I didn't hear anything," says Wally, like he was lying to his brief.

"You cunt," D'Antoni says. There is a short silence. Then D'Antoni calls: "Jack!"

I stay by the curtains and don't answer. Then I hear D'Antoni's steps retreating down the stairs and I know precisely where the steps are going to stop. Poor old Wally. He must have been so chuffed to land this number.

D'Antoni's voice is now almost a whisper, but it carries quite clearly up to where I'm standing, amplified as it is by all of Gerald and Les's poncey stonework.

"You cunt," D'Antoni says. "You heard it. You say not. Well, that's fine. You heard nothing. So you won't care whether or not you go outside and prove to me that you heard nothing because there ain't nothing out there to hear. O.K?"

"Hang about," Wally says. "I mean, I know *I* didn't hear nothing, but I mean, *you* did, you said you did, didn't you, and I mean, well maybe you did, didn't you, so, I mean to say, why should I go? I mean, I didn't hear nothing. You're the one what's hearing things."

Even D'Antoni's breather, a mixture of the furious and the paranoid, carries upwards into my ears. There is another silence which D'Antoni breaks by saying:

"Out."

"What?"

"Out."

"Look, do me a favour — "

"Take this and get out."

"It's dark out there. I don't know where the torch is gone."

More silent fury from D'Antoni.

"Listen, there's somebody out there, the last thing you need is lights. You see that, don't you? I mean, you do understand what I'm saying?"

The silence from Wally indicates that he does, in fact, understand.

"So take this," D'Antoni says, "and get out there."

A shorter silence from Wally this time.

"I don't like them," he says finally.

"What?"

"Them," Wally says, "I never have done."

"You don't like these?"

"No. Never have."

This time it's the turn of D'Antoni's silence.

"Jesus Christ," he says. "Jesus Jesus Christ."

"Can't help it," Wally says. "It's my up bringing. My old Mum used to say I could be as bent as a West Ham forward as long as I never carried nothing. Just sort of stuck, that's all."

"Jesus Christ."

This time they share the silence between them. It's broken by a call from D'Antoni.

"Carter!"

It's time for a bit more stage management so I turn round and slide the window to as hard as I can and stand behind the curtains

56

and wait. A moment later D'Antoni speaks, whispering even softer than before.

"You see," he says to Wally.

Wally doesn't answer, being disinclined to see anything whatsoever.

"They're in," D'Antoni says. "They could be inside the villa."

Wally begins to say something in reply but from the sound effects I gather that D'Antoni has bustled Wally out of the hall and back into the lounge, out of range of anything that might come at them from upstairs. So I gently slide the window open again and nick out onto the balcony and feel my way along to the first open equivalent of my own bedroom window and slip inside. Although it's dark I can gather it's pretty much on the same lines as the one I've got so I walk over to the bedside cabinet and pick up the local colour and creep over to the bedroom door and very slowly and very quietly pull open the woodwork.

Not even the sound of heavy breathing makes an impression on the silence. The only noise is the faintly obscene trickling of water from the mouth of the stone fish.

I move to the balustrade and look down at the fish. From where I am the fish appears to be looking up at me, the stone made fleshy by the sheen of the water, and the lips look even more like Gerald's than they did earlier. So I weigh the local colour in my hand, take aim, and heave. It's perfect. Pure *jeux sans frontières*. The porcelain hits the stonework smack in the mouth. The fish appears to scream but in fact it's Wally wondering where his dear old Mum is, and then the scream is cut short by three, four or perhaps even five shots hauled off in the general direction of the fountain and, much as I'd like to, I don't hang about to contemplate the damage which may have been done to the oracle; instead I leg it back across the bedroom and out onto the balcony and as far as the wrought iron work. I look down and instead of half-mountain half-patio, it's all patio, so in fact it's only a minor operation for me to lower myself off the upper level to the point where all the split-levels coincide. I dust myself down and straighten up and listen to the sound of the shooter racing away from mountain to mountain. When there are no more echoes I take a step towards the windows, but before my sole touches the stonework another solitary shot breaks out into the night. Now, I know I'm on my holidays; that so far it's been the biggest fuck-up since our Man got the dates of Wake's Week wrong; that, in a sense, I'm enjoying myself at the expense of others by way of compensation; and that, due to the manner in which I was borne to this situation, I owe nobody nothing whatsoever, the single shot making me hang about for a moment or two.

First, since I vicariously put the porcelain on what I saw as Gerald's lips, there's been no other sound to cause D'Antoni to haul anything off at; and, on top of that, if I'm any judge of human nature, one shot would not be enough for D'Antoni; the clip in the butt of his Teddy Bear substitute holds thirteen, and since when did one atom bomb suffice when you could have the pleasure of Nagasaki as well? The remarks D'Antoni directed at Wally earlier re-enter my consciousness. Wally's refusal to scour the grounds with D'Antoni's other shooter could be reason enough for D'Antoni to give one single burst to his paranoid. So I put my foot down and reach the window and lie flat on my stomach and slide the window open very slightly and call through.

"Wally?"

There are no shots. Nobody answers. I press myself even lower.

"Wally?"

This time something is said, but I don't know what, or who by.

"You all right, Wally?" I say.

"You all right, Jack?" Wally says.

"Yeah, I'm all right, Wally," I say.

"Jesus Christ," D'Antoni says. "Jesus Jesus Christ."

"You on your own Jack?" Wally says.

"Hang about. I'll just check," I tell him. I let them wait for a moment and then I say: "Well, yes. Apart from this geezer what's out here with me. Says he's from the phone company. Come to see about the phone what's off, hasn't he? Heard the lines were down because of all that rain we've been having, know what I mean?"

Joint silence drifts out of the gap in the glasswork. Eventually it's dissipated by D'Antoni.

"You cocksucker," he screams. "You mother. You fucking cocksucker."

I press myself even flatter than before, but I needn't bother because D'Antoni relinquishes whatever place he's been squeezing himself into and crashes through the blind darkness in the direction of the window.

"You mother," he screams. "I should take you out right now. Why don't I take you out. Tell me, tell me – "

I roll away from the window's access and slip to my feet and lean against the part of the outside which is not glass and wait for D'Antoni's entrance into the open air.

There really is nothing to it. I mean, the way I feel after the day I've had, you'd think it might have taken a little extra effort, a slight withdrawal on hidden reserves. But no, it's easy due to D'Antoni's paranoia and somehow that makes the day even more depressing than I'd imagined it could be.

All I do is to use the drunk disarming routine. Christ, the way D'Antoni's laid himself wide open, even Wally could see to it. So when I've got D'Antoni's shooter in one hand and his collar in the other and he's pressed up against the villa wall I say to him:

"Why the single shot?"

D'Antoni looks at me the way a drunk looks at an empty glass.

"What?" he says.

"What were you shooting at that last time?"

"I wasn't. The one I gave Wally went off."

I smile to myself and let go of him and walk into the lounge.

"See to the lights, Wally," I say into the darkness.

There is a slight scrambling and a minute later the soft house lights go up. Wally is like an air-brushed shadow, the gun he's holding metallic and streamlined in relief.

"Give it back to the nice man, Wally," I say to him. "I think he'd rather shoot himself on purpose than have you do it by accident."

I walk past him and up the steps and into the hall and have a little look at the fish's face. I'm delighted to see that D'Antoni's bullets have taken large lumps of stone out of the fish's fleshy stone lips. It looks even uglier than before, and therefore even more like Gerald. After I've inspected the fish I walk back up the stairs and into my bedroom and start to lay out my gear. Even though I'm not staying, I don't want my mohair crushed up any more than it already has been. I'm in the process of hanging it up in the wardrobe when D'Antoni appears in the doorway. I carry on smoothing out the creases.

"I suppose you thought that was real funny," D'Antoni says.

"Yes, Ollie," I say.

"What?"

I shake my head and go back to the bed and pick up a couple of shirts and carry them over to the wardrobe.

"We could all be lying down there with our dicks hanging out of our mouths, if they'd been outside."

"If who'd been outside?" I ask him. "The Eumenides? The Dagenham Girl Pipers? Snoopy and the Red Baron?"

"You'd be in no doubt if they were out there," D'Antoni says. "There'd be no way."

"Yeah," I say, hanging the second shirt. "Well there's fuck all out there, and after tonight the matter will be purely academic as far as I'm concerned.

"And when you get back," D'Antoni says, "it'll be academic to the Fletchers?"

"Oh no," I say. "It'll be much more down to earth, that will."

D'Antoni walks over to the bed and picks up his shooter and looks at it. "Nobody ever took that away from me before," he says.

"You mean nobody ever tried?" I say walking through into the adjoining bathroom

I turn on the taps and start to get undressed. D'Antoni now appears in the bathroom doorway and watches me. He's beginning to give me the fucking creeps. I get into the bath and lay back and when I look up again a shadow has appeared behind D'Antoni and the shadow is Wally, peering over D'Antoni's shoulder, far enough back to be safe. I look at them both and they both look back at me.

They don't say anything and neither do I. So I reach for the soap and start washing myself, looking up from time to time to see that they're both exactly as before, standing there very interested, watching me take a bath.

When I've finished I get out and dry and powder myself and put on my midnight blue dressing gown and walk out of the bathroom which entails D'Antoni and Wally having to move slightly to allow the operation to be a success. The next event for them to enjoy is me lighting a cigarette then picking up my copy of *Men Only* and lying down on the bed and beginning to read. Eventually the silence is broken by Wally.

"I get you anything, Jack?" he says.

"Yes," I tell him. "When the fellow comes round with the hot-dogs, you can leave out the onions on mine."

"You feeling hungry, then?" Wally says.

I shake my head and turn back to the magazine.

"I can do you whatever you like," Wally says. "I got just about everything."

I carry on reading.

"Got some nice steak," Wally says.

"The butchers haven't been affected by the rains, then?" I say, not looking up.

"What?"

"Never mind. Tell you what you can do. You can go and put the kettle on and fetch me a nice cup of tea, all right?"

Wally brightens up.

"Will do," he says. "You like one, Mr D'Antoni?"

"Coffee," D'Antoni says.

Wally hurries out of the bedroom. I carry on reading the magazine.

D'Antoni stays standing where he is. Then after a while he goes over to the window and makes sure the curtains are pulled tight together. When he's done that he goes out of the bedroom.

I lay the magazine down and lean my head back against the wall and close my eyes. I try and make my mind a blank in preparation for sleep but my mind's eye keeps coming up with photo-fits of Gerald and Les and with their faces in the front of my consciousness I start to boil up again about the whole fucking situation. Those eggs. Well this time the liberty taken has been too large. There's no way there's any obligations for me to fulfil in this instance.

Wally reappears carrying a tray as if he's transporting the crown jewels for me to pick a couple out of. He sets the tray down on the bedside table.

"Here we are, Jack," he says and starts to do the honours.

"Where's D'Antoni?" I ask him

"Dunno, do I?" Wally says. "Probably sellotaping all the windows together."

I look at him

"You don't seem very worried, considering," I say to him.

"Well, I mean to say," Wally says, handing me my tea, "they're all the bleeding same these yanks, isn't they? All mouth. One hundred per cent spill. I mean, I don't know what he's doing here, but whichever way you look at it, there's no chance anybody's going to turn up here with machine guns, is there? I mean, that's probably why Gerald and Les let him come here, they thought, so what, what's a fornight's room and board? I mean, they probably never even bothered to tell you seeing as how there's nothing to break sweat over. I mean, they'd not risk you getting knocked off on account of a berk like this one."

"Oh no," I say to him. "They'd never do a thing like that. Not to me."

"That's right," Wally says, the world suddenly beginning to appear to veer back towards its proper axis.

I take a sip of my tea.

"I mean," I say to him, "I don't suppose it's occurred to you what he might be running away from?"

The world tilts again

"What?" Wally says.

"How the fuck should I know?" I tell him. "I mean, we just don't know, do we?"

"No," Wally says.

"And that, apart from being told fuck all about anything, is why I'm flying back to Blighty in the morning.

Wally starts stoking himself up again.

"Hang about a minute, Jack," he says. "I mean, what about me? What if some geezers do turn up? What happens to me? They're not going to stop at him are they? They're not going to say be a good boy, Wal, keep stum like a good bloke, now are they?"

I regret opening up this particular avenue in Wally's mind.

"Well, we don't know, do we?" I say to him. "Maybe you're right: what you said earlier. Maybe he's full of shit."

"Yeah, and maybe he isn't."

The conversation is brought to an end by the reappearance of D'Antoni. He comes into the bedroom sideways and that is because he is carrying a tubular steel poolside lounger, already opened out. Wally and I watch him put the lounger down in the middle of the room. When D'Antoni's done that he straightens up and looks at us, then goes out again.

"What the fuck's he playing at?" Wally says.

I look at Wally.

"Wally," I say to him, "you ever thought of going on Mastermind?"

D'Antoni comes back again with a sheet and a couple of pillows and the jug of champagne and a glass. He dumps the sheet and the pillows on the lounger then walks round the bed to the marble cupboard and puts down the champagne and the glass and points at the remaining cup on Wally's tray. "That mine?" he says.

"Yes, Mr D'Antoni," Wally says.

D'Antoni picks up the cup and takes a drink. He winces and says: "Tastes like the inside of a hustler's mouth after a long night."

He replaces the cup and picks up the jug and the glass and goes back to the lounger. He lowers himself down until he's balancing his backside on the edge then he pours himself a drink and takes it all at one go. Then he pours himself another one and does the same with it that he did before. After he's done that he pours himself another one only this time he only drinks four-fifths of it. With his free hand he juggles a packet of cigarettes and a lighter out of his shirt pocket and manages to light himself. When that's over he looks at me and Wally, blowing smoke out at regular intervals.

"Well, this is cosy," I say after a while.

D'Antoni just keeps looking in our direction.

"Sort of reminds me of when I was in the Scouts," I say. "All boys together." D'Antoni still doesn't say anything. I light up a cigarette of my own and then I say: "Just carry on as if I'm not here, all right?"

No answer.

I smoke my cigarette and when I've finished I put it out in the saucer of my tea cup. Then I sit up slightly and take off my dressing gown and when I've done that I re-arrange the pillows and lie down in the bed. Wally stays standing where he is.

"Goodnight, Wally," I say to him.

Wally looks down at me but he can't manage to think of anything to say.

"It's all right," I say. "Don't bother to tuck me up. I'll be all right."

Wally stays as he is.

"Goodnight, Wally," I say again. "Switch the light out before you go, will you?"

This time Wally gets the message. He leans over and clicks off the wall light and then in the darkness I can hear him pick up the tray.

"What time you want calling in the morning, Jack," he says.

"Don't worry," I tell him. "I'll be awake bright and early. Don't want to miss my plane, do I?"

There is a silence from Wally's shadow, then I hear him move off towards the door. D'Antoni says:

"You going to bed now, Wally?"

Wally stops moving.

"Well, I was, yes," he says.

"Get one of the other loungers," D'Antoni says. "You're sleeping in the hall."

"Hang about," Wally says. "I won't get no sleep with that bleeding fish dribbling away all night."

"I mean up here," D'Antoni says. "Outside the door."

"Stroll on," Wally says.

"Don't be too long," D'Antoni says.

Nothing happens for a moment, then Wally resumes his progress to the door. When he gets there he says:

"Well, why can't I sleep in here with you two, then?"

D'Antoni doesn't answer him.

"Jack?" says Wally.

I don't answer him either.

Eventually Wally goes out of the room. Nothing happens for a while. Then D'Antoni says:

"You asleep?"

"Oh yes," I tell him. "I been driving them home for hours. It's the mountain air."

"You're going back tomorrow?"

"If a twenty-nine bus ran past the gate of this place I'd be on my way now."

"And what do your bosses say when an employee of theirs refuses to fulfil the obligations of his contract?"

"Normally they'd tell him he took a dead bleedin' liberty and then shoot off his kneecaps just so he'd remember why he didn't get a Christmas card next Christmas."

D'Antoni laughs.

"Yeah," he says.

There is a short silence.

"But not in your case," he says.

"No," I tell him, "not in my case."

"I kind of got that impression earlier," D'Antoni says.

There is more drinking in the darkness and then I hear D'Antoni's swallow as it goes all the way down, and the noise of his swallow coincides with the sounds of Wally fixing up his set of camping equipment on the landing outside.

"I could always make you stay," D'Antoni says. "I mean, how about if I did that? I'm the one with the artillery, when all's said and done."

"That's a fact," I tell him, sliding down a little farther between the sheets.

"I could keep you here as long as I liked," he says.

"And of course I'd just naturally let you and your toys stay together, just like last time."

There is a creak as I hear D'Antoni get up off the camp bed and then I can hear him moving around aimlessly in the darkness, propelled by the workings of his mind.

"Jesus," he says at last, after another long swallow, "here I am. I mean, what the Christ am I doing here? I never been out the States in my fucking life before, except to Canada one time. And here I am. In the middle of nowhere, on an island in the middle of a nowhere fucking ocean, with a couple fucking creeps who I don't want to know, just waiting to get off this fucking place."

I turn onto my back. My sentiments exactly, I think.

The creak occurs in reverse as D'Antoni sits down on the camp bed again. There is silence out in the hall. Wally has finished his manoeuvres. There is a sort of non-noise as I sense Wally drift into the bedroom. Then more silence.

"You all right, Jack?" Wally says eventually.

I swear to myself then I push myself upwards and find the light switch and flick it on.

"Look," I say to Wally. "Why don't we do the job properly? Why don't you go and make a midnight snack and get hold of a pack of cards and we can all pretend it's like it used to be, under canvas with the bleeding wolf cubs."

"I was only asking," Wally says, giving his impression of not actually being in the room

D'Antoni passes between us, gargling some more champagne, looking at neither of us.

"I should've known," he says. "Those two cocksuckers. But what choice'd I have? I get off the plane and who else could I contact? They're the only ones, and I get this. I should have got straight back on the plane, taken my chances. I sure as hell got no cover here. They can walk right on in and take all the time there is. The creep'll probably show them to my room and ask for a tip before they splash him all over the plaster. Jesus Christ."

I sit up in bed and lean back against the wall and fold my arms. Wally looks at me and tries to express something that is apparently on his mind but without actually saying anything. I stare back at him. Wally keeps flicking his head in D'Antoni's direction and then back at me but as I give him no response he gives up before he breaks it. D'Antoni's doing his own share of head shaking as well, but after a while he gets back on the lounger and pours himself some more of his drink and drinks it. I wait a while before I say anything.

"Both finished?" I ask them.

They both look at me.

"I mean," I say to them, "you've jacked it in for the night? You've just about tired yourselves out?"

Wally just looks at me and D'Antoni doesn't look at anybody; the champagne and orange juice is almost finished. D'Antoni takes another large guzzle and then puts down his glass and lies full length on the camp bed.

"There's nice," I say.

Wally stays where he is.

"Why don't you go and get your head down as well, Wally?"

Wally looks at D'Antoni, then back at me, the way he was doing before. I take no notice of him and switch off the light and slide back down between the sheets. In the darkness there is the sound of D'Antoni's breathing and nothing at all from Wally because he hasn't moved a muscle, he's still standing exactly where he was when the light went out. Fuck him, I think to myself. He can stand there all through the night as far as I'm concerned. Then there's a slight rustling and there's warm breath on my face because Wally's squatting down at the bedside and he's talking to me in a low voice.

"Listen," he says, "Jack, you can't clear off in the morning. I mean, you can't leave me on me own. Supposing some bastards do turn up? I mean, like he says, they ain't going to ask me what time the next bus leaves after they've knocked him off, are they?"

"Go to bed, Wal," I tell him.

"But Jack," he says, "I'll be in dead lumber, won't I? If they turn up, I'm as dead as he is."

"How dead do you think you can get?" I ask him.

"Beg pardon?" Wally says.

"Go back to bed, Wally," I tell him.

"But Jack — " Wally begins, but his protest is cut off by a cracking fart from D'Antoni, followed by a few mumbled words from the back of the American's throat.

"Oh, for fuck's sake," I say, but before I can lever myself up completely Wally is scuttling on his way towards the door. I lean on my elbow for a while, staring at the slightly less darker patch where the curtains are. While outside on the landing there are the sounds of Wally presumably settling down for the night. I shake my head in the darkness, but of course that will have as much effect as a duck breaking wind on the water, a futile gesture in the surrounding darkness of the mountains, an unseen release to my feelings. I stay like that for a few minutes longer, then I lower my weary bones back onto the sheets and close my eyes.

I'm just nodding off when I'm brought back to the land of the living by a voice from the landing.

"Goodnight, Jack," Wally says. "Anything you want, you know where I am."

Chapter Seven

It's raining, and there's this delicious smell, a smell of frying fish and damp raincoats, and this terrific sound, the splashing of chip fat and the beating of rain on Akrill's plate glass window. I'm back in Villiers Street and I'm only third in a full house Saturday-night queue and at home there's Man waiting with the wireless tuned to Saturday Night Music Hall. The mixed sound of the beating rain and the splashing fat gets louder and louder and the heat from the chip machine gets louder and then I wake up and I realize that the heat from the frying chips is the breath of Wally on my face and the frying sound is the hissing noise he's making and maybe the chattering of his teeth could account for the noise of the rain, but I couldn't be too sure about that, not that I really care because I'm much too preoccupied with taking hold of Wally by his scrawny neck prior to putting one on him, but I don't get round to doing that because somehow the tone in Wally's strangulated voice makes me hold off until I listen to what he has to say.

"Jack, for fuck's sake," he croaks, "Listen. There's some fucker outside. What I mean is, some fucker's trying to get in."

In the darkness I squeeze my eyes tight shut as an aid to concentration. And when I've concentrated I say to him: "Listen, you fucking chancer. All you fucking well heard was the sound of your bottle disintegrating."

"I didn't. I didn't. Somebody's outside."

I begin to reach up for the light but Wally's eyes, like those of a shithouse rat, have sussed out my projected action and before I know what's happening he's lying on top of me, gripping my wrist.

"Jack, no," he says. "Don't do it. They'll see."

I shake my wrist free and try and push Wally off the bed but he grips me like a demented leech and we both go off the bed, sheets and all, and as we cockle over the coffee tray is caught by Wally or the sheet and crashes down onto the floor. The noise is so startling that it temporarily stills our own and our movement. We listen to the darkness. The only sound is that of D'Antoni's breathing drifting off the camp bed.

"Listen, you cunt," I begin, but Wally cuts me off.

"No, wait," he says. "It's right. I heard somebody. I mean, I couldn't sleep out there, could I? Felt like Morden after the last train'd gone, didn't I? So I'm just lying there on my back looking up at the darkness when I hear somebody walk up the front steps and try the sliding doors. The whole glass shuddered. So I got off my pit and went to the edge of the gallery and Christ if it doesn't happen again. Straight up. So I come in here and tell you, don't I?"

I lie there in the darkness and give Wally's theory a little listen and I'm just about to tell him my views on everything when what Wally's just said happens again. The shuddering sound drifts up into the gallery and along the landing. Wally's in too much of a state of macaroni to tell me I told you so. I manage to unfurl the sheet off me and I scramble about and on the floor find my dressing gown and then I stand up and follow the sound of D'Antoni's breathing. When I get to the camp-bed I carefully take the big shooter from his holster and reflect on how D'Antoni's managed to live so long. Then I make for the lighter darkness of the door that leads onto the landing and walk along the parquet work to the gallery rail. Down in the lower reaches the fish is still dribbling away but apart from that there are no other noises. Somewhere there must be some kind of light source because a couple of pallid reflections dance slowly in the plate glass as a result of the recent shudderings; but there's certainly not enough light to reveal any movement I might make to any observer outside so I start to puss-cat down the steps. When I get down to the hall level I wait for a moment and have another listen. Nothing. So I take another step forward and just as I do that there's more hissing from up in the gallery. I turn and look upwards and I can just make out Wally's vague shape craning over the rail.

"Jack," he croaks. "They're up here. They're outside the bedrooms up here."

I go back up the steps.

"You what?" I whisper.

"Up here. They're trying the bedroom wossnames."

"Windows?"

"Yeah, them."

"Which one last?"

"The one next to yours, wasn't it?"

I go back down the hall and into the bedroom next to mine. Like everywhere else, the curtains are drawn right across the expanse of plate glass. The bedroom is roughly the same size and plan as my own so I walk across to the windows and stand there an inch or so away from the curtain and listen. Whoever was there isn't there now because they've moved along a room and they're trying the windows to that one and whoever it is isn't doing the best job in the world of keeping quiet about it. Very carefully I find the gap in the curtains and slide my hand through and locate the bolts on the sliding glass and ease them out. I listen for a moment. Whoever is outside is still having a go at the other window. Even more carefully than I slid the bolts, I exert some pressure on the window and it glides noiselessly open a few inches. Cool mountain air sidles in through the crack. The sounds from outside have ceased for the moment. I slide the window open a bit more and it's as noiseless as before. It's now wide enough for me to step through. If I want to. The attention the other window's been getting starts up again. Very slowly I poke my head through the gap. I can just make out a shadow shaking at the handles of the next window. There only seems to be one shadow but that's something I can't be sure of so I straighten up and stand there and wonder what the Christ I'm going to do about it but as it happens I don't have to come to a decision because the sounds from the other window stop and there's the new sound of footsteps returning to the window I'm at. I step smartly out of the gap and stand shielded by the curtain, not moving at all. The footsteps stop and there is a short surprised breath from beyond the curtains and also I notice something else, and that is that there's not only the aroma of the assorted mountains drifting in through the gap, there's the smell of a rather cheap perfume, cheap and nasty but nice. Then the figure that's wearing the perfume steps through the gap and into the bedroom and all I have to do is to reach out and grip the figure's arms behind its back and slap a hand across its mouth and while all the threshing and squirming and suppressed squealing's going on I call out to Wally, wherever he is.

"Wally, the light."

A shadow scuttles in from off the landing and almost immediately the bedroom is suffused with the kind of glow my bedroom was suffused with and now I can see the figure I'm wrestling with and as I take it in it occurs to me that I wouldn't mind the best of three falls with this particular opponent. The reason being that she's got beautifully cut short black hair, she's got a body that flatters the blouse and the satin trousers rather than the other way around, and in spite of the way I'm squashing her face I can tell that she and everyone whoever gazes on it will be more than happy with the way it's arranged and the effect that arrangement has. But what, at the moment, is unavoidably more interesting is Wally's reaction to the intruder.

"Jesus fucking Christ," he says. "What you doing here?"

As he speaks he walks forward towards me and the girl, looking for the first time tonight as though he's got a set of balls. The girl stops struggling but she doesn't relax and neither do I except to take my hand away from her mouth.

"What the bleeding hell's going on?" the girl says, looking at me as if I need to blow my nose. "Just what is this?"

"What do you mean, what is this?" Wally says. "What is *this*. Just what the Christ you think you're doing? Eh? I mean, what are *you* doing?"

"What's it look like I'm doing?" she says. "Trying to get in the flaming villa, wasn't I?"

"Listen, don't come the snot with me," Wally says. "I'll haul you one off if you're not careful."

"Yes, I expect you will, seeing as how you've got somebody to hold me first. Just your drop, that is."

And as the girl says, Wally's drop it appears to be, because he starts to do just that so I let the girl go and she's fast enough to dodge the swinger, leaving me to catch Wally's wrist in my hand and get a grip on him.

"Ease off, eh?" I tell him. "Evens?"

Wally looks at me, then relaxes. I let go of his wrist.

"Well," he says. "I mean to say."

I look at the girl. She's massaging her wrists where I was holding her. She looks back at me and she hasn't grown to love me any more over the last minute or so.

"Well?" Wally says to her. "What about it?"

"What about what?" the girl says.

Wally takes a step forward but I speak to him and he stops.

"Wally," I say to him, "when are you going to introduce me to the young lady?"

"Young bleeding lady?" Wally says. "My arse she is."

"Charming," the girl says.

"Listen, my girl, the day I call you a young lady's the day you start behaving differently from the way you been doing the last seventeen years, all right?"

I take out a cigarette and as I'm lighting up I say to Wally: "I take it, then, Wal, that this happens so to speak, to be your off-spring."

"Too bleeding right," Wally says.

"I wish I could say there's a family resemblance, but I'm glad to say there isn't," I tell Wally.

Wally and the girl glare at each other. I blow out some cigarette smoke. The girl turns her attention back to me.

"Could I have one of those?" she says, indicating my cigarette, her expression the same as it's been since I took my hand from her mouth.

"You smoke, do you?" I ask her.

"When you start smoking, then?" Wally asks her.

"What for?" she says.

"What you mean, what for?" Wally says. "Since when could you afford packets of fags on your grant, then?"

The girl gives Wally the kind of condescending smile she'd reserve for a twelve-year-old in a blazer who'd just tried to chat her up.

"I don't necessarily have to *buy* them, do I?" she says.

"I see," Wally says.

The girl snorts and the snort coincides with taking a cigarette from the packet I'm extending to her. She then makes a big production of putting the cigarette in her mouth and accepting the light I offer her and when she blows the smoke out it's like the last time I saw Natalie Wood in 'Rebel Without a Cause' on T.V.

"So," Wally says, "let's get back to starters. What the bleeding hell you doing here?"

The girl blows out some more smoke and says:

"Come for me Christmas vac., haven't I?"

"You what?" Wally says.

"Christmas with Daddy, isn't it?" she says. "Dear Octopus time, isn't it. Family ties and all that."

"Christmas holidays?" Wally says. "Christmas holidays? You're supposed to be in college another couple or three weeks at least."

Another puff of the cigarette.

"Yes, well," she says.

"You been slung out?" Wally says. "That's what it is. You been bleeding well slung out. Jesus. I knew it. First off, when you first got the idea in your head, I knew it wouldn't last, one way or another. Bleeding art school. I ask you. All your mates making themselves forty quid a week as temps and throwing it all over the place on the gear but you were so bleeding right, weren't you. What you really wanted to do, wasn't it?"

"I haven't been slung out. I finished my exams, didn't I? After you've finished them, there is bugger all to do, is there? I mean, you just hang about, doing darn all. So I just left early. Lots of us did. Nobody cares."

"Oh no," Wally says. "Remember you said that when you're out on your arse after you get back."

The girl gives him her smile again.

"Anyhow," Wally says, "what you mean turning up without warning? Why didn't you let me know you was coming?"

The girl shrugs.

"Why should I?"

"Cause it might not be convenient, that's why. The Fletchers might be here. They might be entertaining or something. This isn't my place, you know."

"Really?"

"If you turned up and the Fletchers was here they'd be well pleased."

"They would. The thinner one's always fancied me."

"Less of that."

"Fetched after since I was twelve, he has."

"You got a good opinion of yourself, you have."

I decide to let the family discussion run its course without me. The brilliance of the exchange is making me feel thirsty so I cross the bedroom and switch on the landing light and go downstairs and into the lounge and pour myself a glass of champagne, and I stand in the middle of the room drinking it and while I'm doing that I reflect that at this time of night, back in the smoke, I'd be having the same kind of drink, in a different kind of quietness, in the club, after all the punters had taken their last illusions home with them. And there'd be the soft comfortable sounds of the staff taking care of their clearing up, and I'd be sitting at my table, perhaps with Con or with Audrey, not saying much, perhaps discussing the merits or not of the Hammers' new goalkeeper, or how funny it was to learn that George Clark had been found a danger to shipping near Putney Bridge, how surprising, who would have thought it, that kind of thing. And then after the conversation, and the champagne'd finished, I'd leave and take the slow ten-minute, near-dawn walk across Soho to my flat, picking up the papers on the way, and when I got in, I'd put some bacon in the pan, and while that's sizzling slowly, I'd have a quick shower and then I'd get into my pit with my bacon sandwich and the papers and a pint mug of tea and I'd spend an hour drifting towards drowsiness, a mood orchestrated by the sound of the hotel dustbins and rest of re-emerging Soho, and to wake five hours later to the mid-morning thin London brightness streaming in through the flat windows. But instead I'm here in the splendid silence of the mountains (the image of which will be carried back a million Kodachromed times to Blighty), listening to the droning whitter of a family domestic drifting down from the Spanish heights, sparring with the nail-driving of a tenth-rate member of the Brotherhood. So I pour myself another glass of champagne and walk over to the window and draw back the curtain and look out at the mountains. It's not yet quite dawn and that transitional thick uniform blueness flattens out all the different angles and perspectives, making the aspect look like a sketchy backcloth on BBC 2.

While I'm taking in this mind-reflecting monotonous aspect the sounds of Happy Families starts filtering down the stairs and the next thing I know the young bird has entered the room and has found the drinks and is pouring herself some champagne. Her entrance is closely followed by that of Wally, who's opening line is this:

"I want to know how you got up here, that's what I want to know."

The girl takes a sip of her drink.

"I got a lift, didn't I?"

"A lift? At this time of night? With a bleeding wop?"

"No, not with a bleeding wop."

"Who with then?"

"Some students who were on the flight. They'd hired a car and they were going past here because they're camping over at Solla, aren't they?"

"All fellows, were they?"

"As far as I could tell. I mean, I suppose if I'd gone into the bushes with them I could have found out, like they wanted."

"What?"

"Oh, for Christ's sake," she says, taking another drink.

"They asked you to go into the bushes?"

She looks at me in despair.

"What do you do," she says, "in the face of such monolithic gullibility?"

"Where I come from," I tell her, "what you do is that you very likely get a smacked arse."

The girl turns on the look from upstairs again.

"And where would that be?" she says.

"From under a wet stone?"

"Listen — " Wally begins, but I cut him off.

"It's late, Wally. Let's cut it all out, shall we?"

"Oh, Top Cat, this one, is he?" the girl says.

"Listen, Tina, this is Jack Carter. Know what I mean. Just leave it out, eh?"

"Oh yes? I heard about you."

She pours herself another drink.

"You're the one that does all the damage but never gets his name in the papers, isn't that it?"

I just look at her and say nothing.

"Down our way you never buy a drink, isn't that right?" she says.

I still say nothing.

"You on your holidays as well, are you?" she says.

That was the general idea, I think to myself, a happy holiday at the villa of your choice, under still warm Spanish skies in November, drinking Sangria with new-found friends while the friendly staff attend to your every whim.

"Wally," I say, "I'm going back to my pit for what's left of the night. If anybody else turns up, like, say, the Band of the Coldstream Guards, just leave me out of it, all right?"

I down my drink and walk out of the room and back up the stairs and into the bedroom. D'Antoni is still as he was left, feet apart, mouth apart, a human flytrap, miles apart from the reality of him being in the fantasy world of the Fletchers' villa, miles apart from the real or imagined anxieties about the arrival of his own personal Furies. I wish I was as many points removed from my present, and none the less for the fact that when, for the third time that night, I get my head down, it's lifted once more by the moth-like presence of Wally flitting by my bedside and whispering words of seduction. This time, he's back on the theme of personal safety.

"Jack," he says for openers.

So for openers I raise myself off the pillow and throat him and he coughs and splutters and I say to him:

"Wally, you really are pushing the good luck you've had all your life."

Wally's sweaty hands grip my wrists and try and force them off his neck; of course there is no danger of that but I don't really feel like taking Wally's lifeless form out of the bedroom and onto the patio and hurling him into the chasm and then going back to bed for the extra hour and a half. So I let go of him and I let him massage his neck and get his breath back in order for him to lay on me whatever he considers urgent enough to put his life in my hands.

"I'm not taking liberties, Jack, honest I ain't," he says, "but I got to put it to you, straight up, you can't troll out of it, not now."

"Oh, yes?"

"Not now, not now Tina's here. On account of, well, if the geezers turn up, she's going to be for it as well, ain't she? They ain't going to leave her out of it, are they?"

"You leave her out of it, Wally," I tell him. "You leave her out of it by sending her back on the plane with me in the morning. That's the way she gets left out of it."

"How can I do that?" he says. "I'd have to tell her what for, and Gerald and Les'd nail me up if ever I did that. You know what they'd do."

"How the Christ do you think they're going to find out?"

"D'Antoni'd tell them Tina'd been and gone in a day and she'd left with you. They'd work the rest out for themselves, wouldn't they?"

"You're giving them a lot of credit, Wally?"

"Jack, you know what they're like."

I had to admit, yes, I do know what those bastards are like, but I only admit it to myself, not to Wally.

"Jack, you can't leave us in the shit," Wally says. "I know you been dropped in it yourself, but, I mean to say."

I lie back on my pillow and stare up at the dark of the ceiling.

"What's she doing now?"

"I put her in the next bedroom. It adjoins your bathroom."

I don't say anything.

"Jack?" Wally says.

"What she have to say about the camp bed on the landing?"

"I told her I was kipping down there as I was listening out for you to arrive."

"She wear that?"

"Course she did."

"And what about the Sleeping Beauty?"

"Haven't told her yet, have I?"

"He'll be well pleased when he gets back from Paradise."

"He'll be better pleased if he knows you're staying."

I don't answer.

"Jack?"

"Wally," I say to him, "there's only two things I'm going to guarantee right at this precise moment in time. One, I'm going to get some sleep and you're fucking off out of it and back to your pit on the landing."

"Jack – "

"Wally."

After a moment or so the shadow of Wally shuffles away from my bedside. I close my eyes and I blank everything out of my mind and wallow in the wonderful relaxed tiredness that's going to usher me into the arms of Morpheus, but like sometimes during National Service, particularly one time in winter, in Oswestry of all fucking places, I'd been on duty all night, just aching for my pit, sometimes nodding off for a half minute and dreaming I was actually between the blankets, only to jerk back into the reality of the ice cold – I remember, when I'd finally signed off, and actually got between the blankets, that I was buggered, really dead, but sleep wouldn't come. The more I'd urged it, the less likely it got that it would come, and in the end, I'd dropped into a deep sleep about five minutes after my official kip was due to be up. And now it's the same fucking issue, can I as hell as like get off. D'Antoni's rasping and Wally's thrashing about on the other camp bed fills the front of my head. And coupled with that, I can hear Tina moving about in the bedroom beyond the bathroom, sorting her gear out. And then eventually she gets herself sorted and decides to use the bathroom, of which she makes full use for approximately three quarters of an hour. Bottles are placed, clinking on the ceramics, tissues are torn, taps are run, the toilet is flushed approximately twenty-five thousand times. After that she seems out of ideas and finally decides to go to bed and by that time I've given up on trying to sleep and I'm sitting in a cane chair, wide awake, smoking cigarettes, watching, in the half light, to pass the time, the slight un-symmetrical movements of D'Antoni's open mouth as he inhales and exhales his sleep of the unjust. Finally even that loses its fascination so I get up from the chair and go over to the curtains and part them a little way. The mountains are now ochre – sharp in the dawning of the day. Boring, but ochre – sharp, nonetheless. I look at the nothingness. You can take in the whole panorama, from right to left and in between, there's nothing in the landscape to relieve the monotony, to hold the attention.

I light another cigarette and at that point D'Antoni awakes. Although I have my back to him I'm made aware of the event by

D'Antoni crying out at his moment of consciousness.

I turn and look at him.

He's propped up on his elbows, one hand squirming across his chest for the butt of the automatic and his head is flicking from side to side like a fish trying to get a hook from its gills. His eyes are squitty from the amount of champagne he's sorted but the lids are not bunged up enough to prevent his eyeballs swivelling about like Catherine Wheels, trying to spin to some kind of focus, to get him to some kind of reference point about who he is and where he is and why he's who he is and where he is.

I smoke my cigarette and watch while D'Antoni co-ordinates himself, while he manages to release the automatic from its holster, while his eyes slow down and come to rest on his surroundings and his situation and finally on myself. And when his gaze has settled on me he holds the pose, as if by concentrating on me the reality of his situation will achieve a sharper definition.

All I do is to carry on smoking my cigarette. Eventually D'Antoni manages to speak.

"What's wrong?" he says. "What's happening?"

I don't answer him. Let him sweat.

"What's wrong?" he says again, only this time his words are accompanied by actions, those being to try to get off the camp bed, but of course he's not sufficiently together to execute it properly so he and the camp bed go over in a swirl of sheets and cursing but no sooner has he hit the deck than he's on his feet, still with a grip on his shooter, looking at me as if somehow I'm responsible for his falling out of bed.

He shakes a sheet from round his shoulders and advances towards me, arms at full slope.

"You bastard," he says. "What goes on?"

I spread my hands.

"Nothing at all," I tell him. "Not as far as I know."

"What's the idea of standing over by the window?"

"I couldn't sleep. I thought I'd see if the boring view might help."

D'Antoni looks at me, then he backs off and sits down on the end of my bed.

"I feel terrible," he says. "I feel like the cat's crapped in my mouth." He stands up and staggers towards the door.

"I got to get some sleep on a real bed," he says.

He bangs against the door jamb and goes out onto the landing and somehow manages to avoid Wally's cot and staggers off to find his bed. Suddenly I'm overcome with the sleepiness I've been waiting for, so to myself I say sod it all and I put out my cigarette and crawl into my pit and I don't have to anticipate the feeling because the minute my head's down my eyelids are heavy as flagstones and my mind begins swimming away from me, but unfortunately it doesn't get far from the shallow end because the most God-almighty shrieking starts up as though it's never going to stop, and that's followed almost immediately by Wally cockling out of his camp bed and trying to decide what the noise is and where it's coming from. As I've already sussed where it's coming from and I'm totally awake again I get out of bed and walk through the bathroom and switch on the light and open the other adjoining door thus illuminating the scene in front of me, which is this: Tina, her shoulders on the bedroom floor, her legs thrown wide still up on the bed, and D'Antoni, his torso straddling Tina's, one hand gripping her throat, the other grasping the automatic, thrusting it into her left breast making it rather less symmetrically attractive than when I was struggling with her earlier on. But what does add a certain attraction to the scene is that Tina is stark naked, waving and kicking her legs at whatever parts of D'Antoni are accessible, at the same time trying to grasp whatever hair D'Antoni has left on his head; from where I'm standing she'd be better off going for the hairs on his chest. Now, coincidentally to my opening the bedroom door, Wally appears on the scene, and his reactions are very interesting because whereas before, when D'Antoni mentioned Dunkirk, Wally was prepared to have a go and put his head on the block, now that he's confronted with the spectacle of his naked daughter, legs akimbo and bollock naked underneath the heaving form of an American mafiosi, he hesitates, weighing the consequences in the balance, and by the time he's decided he should act in the role of the father, other things have happened to cause him to take several steps backwards, away from the forward motion he'd decided to execute; the other things being, that when I opened the door, and the shaft of light illuminated D'Antoni, which coincided with Wally's arrival on the scene, D'Antoni obviously came to the conclusion that the naked girl, the shaft of light, the swift appearance of two other figures, all put together added up to a set-up, and that had caused him to loose off a couple of unprecise shots from his automatic, resulting on three other things; Wally's retreat, my slamming shut the bathroom door, and louder and more hysterical screaming from the girl.

"You mothers," D'Antoni screeches. "You bastards, you set me up."

A couple more random shots hit somewhere or other and I lean against the bathroom wall and close my eyes and open them again as if in that way I might get to a state of waking. But it doesn't work; I'm still back in the current dream-like situation, and that's underlined by the presence of Wally, who's scuttled round from the landing and through my bedroom and now he's framed in the bathroom door behind me.

"Jack," he says, "the cunt's bleeding barmy. He's just bleeding barmy."

D'Antoni's voice filters through the woodwork.

"You think I'm stupid or something?" he shouts. "You think I don't know? Hey?"

Another shot crackles from behind the door. The screaming from Tina is constant.

"Jack," Wally says, "you got to do something. What'll he do to Tina?"

I give Wally a look and then I call through the door.

"D'Antoni, listen. You've got it all wrong. Let me explain."

D'Antoni laughs. Tina stops screaming. D'Antoni says: "You must think I'm really sweet."

"Listen," I tell him. "That's Wally's daughter. She turned up while you were asleep. You just got in the wrong bed."

"You bet I did," D'Antoni says.

"For fuck's sake," shouts Tina. "What in fuck's name's going on."

"Shut up," shouts Wally.

Now it's my turn.

"D'Antoni, it's right. We didn't know she was coming. Nobody did. Just leave off and listen to what we're saying."

Tina speaks.

"Get your bleeding hands off me."

"Leave her alone," Wally shouts.

Then there's silence, because nobody appears to be able to think of anything else to say.

Time passes.

Then the bathroom door bursts open.

I don't have to look behind me to know that Wally has disappeared into the safety of the darkness in my bedroom. D'Antoni is stark in the bathroom's light, as though he's just been overdeveloped in a photographer's acid bath.

"All right," he says. "Tell me again."

His eyes are bulging and his face looks as though he's experiencing maximum Gs, but apart from all that I know I'll be preaching to the converted. Even so, I'd still rather do the polka on a stack of eggs, because the automatic is waving about like a stamen at pollination time.

"Look, it's like I say," I tell him. "She turned up while you were sacking it. You were well away so we didn't bother to wake you up. All right?"

"Why'd she come?"

"She's on her holidays. School's out, and all that."

"Why's she come here?"

I shake my head.

"Wally's her old man, is why. The caretaker. Perks. Got it?"

D'Antoni looks at me as if I'm a figment of his imagination, but nevertheless what I've said seems to reassure him somewhere at the back of his mind, wherever that may be. So when, as a result, the automatic drops to his side, I take him by the shirt and slam him against the wall and slap him around the face a couple of times and when that doesn't have the desired effect either on him or on myself I give him a knee in the crutch and as he gags and jacknifes forward I give him a wide clenched one at the side of his head which sends him grasping at the shower curtains, but by the time he gets to them there's no strength left in his fingers to clutch onto them with, because he's unconscious, and unconscious is how he finishes up in the bottom of the shower, that state having been achieved by a little encouragement from the porcelain that has come into contact with his left temple.

After that has happened, nothing happens for a while.

Through the re-opened door, I can see that the girl is now totally on the floor, staring through into the lighted bathroom at the memory of the events that have just taken place. Her train of thought is broken by the appearance in her bedroom of Wally who even though the action is now over has taken the trouble to avoid the bathroom and has gone round via the landing.

"You all right, girl?" he says.

Tina looks at him.

"You all right?" he says again.

"What the bleeding hell's going on?" says Tina.

"Never mind about that. You all right?"

"Never mind? Never bleeding mind? Christ. Bullets going off and I'm half strangled and never mind? God, I always knew you were involved with some barmy bastards, but this — I mean, I know it's only your only daughter, and this kind of thing happens every day, but you might have tried to row me out of it."

"I was about to but the bleeding shooter started going off, didn't it?"

"Oh yes, it did, didn't it? Look after Number One. Real fatherly instincts, those are."

"I didn't want to do anything to make things worse, did I?"

Tina laughs and stands up.

"You made things worse all your life. Why change at your age?"

Wally looks through into the bathroom and takes in what I'm taking in, which is not only the admirable character of the naked young lady in front of me.

"Look," Wally says to her, "you just get some clothes on, will you?"

Tina looks at him.

"That's all you can think of?" she says.

"Well, it ain't right, is it?"

"Oh, fuck off," she says.

Tina turns away from him and leans over the bed and starts straightening the covers.

"You what?" Wally says.

"You heard," Tina says, not looking up from what she's doing, but the next second she has to because Wally's strode over to her and spun her round and hauled her off a couple round her ears. It really isn't her night. But considering what's happened to her so far she's shown much character, and now instead of taking what Wally's handing out she gives him a couple back. It surprises Wally no end, causing him to step back against the bed, and he has to sit down, very undignified. At the same time Tina walks away from the bed and into the bathroom, past me without looking at me, and through into my bedroom, slamming the door behind her. Wally gets up off the bed and comes steaming through after her but I stand in his way.

"Wally," I say to him, "give me a hand with the geezer, will you?"

Wally looks at me. I bend over and start hauling D'Antoni off the bottom of the shower and of course Wally has to do the same. We carry D'Antoni through into Tina's bedroom and dump him on the bed. Wally scratches his chest and looks down at D'Antoni.

"That's bleeding torn it, ain't it?" he says. "I mean, what the Christ's he going to be like when he comes round."

"You'll find out," I tell him.

"What you mean?"

"Because you're going to sit here with him until he does."

Wally looks at me.

"What you going to be doing?" he says.

"First of all I'm going to have a few words with your charmer of a daughter," I tell him. "After that, I haven't made my mind up."

Wally gives me a different kind of look. I pat him on his face.

"Don't worry, my old son," I tell him. "I'd probably be too tired for that, anyway."

I turn away from him and open the door to my bedroom and close it behind me.

The curtains have been drawn a little wider and now the dawn is bright enough to illuminate the fact that Tina is sitting in my bed, knees drawn up, looking out at the dawn light, smoking one of my cigarettes. As I close the door she inhales and the orange tip glows in the blueness of the room. The sound of the door closing doesn't make her move in any way.

I walk round to the side of the bed where the cabinet is. She's taken all my cigarettes out of the pack and they're strewn all over the marble top and she's using the pack as an ashtray, perched on top of her drawn-up knees. I take a cigarette from the cabinet top and pick up my lighter and light up. Although I've pushed through her line of vision she doesn't waver from gazing out at the mountains. I put the lighter down on the marble.

"All right?" I ask her.

She looks up, blowing out smoke.

"Oh yes," she says. "I'm bleeding smashing, I am."

"What happened?"

"You saw what happened. Or do you want an action replay?"

I shake my head.

"No, I mean, I just wondered what he said when he stumbled in on you. Like, I imagine you were terrified, weren't you?"

"No," she says. "I wasn't terrified: I thought it was you."

I smile to myself.

"It's just that the gentleman isn't himself. He didn't expect to find you in the bed. So he over-reacted."

"How do you think he would have reacted if he'd have found

what he wanted to find?"

"I beg your pardon?"

She smiles at me. There is a silence. Eventually she says: "I mean, who the fuck is he? What's he want to go around acting like that for? Shooting bloody guns off."

"He's just staying here a few days. He's been drinking. He didn't know where he was."

"So when he's drinking he starts shooting. Course. Simple, really." She stubs her cigarette out and leans back against the wall clasping her hands to the back of her neck, an action that displays her titties to extremely good effect. She looks me straight in the eye and says: "For a second or so I thought it might have been you."

I look back at her and say nothing.

"You know, in the other bedroom," she says.

"Oh, yes?"

"Yes," she says.

"Why should you think a thing like that?"

She grins at me.

"You want me to tell you what you already know?" she says.

I don't say anything.

"Come off it," she says, still smirking away.

"You need your arse smacking," I tell her.

"Promises, promises."

I look at her and shake my head.

"I know Wally's not the most perceptive geezer in the world," I tell her, "but I don't think even he believes the guff you gave him about why you're here."

"Why shouldn't it be the truth?"

"No reason. Except that it isn't."

"So what is?"

"You've been slung out."

"Oh yes? And why should a nice girl like me be thrown out of a place like that?"

"I wouldn't know, would I?"

"I mean, it'd have to be something pretty bad to get slung out of an art school these days, wouldn't it?"

"I wouldn't know."

"Wouldn't you?"

"I never did finish my thesis on Further Education."

"Oh, you have heard there's such a thing."

"Vaguely."

"And what about your education? When did that finish? Or did it ever start?"

"I learn something every day."

She gives me the look my remark deserved.

"The one I expected was the one about being raised in a hard school," she says.

I smile to myself and while I'm doing that there's a knock on the other side of the bathroom door, followed by Wally calling my name in his low shifty voice.

"Jack?"

Immediately Tina says, in an urgent voice, loud enough for Wally to hear: "Quick, put your trousers on, it's my old man."

Then she falls over sideways and breaks up, face buried in the bedclothes. The bathroom door opens and Wally makes another entrance. This time he's really torn until he sees his little girl's been having him on.

"Yes, Wally?" I say to him.

"Er, it's the geezer," Wally says. "I think he's stirring."

"Oh, really?"

"Well, I think he is."

"Go and have another look, then."

"Supposing he starts hauling off with his shooter?"

"Well you won't have the bother of having to come back and tell me because I'll hear it, won't I?"

The girl's still having hysterics into the bedclothes.

"I'll knock seven kids of shit out of you later on," Wally says to her, turning back to the bedroom.

Tina sits up and wipes a tear from her eye.

"What a twit," she says. "But then, he always was."

I lean over and grab her by the wrist.

"Yes, and he's your old man and he was always that, too," I tell her. "So show a bit of respect."

She shakes her wrist free. "Respect for him? You're joking. Let him earn it. He's been like this all his bloody life, a frightened little crawler. He makes me sick."

I grab her wrist again.

"He's still your old man."

"In name only. He's here all the time, isn't he, and I've always lived with my auntie Lillian, so what sort of a family feeling does that generate?"

"He done what he had to."

"No he never. He didn't have to come out here. He came out because he wanted to. He couldn't believe his luck, dropping in this one. I didn't even enter into it. He gets himself pensioned off lovely and I can bleeding well whistle as far as he's concerned."

I let go of her wrist. I have to admit that there isn't a word she's said that isn't true and that my opinions and her opinions of her old man are approximately on the same level.

"Anyway," she says, "where do you come off telling me how I should carry on?"

I pick up the cigarette packet and stub my cigarette out.

"Forget it," I tell her.

"Full of the old-style values, aren't we?" she says. "Who did you vote for last time?"

"I said forget it."

I light another cigarette and go and sit myself carefully down on the edge of D'Antoni's camp bed. Tina looks at me.

"What do you think you're doing?"

I don't answer her. Instead I lift my feet off the floor and lie down on the camp bed and carry on smoking and do some more ceiling staring.

"You going to stay there all night?" Tina asks me.

"There isn't exactly a lot of it left," I tell her.

Wally's voice drifts in from the far bedroom.

"Jack?"

"What, for fuck's sake."

"I don't think he is coming round."

I close my eyes and don't answer.

Apparently Wally has no other information for me.

"Oh, well," Tina says, "I think I'll get my head down. If you see what I mean."

There's the sound of her sliding down between the sheets and making exaggerated snuggling noises, soft and feminine, at definite odds with the character that has so far been demonstrated. Just goes to show that having no parents to speak of can't always be bad, I think to myself. I finish my cigarette and stub it out in the packet. Then I lie down on my back again.

The snuggling sounds continue from my bed and it's making me feel, well, ready for sleep, I can tell you. In the end I say to her: "Leave it out, will you?"

'Mmm?"

"I said leave it out."

"Just tell me what it is you particularly want leaving out and that's what I'll do."

"Leave it out." I clench my teeth. "Listen," I say.

"I'm listening."

"Look, forget it. Just go to sleep and forget it."

"I tell you what: I promise I'll forget it if you promise to forget it. Do you think you'll be able to do that?"

"Remember what I said about smacking your backside?"

"Never stopped thinking about it."

"Well don't think it'd be as pleasant as you might imagine, I can tell you."

"You don't know about that, do you?"

"What you been studying, for Christ's sake. Do your thesis on Medieval Flagellant Engravings, did you?"

"Maybe I would if – "

"– if you hadn't got the elbow."

This time she doesn't answer. Instead she does a shuffle in the sheets and then all is stillness and silence and thank Christ for that. I lie there for ten minutes, tense, just waiting for nothing in particular, just something else that'll stop me having at least half an hour's kip, like my pyjamas catching fire or D'Antoni shooting Wally dead, or the whole fucking villa sliding off the top of the mountain and disappearing down the chasm. The ten minutes extend to fifteen and I'm just beginning to believe in Fairy Godmothers when of course it has got to be Wally who shatters my illusions, his voice materializing above my head like something from a fake seance.

"It's no good," he says. "I can't bleedin' stand it."

I don't say anything.

"It's like keeping a flaming vigil, only you know at some point the corpse is bleedin' well going to wake up."

I close my eyes.

"I mean," Wally says.

Very quickly I get up and the cot tips over and I walk out of the bedroom and downstairs to the enormous lounge and I cross it and part the curtains and slide open the windows and walk out onto the patio. The sunlight air has warmth in it even this early and the trace of heat seems to accentuate the silence of the mountains. I walk across the flagstones to the retaining wall that separates the neatness of the patio from the jagged mess of the chasm. I sit on the wall and light a cigarette and look across the breadth of the island to the uniform blueness of the sea, stretching to the horizon, a great big nothing.

Eventually Wally sidles out onto the patio and makes it over to me with the minimum of movement, hoping that I'll be unaware of his presence until he's close enough to engage me with whatever he wants to engage me with. Which is of course, the usual.

"Jack," he says. "You got to stay. You just got to."

I blow smoke into the still air. There is no way I would stay on account of Wally or his brat or D'Antoni due to the way those bastards in London have set me up. But unfortunately I've been set up in another way. And that is by Audrey. When she turns up at the hold and I'm not around to greet her in my own inimitable way she'll wait a while, all right, she'll wait because she's a patient bird but when she's tired of being patient, she's the most impatient bird you'd be unlucky enough to make impatient, in fact she's like something out of the Snake Pit, no regard whatsoever for anything or anybody, and after a while she'd make it up here to the villa and get Wally to tell her the story and Wally, when the wrath of Gerald and Les is pointed in his direction because of my departing, is likely to help himself out of it a little bit by mentioning the nature of Audrey's visit and of her enquiries and what with her in any case supposedly in Hamburg drumming up talent; whatever way you look at it I'd be smiling out of my neck and wearing a red shirt, no trouble; however safe I tried to make myself there'd be no getting away from the razor's edge, and I should know, I've ordered up more than a couple such retribution parties on behalf of Gerald and Les. And so, until Audrey's arrival, when I can explain the situation to her and row us both out of it, which will be in approximately four days time, I will just have to swallow and sit in the fucking sun with this pantomime act and not only just swallow, swallow in front of a brat, a half-arse and a madman.

"Jack," Wally says again.

I flip my cigarette away into the chasm and turn to look at Wally.

"A couple of days," I tell him. "I'll give it a couple of days. But on one condition. You keep out of my fucking way, and when you are in any fucking way, you keep your fucking trap shut, except maybe when it's to tell me dinner is served, all right?"

My reply makes Wally look as if he's just had a face lift.

"Christ, thanks Jack," he says. "I really mean it, I really do."

"Yes, I know," I tell him. "You can show your appreciation by fetching that camp bed out here and you can follow that by bringing me a Bloody Mary."

"Right," says Wally. "Right you are, Jack. No bother."

Wally scuttles back inside and wrestles the camp bed out through the sliding windows.

"Where'd you like it, Jack?" he says.

"On the floor," I tell him.

Wally makes a production out of appreciating my very funny joke and says: "Shall I put it in the shade?"

"Anywhere you like."

"I'll put it in the shade."

I don't say anything. Wally puts it in the shade. Then he goes back inside and a couple of minutes later he comes out with the Bloody Mary all nice and iced up, and he brings it over the wall, by which time I've lit up another cigarette. Wally hands me the drink and says: "There you are Jack; you'll like that one. Dead right this time of day, that is."

I take the drink from him and take a sip. Wally hovers where he is.

"Anything else I can get you?" he says. "I even got bacon and eggs in the freezer, none of your Spanish muck, you can have anything you want."

"Not now, Wally."

"Well, all you have to do is shout. Any time."

"Wally," I say to him, "you like it out here? I mean, do you ever get a bit lonely, like?"

"Yeah, I like it, it's great. I mean, I'm my own guv'nor, in' I, and I have fuck all to do except when Gerald and Les come out; I mean, it's a doddle. Course, I sometimes get a bit pissed off with my own company, but that's to be expected, isn't it?"

"I thought you must do," I say to him. "I suppose that's why you haven't stopped mouthing it since I walked in the door."

Wally actually looks as if I've hurt his feelings.

"I believe the L.S.O. are looking for a good jawbone soloist," I tell him. "I should apply if I was you."

Wally starts a game of pocket billiards with himself. I take another drink and look across the island again. Shining white hotels are like reverse negatives against the deep blue of the sea.

"You get down there much?" I ask Wally.

"Couple of times a week, maybe. Shopping, mainly."

"Go down there for a bit of the other, do you, or do you send out for it, like to the Chinese Chippie?"

"You know me, Jack. Never was strong on all that. Lot of trouble to go to, all that."

"Oh yes?"

"Well, maybe now and then. I mean, I can fix you up, no bother."

"How do you fix yourself up?"

"Well, there's this club, the Picador, you know, the one Gerald and Les got some money in. Biggest in Palma, that is. Very sprauncey, except for the block bookings from the four organizations that make it a bit untidy, but you also get the yacht class in from the harbour, film stars and that. It's fronted for the investors by a geezer called Johnni Kristen, right fucking name that is; I believe he started out in life choreographing some of them post-war, tat-girlie shows what used to tour all over the place. Anyway now he acts as if he's a cross between Lew Grade and Paul Raymond. Majorca's Premier Impressario. A big celebrity."

"I didn't know those two had money over here?" I say to Wally.

Wally doesn't say anything, wondering what sort of shit he's put his foot in this time, and while he's considering that I'm reflecting on those two bastards and their never-ending capacity for deviousness; the point being, they neither of them have told Audrey about it, she being a partner, because if they had, I'd know about it, as Audrey transmits all relevant financial arrangements to me sufficient unto the day when the two of us become the non-natural heirs to the Fletcher Brothers estate. And my reflections lead me to ruminate on how many other little safety deposits the Brothers Grimm have stacked away the length and breadth of the western hemisphere. Well, I think to myself, come the day, the spare sets of books shouldn't be too difficult to locate. It's just that it boils me up that those fuckers, those Mastermind finalists of Brewer Street, should manage to score off me, Jack the fucking lad, their human roll of sellotape, the geezer that keeps them and their operation from falling apart like so much Hong Kong merchandise; all right, so in a manner of speaking it comes under the heading of enlightened self interest, but it stokes me to think of them thinking they're smarter than Audrey without whom they'd never even have had a backyard, let alone an estate.

Wally is still standing there wondering how much he might be figuring in my thoughts.

"So?" I say to Wally.

"What?" he says.

"You were talking about the other out here," I say to him. "And how you get it."

Once more Wally's relief is visible. "Oh, yeah," he says. "That. Well, I mean, it's not generally for me, it's mainly when Mr and Mr Fletcher come over, when they're entertaining, like, or not. What happens is they go down the Picador for a knees-up and bring back some of the cast, you know, the dancers as is supposed to be Spanish what in actual fact comes from Ilford, those of them who aren't averse to earning the odd hundred nicker or so, in whatever manner, or maybe Johnni Kristen's just got on the blower and he sends them up in a Volkswagen bus and the same sort of events transpire."

I don't say anything.

"Why, you thinking along those lines, Jack?" Wally says.

I shake my head.

"It's no trouble. All I have to do is lift the phone."

I give him a look.

"The phone's off, isn't it?" I say to him.

"Oh, yeah, I was forgetting. In this case, I'd just nip down in the Merc and have a word, personal like. I could go anytime you wanted."

I don't answer him.

"Course, there's the Blues. Personally speaking they don't bother me. They got it done out like a warehouse down in the basement. Which of course is what it is. There must be about ten thousand down there, in fifties, what they ship out and replenish from time to time. Even at a tenner a time you can work it out yourself."

"I know the economics of the film industry," I tell him.

"Yeah, course, well you would, wouldn't you."

"Yes, I would."

"Got five hundred shipped in last week. And five hundred out."

"You pass the long winter evening exercising your right arm, then do you?"

Wally actually blushes.

"No, not really, just occasionally run a few through, make sure there's not a dicey batch so there's no come back from the retailers."

"Do me a favour," I tell him. "Those goods always come over mint condition. Ray Creasey sees to that."

Wally shuffles about a bit. I smile at him.

"I got you sorted," I say to him. "I know why you don't bother pulling stuff for yourself from the Picador. You prefer it off the wrist, so there's no sweat in case you can't score your performance full marks, eh Wal? That's why you don't mind being on your own. You got the Blues to keep company with. Isn't that right, Wal?"

By now, Wally's as scarlet as Reggie Eames's shirt after it'd been discovered he'd taken a dead bleeding liberty. But I consider a little bit of jovial sadism isn't exactly out of order considering what I've had to put up with all through the night.

"I bet you run them all day long, don't you Wal. That's why your tan isn't all it should be, eh, Wal?"

"Leave it out, Jack, all right?" Wally says.

I laugh.

"Yeah, all right, Wal, I'll leave it out." I hand him the empty glass. "Just get me another one of these, my old son. No, tell you what, mix me a jug up, will you, there's a good old boy."

Wally takes the glass and registers the fact that he's sulking by going back inside without saying anything. I get up off the wall and walk over to the camp bed and lie down on it. The shade is cool but not cool enough for me to be able to lie down and go to sleep in it; a hundred days out at Cleethorpes as a kid has vaccinated me permanently against goose pimples. Wally reappears with the jug and drags a wrought-iron table across the flagstones to the side of the camp bed.

"There you are," he says, still a trifle formal.

"*Gracias*," I say to him.

This time he doesn't hover about and earhole me about how shit-scared he is about D'Antoni or how delighted he is that I'm staying on or anything like that. He just pisses off back inside and almost immediately, without availing myself of the Bloody Mary, I am off up the Wooden Hill to Bedfordshire, as my old mother used to enjoy saying to me.

Chapter Eight

I am awakened by a splash.

For a moment I am unaware of where precisely in the world I am supposed to be. I open my eyes and I am blinded by bright sunlight which, I realize at once, is why my pyjamas and my robe feel as though I've just stepped from under a shower. The shade has moved but apparently Wally has had the nous to move the wrought iron table to where the shade is and the Bloody Mary jug has fresh ice in it. I walk over to the table and pour myself a drink and when I've done that I pick up the jug and turn round and walk to the end of the villa and turn the corner to find out what the splash has been caused by.

The chasm and the retaining wall make a turn at an angle similar to the right angle the corner of the villa makes, and between the second aspect of the villa and the retaining wall is the swimming pool. Dead centre of the pool, like a doll in aspic, is Tina, floating on her back, a rubber ring round her waist, staring up into the deep blue sky. Floating near her, spinning lazily in the wake of Tina's entry, is one of those inflatable lilos. On the edge of the pool is a towel and that is the only piece of material in sight because Tina hasn't bothered to put on anything except the rubber band or whatever it is that's drawing her hair back from her face, making a ponytail that floats on the top of the water.

I watch her as she swans about, occasionally kicking a lazy leg to change direction, the rubber ring beneath her armpits pushing her tits even higher than ever so that her nipples are pointing skywards at an angle of one hundred and eighty degrees.

Sipping the Bloody Mary and watching the almost prehensile nipples is not in fact an unpleasant way of whiling away the following ten minutes, particularly as the warmth of the sun has by now crystallized the sweat on my soaking pyjamas, causing an aroma that makes me feel a little more at home, reminding me of the kind of smell I wash off in the shower in my flat after I've given Audrey one, or anybody else who might be present at the time, Audrey not being privy to that particular kind of information. Eventually the girl manoeuvres herself into a position from which she can see who's watching her. When she's taken that in, she closes her eyes and lazily does a half circle so that her toes are pointing towards the chasm and I'm presented with a view of the top of her head.

"Enjoying the view of the chasm?" she says.

"I was."

"Dirty old bastard," she says.

"Not so much of the old," I tell her.

"Let's put it this way. Last night we're in the same bedroom, but in different beds. I've been trolling about starkers. The upshot of the situation is that the sleeping arrangements remain the same. Now, that I call old."

I sit down in a wrought iron chair by the pool's edge.

"Supposing I called it disinterest?"

"That's what I mean. Old."

"Your old man wasn't wrong, was he?"

"Has he ever been right?"

"What he said about you having a good opinion of yourself."

"Well you have to, don't you. No bugger else will."

"Depends how you go about things."

"Of course, people have a good opinion of you, don't they? On the strength of how you go about things?"

"On the strength of it, yes."

She makes the other half of the circle and her toes are pointing at me again. Her nipples haven't changed direction at all.

"Oh, yes," she says. "That's something else I was thinking about."

"What?"

"I was wondering if you were one of those persons who got their kicks by bashing other persons about. You know, rather than actually getting down to the other."

This conversation seems to be resonant with vague echoes of the conversation I was having with Wally before I got my overdue kip.

"There are people like that, you know," she says, looking straight at me.

"Oh really?"

"I mean," she says, "they may not necessarily know it, might never occur to them in a million years, but they do."

"They do?"

"Well, like you. Probably enjoyed yourself so much getting a grip on me and bashing that yank about and treating my old man like a piece of loo paper that you hadn't any appetite left for crawling in with me."

"Is that so?"

She closes her eyes again.

"It could be," she says. "Personally, I couldn't give a fuck."

Another half circle, and I get the back of her head again.

I smile to myself and pour some more from the jug into my glass and I take a drink and continue to watch her still closed-eye figure suspended by the reflection of the deep blue sky.

But the peaceful reflection doesn't stay intact for long. It's shattered by Wally doing a Buster Keaton round the corner of the villa. When he sees me he proceeds crabwise along the white plasterwork, looking back over his shoulder to the corner from time to time. When he's finally opposite where I'm sitting he quick-marches across the flagstones like a private trying to avoid a one-stripe.

"Jack," he says, "Jack, the bastard's — "

Then he catches sight of Tina on the surface of the pool and the image drives the information he was about to impart straight out of his mind. Apparently it's driven out everything else as well because all that happens is that his mouth falls open to no effect because no words accompany the action.

"Yes, Wal?" I say to him.

But Wal isn't listening. He walks as far to the edge of the pool as he can without getting his feet wet and then he launches himself another way: "You fucking tart," he screeches at her. "You bleeding' little brass; get out of there and get your fucking gear on."

There's not a ripple on the pool.

"Do you hear me?"

"No."

"Listen — "

Tina starts singing.

"The hills are alive to the sound of music — "

"You don't come out there right now — "

"You'll what? Come in after me? You've spent all your life not getting your feet wet."

"Listen — "

"Get your mate to fetch me. From what I've heard he should be able to walk on water."

"Listen — "

"Oh, piss off."

Any additional dialogue to this exchange is precluded by the appearance of D'Antoni at the same corner round which Wally had made his entrance. Not that it cuts off anything from Tina because she is not facing in D'Antoni's direction, her eyes are still closed, and in any case I get the impression she has nothing further to add to what has gone before. It is Wally, with his shit-house rat's instinct, who terminates the conversation by facing D'Antoni and then shuffling backwards along the edge of the pool, like a man on a tightrope, until he feels relatively secure on the western side of my chair. Why he should worry, except for the fact that he's Wally, I'll never know, because D'Antoni is in no shape to do anybody any harm except himself. At the moment it's all he can do to support himself, one arm at full stretch, against the corner of the villa. He's looking in our direction, but whether he's seeing us or not is another matter. There is a long silence. Tina is motionless in the pool, Wally is motionless by the side of it, and D'Antoni is fairly motionless trying to keep upright at the corner of the villa. The only positive action is myself pouring myself some more from the jug.

Finally D'Antoni detaches himself from the villa and makes it to the edge of the pool and sits down in a chair which is a twin to the one I'm sitting in. Nothing happens for a moment or two. I'm just about to take a sip of my drink when the silence of the mountains is disturbed, and not the only thing that is disturbed, because D'Antoni jacknifes forward in his chair and is violently but briefly sick right into the fucking swimming pool. Several things happen at once; I don't drink my drink, Wally almost imitates D'Antoni, and Tina, for the first time, is upright in the rubber ring, looking at D'Antoni and then at what is gradually floating out from the edge of the pool.

"Oh, for fuck's sake," she says, and splashes her way to the floating lilo and paddles her way to the far side of the pool, where the towel isn't. When she gets there she scrambles out and stands on the edge and gives D'Antoni the kind of verballing he's never heard since maybe he shot the wrong geezer on his first contract, if he was listening. When she's finished she walks all the way round three sides of the pool until she reaches the towel which is about six inches away from my right foot. She picks up the towel and gives D'Antoni some more mouth. D'Antoni just stays as he is, head in hands. Then after she's given him everything she can think of she walks off round the corner, dragging the towel behind her. This time, Wally doesn't say anything to her.

I put my glass down on the flagstones.

"It'll soon go through the filter," Wally says at length.

I don't say anything. D'Antoni says:

"Jesus Christ."

I look at him again. He is no longer bent double. Now he is leaning back in the chair, his head hanging backwards, his face parallel with the sky, his arms hanging, perpendicular.

"God," he says. "Jesus."

Then, abruptly, he stands up. He sways so much I think he's going to bellyflop into the pool. But gradually the swaying slows down until he's more or less vertical. Then he turns around to look at me and Wally. Wally and me look back.

"Is this the end of Rico?" I say to him.

D'Antoni focuses all of his uncomprehending attention on me. He probably never even saw the movie, I think to myself. Then D'Antoni disengages his gaze and visibly seems to snap himself back together. He strides forward and round my chair and grabs Wally by the shirt and says:

"I want scrambled eggs, bacon, coffee, toast, and a lot of fruit juice. And I want it now, O.K?"

Wally nods his head.

"You got all that?" D'Antoni says.

The same from Wally. D'Antoni lets go of him. Wally begins to walk away. "Wally," I say to him, "I'll have the same. Except I'll have the eggs fried and the coffee tea."

"Yes, Jack," Wally says, not breaking step. D'Antoni looks down at me, then at his watch.

"I thought you were going to be out of here by now?" he says.

I don't answer him.

"You staying?"

I still don't answer him. D'Antoni laughs. Then he goes back down the edge of the pool and drags the twin seat to where I am and sits down in it. Then he laughs the same laugh again.

"Bullshit," he says, looking at me with the expression that accompanied the laugh. "A crap artist, I knew it. I knew you'd never have the balls to go against the Fletchers. A bullshit vendor. I saw it, right away. You guys always think you can hide it, but it always shows. I had you figured from the start."

He throws back his head and laughs again.

I light a cigarette and decide against making him eat the jug that contains the Bloody Mary. Instead I say: "You've recovered pretty well, considering you just tried to turn the pool into the Sargasso Sea."

D'Antoni continues to grin at me.

"I throw up," he says, "whenever I tie one on; first thing I do I get out of bed and I throw up. Then I'm fine. Then I eat and after that I'm even better."

"Tonight I'll put you to bed in the bathtub," I say to him.

The smile almost goes.

"Yeah," he says. "I seem to remember that, last night. In the bathroom."

I look at him.

"Yeah, I remember that," he says. "I still kind of feel it." He leans forward, almost confidential. "The last guy did that, he ended his days by way of standing up in a pillar that happened to support a clover-leaf on the outskirts of New Jersey."

"Oh, really?"

"That's right," D'Antoni says.

"Well, I don't think it'd be too good an idea over here. From what I've seen the labour isn't quite so skilled."

"What I'm trying to tell you is — " D'Antoni says. "What I'm telling you — you're a very privileged human being. But the reason is, why I don't take you apart for that, is I need you, in case of certain eventualities. You're all I got and that is better than nothing at all. I just want you to understand my meaning, is all."

I smile to myself. It really doesn't matter, I think. Let him think it. It's too warm to be any other way.

"See," he says. "Where I come from, the crowd of mechanics I'm used to, a guy like you wouldn't even get to hand out song sheets at the glee club. None of you limeys would. Compared to us, you guys are like as scary as the Adams Family. Amateurs. You know?"

"I expect we are," I say to him. "A pity you have to put your life in our hands."

"Right," D'Antoni says. "That's right. But what choice did I have? I had no choice whatsoever. A bastard in the bureau fixed that."

D'Antoni looks at the Bloody Mary jug.

"Here, give me that," he says.

I hand him the jug.

"You got a glass?"

I take a sip of my drink and so D'Antoni takes a pull from the side of the jug, leaving just about enough for the melting ice cubes not to be able to imitate icebergs.

"Why not try that on the pool," I tell him. "It'll clean it quicker than the filter."

D'Antoni takes no notice and finishes off the rest of the jug, cubes and all. Then he sits back and contemplates the mountains.

"Yeah," he says. "A bastard in the bureau. The guy I talked to most. The guy was a genius. You got to give him that."

D'Antoni continues to stare at the mountains.

"Shouldn't have talked to him, then, should you?" I say to him.

D'Antoni looks at me.

"Oh, yeah," he says. "You wouldn't, I take it. You're one of the straight guys, yeah?"

"The only times I talk to old Bill — " D'Antoni's expression causes me to qualify "— is when I'm paying their wages or when they're telling me the kind of thing they get their wages to tell me."

"Sure," he says. "And supposing the Fletchers did a deal with the authorities that served up your head on a platter?"

I look at him without answering.

"Pure public relations," D'Antoni says. "They all figured that because of certain happenings in the State of New York it was time that the Mafia got a sacrificial goat, that goat being me."

He picks up the empty jug, looks at it, puts it down again.

"Yeah, me," he says. "Christ, I never personally had anybody taken out in fifteen years. I'd moved on from that level. Investments, loans, take-overs, stocks and bonds was what I'd moved into. They never even asked me what I was doing, only twice a year. They just gave me the money and I put it to work. I had forty guys working for me. Graduates, most of them; accountants, lawyers, guys with degrees in Business Management. I had 'em all. Then this messy stuff flew up and they needed somebody to be in the papers and on T.V. all the time. But this time they figure some guy off the street ain't good enough, it's got to be somebody heavy. I get wind of all this from a broad who is no longer in the land of the living owing to the nature of the information she imparts. But that's by the by. What I do is I decide to beat the lousy bastards to it by going through various highly sensitive channels that by-passed all sorts of people and led to me doing some kind of deal where I named some really big ones in return for protection like you never seen, a passage so cast-iron Martin Bormann could have used it. I mean the guys I'm with, well, I don't have to tell you the guarantees'd have to be good before I talked about them to anybody. But it's very funny, it really is. The guy I've got to who, believe me, has taken a lot of getting to, the guy I'm going to do all the talking to, he's on the payroll too. I find out because I have a piece of luck. This guy has been playing me along to reassure me before the guys take me out, so I'm under no kind of surveillance. And it's no hassle to get my ass set down over here."

I take another sip of my drink.

"Yeah, me," he says. "Me they wanted to fix."

He shakes his head.

"Well, that's what you get with your crowd of mechanics," I tell him. "You're not safe unless you're handing out songs for the glee club."

D'Antoni just continues taking in the view.

"Still, at least I get my money stashed," he says. "At least I can get to that. Plus what I took out. I got no worries."

I smile.

"Only every morning when you wake up, wondering whether you're still alive."

D'Antoni looks at me.

"When I'm out of here, no way, no way, where I'm going."

I shrug.

"In the movies I've seen, they always catch up with you, even if it's twenty years later, and you're digging your vegetable garden."

"Listen, I told you. Not me. Not this guy. All right?"

I shrug again.

"You know who you're dealing with," I say to him.

To that, there is no answer from D'Antoni. He looks from side to side, then he stands up and shouts at the villa.

"Hey!" he shouts.

There is only the echo from the mountains.

"Wally!"

Wally appears at the corner.

"How long's that food going to be coming?" D'Antoni shouts.

"Couple of seconds. I was just laying the table in the arbor, round here."

"Then lay it again, only inside."

"Yes, Mr D'Antoni," Wally says, and flashes off.

D'Antoni turns round and sees that I'm looking at him.

"It's the flies," he says. "The way they come around, crapping all over your food."

I finish my drink and stand up and walk past him, to the villa.

99

Chapter Nine

D'Antoni's right. After he's eaten, he's much better, by his standards. He's smiling all the time and occasionally cracking jokes that are about as funny as him being sick into the pool.

I pour myself some more tea.

"What time does the paper lad come with the Express, Wally?" I say to him.

Wally shows his appreciation of my funny joke.

"I usually pick up the week's ration when I go into Palma," Wally says.

"Just wondered how the Spurs got on," I say to him.

"Yeah," Wally says, grinning at me and D'Antoni.

"More coffee," D'Antoni says to him.

Wally picks up the coffee pot and makes for the kitchen but before he's a yard away from the table, D'Antoni says: "So where's the broad? The one with the tits and the black black hair, if you get my meaning."

Wally turns round but he doesn't stop moving.

"Tina? Oh, she's about somewhere. If I know her she'd be in the bath."

"She's just been in the pool."

"Yeah, well, you know women."

D'Antoni laughs his laugh and Wally disappears into kitchen.

The dining room is slightly smaller than the other rooms in the villa, which makes it not quite as big as the Savoy Grill. It has the same kind of carpets on the walls as all the other rooms and the arrangement is beginning to make me feel like something out of Alice in Wonderland.

"Well," D'Antoni says, wiping his mouth with a napkin, "at least we now got some ass with which to while away the hours."

"You think so," I say to him.

"That's what I think," D'Antoni says. "No problem with that one."

"Maybe."

"What do you mean, maybe. Listen, I seen broads like that that age before. They know how to turn more tricks than a forty-year-

-old hooker, and enthusiastic with it. We would get broads like that anytime, to entertain associates, and younger. Once, I saw these two ten-year-olds, a boy, a girl, they – "

"Yes," I tell him. "I seen things like that. They make me throw up."

"You're in a minority. Big market in that kind of thing. Lot of people pay big money for it."

"I know." I pour some more tea. "I also heard what happens to some of the kids that took part, to protect some of the senior citizens involved."

"Yeah," D'Antoni says. "Well, those things have to be taken care of."

"Not by me they don't."

"You think I have? Personally? I never had nothing to do with that side of the operation. I just saw some things, now and then."

"Well, on my firm, we don't have that kind of an operation."

"Yeah?" D'Antoni says. "I must know the Fletchers better than you do."

"There's nothing I don't know about the firm."

D'Antoni laughs.

"You should see some of the movies they ship over."

"I don't see every movie the firm makes."

"That's what I mean," D'Antoni says. "Compared to me, you're first grade. I knew where every cent I handled was buried. You're supposed to be their number one man and you don't even know the kind of movies you're making."

I don't say anything.

"A joke," D'Antoni says. "Berll could use you."

"Well," I say to him, "at least I still work for my firm. They haven't decided to give me a free transfer."

"Comes the day they need to, they will," D'Antoni says. "It's the same the world over."

There's no arguing with that, and I'm not going to give D'Antoni the satisfaction of giving him one. Instead I get up and walk away from the table and into the kitchen where Wally has started the washing up. I light a cigarette and watch him for a while. Wally doesn't turn round. He just gets on with the dishes, like a woman not speaking in the course of a barney.

Eventually Wally says: "She turned out just like her old lady, that's what she done." He puts the last plate in the drainer and unties his apron. "The way she goes on you think she'd been mixing with our sort all her bleeding life." He folds the apron up and lays it on the work surface.

"You're out of touch, Wally," I tell him. "Stuck out here in the wilderness."

"I'll be in touch with her when I see her."

"Oh, leave her alone. You're like an old woman."

A voice behind me says: "You should be very happy, then; old man, old woman. Just get the banns read."

I turn round and Tina's standing in the doorway and the novelty is she's wearing some clothes. Only a bikini, but for her it's some kind of breakthrough.

Wally begins marching over to her.

"Leave it out," she says, "I've heard it all before."

Wally keeps on going but Tina ducks round him and makes for the fridge. "What's for breakfast?" she says.

"Listen," Wally begins, but I cut him short.

"Yeah, leave it out, Wally. We know what you're going to say."

Wally lowers his voice and says:

"Listen, Jack, I overheard what he was on about through there. Fuck me, how'd you feel, if it was your daughter was being discussed like that? Eh?"

"Don't worry," I tell him. "She'll be looked after."

"You mean that?"

Tina's crouching down and looking in the fridge.

"I can look after myself, thanks," she says.

"You just keep out of his way," Wally says. "He don't need no provoking."

"Who don't?"

Now it's D'Antoni's turn to appear in the doorway. He's looking at Tina's arse as she's bent by the fridge.

"I said who don't?" he says.

Wally doesn't say anything. D'Antoni doesn't take his eyes off Tina, and even when she stands up and turns to face us his gaze stays riveted on the same level of her body.

"You going to cook my breakfast, then?" Tina says to Wally.

"Cook your own bleeding breakfast," Wally says.

"I'll cook your breakfast anytime, baby," D'Antoni says.

"No thanks," says Tina. "I like my eggs hard."

Later on I'm sitting out on the patio under a Cinzano-style umbrella, wondering how the fuck I'm going to stop going barmy during the next three days when Wally comes funnelling out of the villa and says to me: "He's acting up again."

"What?"

"D'Antoni. He says he wants you inside."

"What for?"

"I dunno. In case, he says."

"Tell him to fuck off."

"He says if there's anybody around looking for him and they see this place is inhabited they'll just naturally investigate."

"He should have thought of that this morning when he was puking in the pool."

"Jack — "

"Tell him to fuck off."

"Jack — "

I close my eyes. Eventually Wally goes back into the villa. A moment or so later D'Antoni's voice comes drifting out of the villa.

"Carter!"

My eyes remain shut.

"Carter."

"Fuck off."

There's a silence. The next time D'Antoni speaks his voice is closer. About six inches from my left ear.

"Listen you fucking creep," he says. "If there's anybody comes along out there they're going to know somebody's here."

"And if they're as thorough as they're supposed to be and the place looks as if it's empty and shut up then they'll come down and take a look anyway."

"Yeah, but if we're all inside we got the edge on them. That way we stand a better chance of seeing them coming."

"How? With the fucking curtains drawn?"

"Look — "

"No, you look. Either way it makes no difference. They've got to be sure before they start popping off and to be sure they've got to get close, know what I mean?"

"You know they already invented telescopic sights?" D'Antoni says. "I suppose you heard about those things?"

"The only way they can get a line on this particular piece of patio is by getting sherpas to carry their equipment."

"They just could, you know that?"

I don't answer him. I just keep my eyes shut and wait for him to go away. It takes a long time, but in the end, he does.

I go inside when it starts to get too warm for me. I go into the bathroom and take a quick shower and after that I'm strolling down the stone steps to get to the lounge and the drinks when Wally interrupts my progress by appearing at the bottom of the stairs.

"Jack," he says. "You got to do something."

"Oh, yes?"

"They're playing patience."

I look at him. "They're playing patience," I say to him.

Wally advances up the steps a little bit.

"Yeah," he says. "They're playing patience and they're getting pissed to the gills."

"They're playing patience and they're getting pissed to the gills."

"Yeah. On that champagne mixture."

I look down at my feet and then back at Wally.

"Wally," I say to him, "you really do have a load of problems, don't you? Every moment, something new to worry about. I don't know how you manage, one day to the next."

I begin to walk past him.

"No, listen," he says. "They're playing strip patience. With two packs. The one who gets out last has to take something off."

"That don't give Tina much a chance, then."

"You don't get it. She ain't lost yet. It's D'Antoni that's losing. He's down to his fucking underpants."

"Well, he's wearing the right pair then, isn't he?"

Wally looks blank. I walk past him and down the last few steps and into the lounge and I discover that Wally hasn't been at the cooking Jerez, the game he's just described is still in progress. Tina and D'Antoni are getting pissed to the gills, only Tina's gills seem to be situated somewhat higher than D'Antoni's as her concentration is more together than D'Antoni's, although he's more than making up for the softness in his head, judging by the hardness elsewhere, and to paraphrase the words of the lady, that't not a gun he's got in his underpants.

I cross the floor and make myself a drink and carry it over to where the game is. The two of them are kneeling on the floor like Buddhas, looking down at their own facing lines of cards like retired generals replaying the Battle of Waterloo. Tina has two aces out and an empty space waiting for one of the two kings showing. But this time D'Antoni looks as if he's better placed as he's showing three aces and all the cards he's got face up are movable, and as I sit down on the arm of a leather settee D'Antoni is in fact engaged in moving the rows. Tina flips three cards from the top of her deck and comes up with a black five which she needs at the moment like she needs a Valentine on February 14th. But as I sit and watch, the thought I have, going on Tina's previous behaviour, is that she wouldn't give a fuck if she had to take her bikini off; all she's really interested in is getting D'Antoni down to the buff, because that's the kind of girl she is.

While D'Antoni's moving his cards, Tina pours some more champagne and orange juice from the jug into their glasses, but I notice D'Antoni gets about twice as much in his glass as Tina does, and while he's flipping three of his cards, Tina flips three of hers and considering she's the age she is and the amount she's had to drink she very neatly palms the Ace of Clubs from the middle to the top, which very neatly releases the two of hearts off a face-down row and after that, when she's turned up the naked face-down card she can move a few more around to her advantage. Meanwhile D'Antoni is merrily flipping through his cards failing to notice that he has a black nine and a red ten waiting to go and although Tina has noticed it, naturally she isn't letting on. I smile to myself, and he prizes himself he's a numbers whizz-kid.

They carry on flipping through their cards. D'Antoni susses out the black nine but that doesn't do him any good as all it releases is a six of hearts and although he's up to the four on his Ace the five isn't in his deck and it isn't showing.

"Looks like maybe this one'll be a draw," D'Antoni says, taking another drink.

Tina looks at the lay-out of her cards and nods solemnly. Then she puts the palm of her hand to her nose and starts to giggle, and the giggle turns into silent uncontrollable laughter and she begins to rock from side to side.

D'Antoni looks at her.

"What's so funny?" he says.

Tina shakes her head but she doesn't stop her rocking and laughing. In fact she's rocking so much that she over-balances and she steadys herself by putting her hand on D'Antoni's crutch and although D'Antoni jumps as if he's just had the electrode treatment, Tina doesn't actually hurry to move and when she does go through the motions of righting herself she makes it more clumsy than it needs to be by shifting her hand a couple of inches so that D'Antoni gets another grope.

"Whoops," she says, finally getting back to her former position, "Sorry about that. No visible means of support."

The hand goes to the face again and again the giggling starts. Then she goes through a pantomime act of pulling herself together and when she's done that she makes a po-face and flips through three more cards – and would you believe it the final ace she needed turns up on top, and when she lays it out it releases all sorts of goodies for her and it seems she's going to have a great deal of bad luck in order for her not to complete her game. On the other hand, D'Antoni appears to be stuck as he begins to flip through the remainder of his deck after not laying anything out the last two times, and he's beginning to think that perhaps the outcome will not be a draw after all, and for a while he just sits there watching Tina move her cards around.

"Now then," she says, when she's moved as many as is presently possible," I wonder if I'll get it out or not? Do you think I'll get it out, mm, D'Antoni?" D'Antoni and Tina look at each other, D'Antoni blank, Tina smiling sweetly. Then D'Antoni starts going through his deck again.

"What happens when the natural course of events takes place?" I ask nobody in particular.

"Fuck all," says Wally, from the safety of the higher part of the split level.

"Beat it," D'Antoni says, not looking up from his cards.

"Yes, piss off," says Tina.

"Here, leave it out, you," Wally says.

"That's what I intend doing," she says, going into her hysterics routine again.

"Listen – " Wally begins, but he's interrupted by D'Antoni heaving himself up off the floor and making in Wally's general direction.

Wally of course begins to back off, but he's too slow because he's trying to give the impression he's not moving and when D'Antoni gets to him he grabs Wally by his shirt and his belt and hustles him out of the room.

"I hope he flushes him down the bleeding toilet," Tina says, searching through her deck to find a card that will fit with what she's already got on the floor.

"Funny how you can go on people," I say to her.

She looks at me as if she's only just noticed I'm there.

"What you talking about?"

"It's just that after what you expressed about D'Antoni's personality by the pool this morning, I would have thought there was nothing else left to say, let alone getting pissed together half naked."

"What the fuck's it to you?"

"I was just thinking, why don't you give Wally a rest for half an hour. Just let his impending coronary sack out for a while, eh?"

She doesn't answer me. Instead she wangles herself another card out of the pack and arranges the cards on the floor to accommodate the new one. When she's done that she pours herself another drink and while she's pouring it D'Antoni returns and sits down on the floor and looks at his cards.

"I locked him in the basement," he says after a while.

Tina moves a couple more cards. Then she says to D'Antoni, "I don't think you're going to do it."

D'Antoni flips through three more cards, then another three.

"You can't, can you?" Tina says.

D'Antoni looks at the cards on the floor.

"You ain't got through yourself yet," he says.

"No, but you're finished.

D'Antoni makes as if he's going to flip through his deck again but instead he drops the cards on the floor.

"Give in?" says Tina.

"You got to finish first."

"I'll finish first," she says. "I always do."

She surveys her cards and flips three more off the deck and comes up with the red jack she's been needing to move a row headed by the ten of spades, releasing four cards still face down, and typically she's able to clear all four cards and open up another row, and from now on it's downhill all the way, and when it's apparent she can get out she says:

"Do you want me to play them onto the aces?"

D'Antoni looks at her cards.

"Ah, screw it," he says.

Tina pours them two more drinks.

"So," she says, handing him his glass. "You lose."

D'Antoni takes a sip of his drink.

"Your pants," Tina says.

"You already got my pants."

"Oh, do beg pardon. You call them shorts, don't you?"

"Yeah. That's what we call them."

"Well, your shorts, then."

D'Antoni looks at me.

"Shove off," he says.

"What, and miss the main event? Always provided it is an event, that is."

"Move it."

"I'm supposed to be your bodyguard. What could be a more appropriate situation?"

"I'm telling you – "

"You're telling me nothing. While I have to be on the same fucking island as you, you're telling me nothing."

D'Antoni looks at me. Tina says:

"The shorts. I won. Give me the shorts."

"Piss off," D'Antoni says, missing his mouth with his glass, the orange liquid slopping onto the thick curly hairs on his chest.

"Listen," Tina says. "I know what you're fucking banking on with me, sooner or later. If you don't want to fuck up your chances, give me the shorts.

D'Antoni has another shot at getting his drink in his mouth and this time he's more than fifty per cent successful. His eyes are glazed over a little bit, partly due to the booze and partly due to the prospect of getting stuck into what he partly sees before him.

Eventually he says: "Aw, fuck you."

Then somehow he manages to get up off the floor and to stay upright long enough to push down his shorts and step out of them. Then he laughs. "Worth waiting for, hey?" he says.

Having said that he reels backward and plants himself down on one of the leather settees making a sound like a diver hitting the water wrong.

"Yeah," he says.

Tina, at any rate, seems to be quite impressed, although she's not the kind of girl who's going to show it. What she does is to shrug and take another sip of her drink.

"Yeah," he says. "I never got no complaints."

He closes his eyes and smiles.

"Yeah," he says again.

A minute later he's asleep.

"Jesus," Tina says. "I can see my holidays are going to be real rubbish unless I get out of this place."

"You should have seen out the term at college," I tell her. "More variety."

She drains her glass and wriggles across the floor so she's closer to where I'm sitting.

"Oh, I don't know," she says. "This is variety to me. I mean, when the fellers can't actually be bothered to do anything about it."

I stand up.

"Like you said," I tell her, "it's all down to old age."

I walk over to the curtained windows.

"Oh, fuck off," she says.

I part the curtains and step outside.

Outside it's bright and hot, but just the same I walk round the villa and take in the surrounding scenery just in case the remote possibility of D'Antoni being sussed out beats the odds. Knowing my luck at this present time I'm surprised I didn't step through the curtains to be greeted by a minuteman.

But there is, of course, sod all, except for the stillness of the scrubby foliage and the empty silence of the mountains and the uniformity of the sun's heat. I find some shade and squat down and light a cigarette and think about Southend, at the height of the season.

When I go back in through the curtains, the lounge is empty. D'Antoni and Tina are no longer part of the fixtures and fittings. Apart from their absence the only other thing that's different is the fact that Tina's bikini is lying on the floor, both bits draped across the scattered cards. I look at my watch. Ah, well, I think to myself, if I want any dinner tonight I'd better leave Wally locked in the cellar for a while. So I pour myself another drink and lie down on one of the settees and close my eyes.

When I wake up I look at my watch and I see that I've been asleep almost three quarters of an hour. I sit up and light a cigarette. Tina's bikini is glowing gold in the shaft of light that's streaming through the gap in the curtains. I get off the settee and pick up the bikini and go in search of the castaways. I find them in the room D'Antoni was put to bed in the previous night. D'Antoni is doing his usual sleeping beauty impression, and at first I think Tina's doing the same, until I walk to the head of the bed to wake her up and it's then that I notice she's lying there with her eyes wide open.

"It's tea-time," I tell her. "Time to put your dollies away and wash your face and sit down at the table and eat your fairy cakes."

She doesn't move. She doesn't even blink. I lean closer and it's then that I notice her back is covered in bruises.

"What happened?" I say to her.

Still nothing. I lift her up so that she's sitting on the edge of the bed, but her eyes stay the same while I'm moving her.

"All right," I say to her. "I won't say it serves you right. All I'll say is this; just put some clothes on that cover up the damage and go and lie down so's your old man just thinks you've flaked out. You think you can do that?"

She looks at me without any expression. So I lift her off the bed and carry her through the bathroom to my room and lay her down on the bed. Then I sort through her luggage and find a dressing gown. After I've done that I manoeuvre her into her bikini and then I put her dressing gown on her and it's like laying out my old grandad the time I had to, her body all stiff and her eyes wide open the way they are. There's no way of knowing whether I'm getting through to her but I try anyway.

"When Wally talks to you, all you did was come to bed and lie down and you don't know how D'Antoni got into his pit, all right?"

She looks at me but there's no way of knowing. I turn away and start back towards D'Antoni's room but before I get to the bathroom door Tina says: "Lock the door."

I turn to look at her. She's still staring straight ahead.

"The doors," she says. "Lock them both."

She doesn't say anything else. I go over to the main door and lock it and put the key in my pocket, and after I've closed the first of the bathroom doors I lock them too and put the key in my pocket along with the other one. Then I go into D'Antoni's bedroom and sit down on the edge of the bed. D'Antoni's still a million miles away.

"Hey," I say softly.

D'Antoni doesn't stir.

I put my hand on his chest and rock him gently from side to side.

"Hey," I say, a little bit louder.

This time it's completely different. He snaps up like a corpse on a bonfire and automatically feels for the shooter that normally adorns his chest but of course being naked he only comes into contact with his left nipple. His eyes of course are now wide open and seeing my face looking into his, what with the expression I'm wearing, makes him wish he's making contact with something more than a hairy tit--end. And now, as he's upright, it's not necessary for me to grab hold of what hair he's got and jerk him all the way up off the silky sheet. All I have to do is get a grip on one of his arms and push my face an inch or so away from his and speak to him.

"I just saw what you did," I tell him.

For a moment his face is expressionless, then a sly grin creeps over his delightful features.

"Yeah," he says. "She really went for that."

Now it's my turn to smile.

"You think so?"

"What do you mean? She'll be crawling back. Crawling back."

I stroke my nose between my thumb and forefinger.

"She really liked it, did she?" I ask him again.

D'Antoni grins even wider.

"Sure she did," he says. "You know the kind of broad. Gets her kicks with her lumps."

"Yes," I say. "You mean like this."

I grab his wrist and, because of the surprise element it's not difficult to whip his arm so that he's got to be face down on the sheets as an alternative to shattering his arm. Nor is it difficult once astride him, straddling the tops of his thighs, to keep him like that, partly due to the clapped-out state he's in because of the drinking and the sinewing and the beating, and partly due to the fact that I'm now carrying on where the beating he gave Tina left off, going to work on his back and putting the punches in exactly all the right places. It doesn't take very long and it doesn't take very much out of me, but the good work I put in takes just about everything out of D'Antoni because when I've finished he doesn't move, not because he's unconscious, but because even if he blinks he's going to send bruises rippling through the bunches of grapes that are the bruises on his back. I get off him and pick up the shooters off the bedside table and I say to him:

"I know you're not going to answer me, but I also know you'll do what you're told because your mouth is all microphone; you're not going to tell Wally about anything that's happened this afternoon. Tina went to bed. After that I put you to bed. That's all that happened. All right?"

Like I said, he doesn't answer, but I know he'll do as I say because he doesn't want to worry about me as well as the cowboys he imagines are going to appear on a rim of the surrounding hills. What he does do is to stay just as he is, face down and naked, motionless.

Then I leave the bedroom and go down the stairs to the basement to free the Widow Twanky.

I must say, the basement is a blessed relief from the rest of the house. It reminds me of when I was eighteen and just in the smokes, working at the North Star, and it was always a treat to go down to the damp coolness and put a new barrel on and get away from the madhouse upstairs, which on reflection is not a dissimilar situation to the one I'm in at the moment. Except of course at the North Star it wasn't part of my contract to go about unlocking garden gnomes.

It doesn't take me long to discover which door Wally's behind because at the sound of my footsteps he starts banging on the door, but the banging stops as quickly as it starts; Wally's obviously realized it could be either of his keepers.

I unlock the door. Wally's face peers at me from behind slotted angle racking, his face divided in two by a can of film, the can looking like a false nose placed symmetrically as it is right between his eyes.

We survey each other like that for a moment.

"What's going on?" Wally says.

"Nothing's going on," I tell him. "They're both sleeping it off."

Wally emerges from behind the racking.

"Sleeping what off?"

"The booze."

"Oh, yes."

"It's right. D'Antoni fell asleep, so Tina cleared off to bed. I got sick of the sound of D'Antoni's snoring so I hauled him to bed myself."

"You sure?"

I look at him.

"I was only asking," he says.

Nevertheless he trots off upstairs to have a look for himself. By the time I get to the lounge Wally's checking what's going on upstairs. When he reappears he says:

"Her doors are locked."

"So?"

"Why they locked then?"

"How the fuck should I know?" Maybe she didn't want him going in after her."

"You seen her. You really believe that?"

I shrug.

"She was just prick-teasing. Seventeen-year-olds do a lot of that."

Wally sits down, looking very glum.

"I dunno," he says. "I dunno what to think."

I walk over to the window and look out through the gap in the curtains at the other curtain, shimmering away in front of the empty mountains. Behind me Wally mumbles on about what he doesn't know.

"Wally," I say to him. "You got any *old* newspapers lying about the place?"

The afternoon passes into evening. I'm lying on my back on the sofa and Wally's in the kitchen lashing up whatever we're going to be sitting down to tonight. Nothing else is happening. The ceiling is the same as it was half an hour ago. I light another cigarette and I'm just finishing it when there's a slight movement and the now familiar perfume glides into the room. I raise myself up on my arm and look at her. She's wearing white jeans and a dark blue tee-shirt approximately the colour her bruises will be by now. She walks over to where I am and picks up my lighter and cigarettes and carries on over towards the windows.

"You all right?" I ask her.

She lights her cigarette.

"Bloody smashing," she says.

As she inhales, a great shudder goes through her body.

"Well," I tell her, "now you know."

"Yes, now I know."

A minute later Wally comes.

"What's been the matter with you?" he says to Tina.

"I been lying down."

"Yeah, that's what I was worried about."

She doesn't answer that one.

"Why'd you lock the doors, then?"

"To keep the insects out."

Now it's Wally's turn to keep quiet.

I got up off the settee.

"What's that smell you got coming out the kitchen, Wal?" I say to him.

"What? Oh, that. Yes – "

"Smells t'rific. You sure you're not letting anything spoil or anything?"

Wally gets the idea and reluctantly clears off back to the hot stove. When he's gone Tina says:

"What happens when D'Antoni wakes up?"

"Nothing for you to worry about."

She turns to face me.

"How do you know?"

"Well, he came to me, you know, after you'd been together, and he said he felt really terrible about what had happened, didn't know what came over him, know what I mean? Really terrible he felt. Asked me if I would see my way clear to apologise for him, like. Just couldn't bring himself to face you, he said, after what he'd done."

"I don't want the jokes," she says, "I just want to know he's had enough for today. I mean, otherwise I'll go and lock myself in my chalet again."

"I've told you. You'll be all right."

"You really do, don't you? You really think you're all the Super-Heroes rolled together in one costume."

"It's a good thing for you that I do," I tell her, and walk out of the lounge and up the stairs and into the bedroom she's just come down from. I unlock the bathroom door and start to run a bath. The door to D'Antoni's room is still closed and it stays like that until I've been lying in the bath for about five minutes. Then the door opens and D'Antoni appears. He's wearing one of his sports shirts and a different pair of slacks. We look at each other then D'Antoni flips down the toilet seat and sits down.

"That's two I owe you," he says.

I don't answer him. After a while he says:

"But what I don't figure," he says, "is why? Why put your head on a block? Over a thing like that?"

I still don't answer him.

"I mean, I could take you out over a thing like that," he says.

I lie back and close my eyes.

"Hey?" he says.

Another silence.

"Nobody hurts me. You know that?"

I lean forward and run some more hot water into the bath.

"I should cut it off and stuff it in your mouth."

"I though that was reserved for squealers," I say to him.

D'Antoni is quiet for a minute or two. Then he says: "In your case, maybe I'll make an exception."

"All right, only do you mind waiting until I've cleaned my teeth?"

D'Antoni looks at me a little bit longer then he eases himself up off the toilet.

"You know, you're going to be a whole lot luckier if those guys *don't* show up," he says. "I mean, that way, you only get to be shot."

I ignore him again and all that's left for him to do is for him to make his exit. After he's gone I just lie in the bath for about half an hour, my mind as blank as the silence of the mountains.

Chapter Ten

Dinner.

I suppose you've got to hand it to Wally. He's done a huge Spanish prawny dish with fried rice and he's done it a treat. Under different circumstances it would be a Meal to Remember, one of the Great Meals. But as things are, it's about half as jovial as things were during the Last Supper. D'Antoni spends the whole time alternating between looking at me and looking at Tina, his expression the same for both of us, a sort of hate-filled contempt expressed by a smirk. And Wally of course, in between dishing up, he's wondering what the fuck the looks mean, if I've been straight with him or not, and he spends more time biting back his questions than eating his dinner. D'Antoni is still stoking himself up on the booze, but like I say this time it's not causing him to have the verbals; it's just making his expression smoulder even more grotesquely. Tina looks a little better than she did this afternoon but she's putting as little effort as possible into moving her knife and fork about. On the other hand, I notice that she doesn't seem to be having any trouble in lifting her glass.

So as the atmosphere is laying heavily on my tits, the minute I've finished eating I get up from the table and go through into the lounge and sit down and light a cigarette and pick up an old Express off a pile on a nearby table and for the fifth time I read how Liverpool knocked out the Hammers in the fourth round, as if I cared. By the time I've almost finished D'Antoni appears, bringing his anaesthetic with him.

"You checked everything outside?" he says to me.

"Yes," I say, folding up the paper. "I checked everything. Everything's fine. I've land-mined the road all the way to the airport and the mountains are all dynamited. I left the plunger on your bedside table, all right?"

D'Antoni takes a drink.

"O.K. Give me all that crap. I do it myself, O.K?"

He starts moving towards the windows.

"Gone a bit chilly out," I say to him. "Mind you don't catch cold."

I pick up another paper but before I can sort out the sports page the lights go out. Then I hear D'Antoni making his way across the room. A few seconds later the curtains part a little bit and let some post-sunset light into the room. Then there's the familiar sound of the window being slid open. D'Antoni manages not to stumble outside. After he's disappeared I sit there in the dark passing the time by trying to listen to D'Antoni's progress. Maybe he'll imagine one of the mainland-bound jets has got machine guns sticking out of the portholes and while he's shaking his fist at it he just might fall over the wall and into the canyon below. In fact I'm just thinking I might go out there and give him a helping hand when suddenly the room's full of light again and when I've got used to it I can see that Tina's the one that's pressed the switch.

"What's this?" she says. "Meditation time?"

Even if I was going to answer her I'm not given any time because D'Antoni re-enters through the windows like a Widnes forward playing against St Helens. He hurtles across the room and snaps off the light without having to push Tina out of the way because the minute she saw him coming through the curtains she moved in the opposite direction even quicker than the way D'Antoni made his entrance. Then I hear D'Antoni making his way back across to the window and his progress is illustrated by a description of his grasp of the situation.

"You bastards, you're gonna set me up," he screeches. "That's what you're gonna do. Set me up, you mothers."

The window is slammed to and there's the sound of the heavy curtains being over-lapped.

"I was standing right in the light," he screams in the darkness. "There would have been no problem. They could have fixed me with a pea-shooter."

"It was just our way of making sure," I tell him. "Saves looking. Now we *know* there's nobody out there."

"Listen, I wasn't even carrying out there. I wasn't even protected."

The source of Tina's perfume is a little bit closer to me in the darkness. I can hear D'Antoni moving back across the room. Then the lights go on again and now D'Antoni's moving towards where I'm sitting.

"That's why you took them, wasn't it?" he says. "So it shortens the odds. Makes no difference if they take me out or not, ain't that right, hey?" He stops a foot or so away from me. "You better give me that stuff back," he says. "Otherwise – "

"Otherwise you'll what? Break my back?"

D'Antoni looks at me for a while then he turns away and makes for the booze. When he's made his drink he says:

"Jesus. I'd be safer calling a press conference and just telling everybody where I am."

"Then why the fuck don't you do that and give us all a rest?"

He doesn't seem to hear me because he says:

"I should have done what Wally did. Gone down south right away. I should never have done what I done."

I get up and say to Tina:

"Wally still in the kitchen?"

She nods.

"Well I'm going to bed. If I was you I'd go and help him finish the washing up."

"If you're going to bed, so am I."

I shrug.

"In that case, tell Wally what you're doing. I don't want him waking me up more than a dozen times tonight."

I walk out of the lounge, leaving D'Antoni pouring himself another drink. When I get to the bedroom I put on my pyjamas and lie down on the cot and look at my watch. It's only a quarter to ten. Well, I think to myself, you're supposed to do something different when you're on your holidays. About five minutes later the Mystery Tour Operator appears in the doorway.

"He's at it again," says Wally.

I don't say anything.

"He's on his third bottle of champagne. That's not counting the wine he had."

"Then we should have a peaceful night."

"It's what he might do before he sparks out."

"He won't do fuck all."

"He wants me to stay with him."

"So stay with him. Then when he's flaked out you can have a good night's kip in your own pit."

"Can't you come down?"

"I thought you'd be happier me playing Fairy Godmother to your offspring." There's a silence while Wally tries to figure out the lesser of two evils. Then there's the sound of water running down the plug-hole.

"Well, I'll go down then."

"Yeah. Don't want him coming looking for you, do we?"

Obviously not; Wally disappears downstairs.

A minute or two later Tina comes out of the bathroom. You got to hand it to her, she knows what it's all about. She hasn't bothered to get into her nightie or anything, well, of course she wouldn't, would she, and in any case there's nothing to hide I haven't seen, but she's very clever; she is in fact hiding it, because she's put on a pair of brilliant white knickers and over the crutch is a transfer that says 'Do it Now,' and of course she's well aware of the fact that having already given her special attraction a previous airing, the wrinkling satin of the pants somehow draws to it an added attraction, which she doesn't detract from by sitting on the edge of the bed, her legs open, while she dries her legs and her back and eventually her tits, and while she's doing all this she's looking at me all the time, and in the look she's expressing something that's usually seen in the face of a stripper who isn't entirely doing it for the money. Now, as far as I'm concerned, I can normally take or leave this kind of behaviour, being as I am in the line of business I happen to be in, where this kind of situation, wherein a young girl from one of the clubs imagines she can advance her career more than somewhat, occurs much more often than does three aces out against three threes. In the normal course of events, I would remind the piece of the existence of Audrey Fletcher, pat her on the bum and send her on her way. Of course, from time to time, I would pat her on the bum without reminding her of the existence of Audrey Fletcher, but those times are very few and far between, the nature of Audrey being what it is. If I ever digress as far as Mrs Fletcher is concerned, it's usually with persons that operate as far off her patch as possible. But in this situation, where it is just gone ten o'clock in the middle of nowhere and Audrey's miles away, those white satin knickers and their message redolent of Norman Vincent Peale are affecting me in a way that the frequent full frontals have failed to so far, and the gaze, too, is an outward shorthand for what it might be like once the knickers have been thrown out of the window.

"A new pence for them," Tina says, rubbing the towel against some strands of hair at the nape of her neck.

"For what?" I ask her.

"Your thoughts'll do for starters."

"I was just wondering how the Spurs went on in the replay what they was playing last night."

"Is that what you do to keep your mind off it? Think about a bloody silly game?"

"Better than some games I can think of. I would have thought you'd have had enough of the other sort."

"My back's sore. Nothing else."

"If your back's sore, I should keep off it for a bit, then."

"You don't always have to be on your back."

I don't answer her. She drops the towel and arches her back and locks her fingers behind her neck.

"Jesus Christ," she says. "I feel really stiff."

She looks at me.

"You don't, obviously."

She shrugs and starts to make as if she's going to take her pants off. She's great, she really is, because what she does is to slip them down her thighs a little bit, then makes a tutting noise and picks up the towel and begins to dab at her hair again, as if she's overlooked a little bit.

"All right," I say to her.

I get up off the cot and lock the bedroom door and the bathroom door. Then when I've done that I walk over to the bed and stand in front of Tina. For a moment or so she pretends not to notice me. Then after she's gone through that routine she looks up at me and says:

"That your after dinner exercise, was it?"

"Part of it."

"Another part to come, is there?"

"Yes," I tell her, undoing my pyjama cord, "this part."

The pyjama trousers reach the floor. Tina looks at me, but this time not in the face. Still doing that, she begins to pull her pants the rest of the way down, but before she can get very far I reach out and stop her; holding her wrist. She looks up at me.

"That's something I like to do myself," I tell her, releasing her wrist and transferring my grip to the satin her open thighs is stretching tight as a whip. She lies back on the bed, her legs bent double, her knees in the air. I drop the fragment of satin on the floor, and put one knee on the bed, between her legs. Just as I do that there's a knock on the door, followed by the sound of Wally's voice.

'Jack," he says, "you're wanted."

I can't think of an answer to that so I don't give him one. On the other hand, I don't give Tina one either, because we both remain poised in the positions we were in before the knock on the door.

"Jack," comes Wally's voice again. "You're wanted. On the blower."

Now, normally, the Sydney Tafler dialogue alone would be enough to get on my nerves. But coupled with the fact that he's preventing me doing just that, he's mentioned the telephone what's supposed to be off, due to the heavy rains, and all that. So I abandon my position supplicant and draw up my pyjama trousers and when I've tied the cord I go over to the door, unlock it, close it behind me, and take hold of Wally by his throat and walk him backwards across the landing until the opposite wall prevents me taking him any farther and before he can gargle out any questions I say to him:

"I'm what?"

"The blower," he croaks. "You're wanted on it."

"I'm wanted on it," I say to him. "Now that's very interesting. Not only because the phone is U.S., but also, who, I ask myself, could be wishing words with me on this island, at this time of night, eh Wally? Couldn't be a wrong number, could it? Couldn't it be a fortunate false alarm, eh? Or could it be Gerald and Les, phoning out of a deep sense of concern for my safe arrival? Couldn't be that, could it, Wally?"

He shakes his head.

"No," he says. "It ain't that. It's Mrs Fletcher what wants you."

I give him the kind of look he can do without right now.

"Mrs Fletcher?"

Wally nods, too many times. I close my eyes. Fuck me, I think to myself. This is all I need. I know she's barmy, but I didn't think she'd be barmy enough to pull this one, to put a mouth like Wally onto the fact that Audrey's making contact with me on the same island where she happens not to be meant to be. My first instinct is to want to give her what is usually reserved for birds that perpetrate this kind of behaviour, but on reflection it occurs to me that once Gerald gets wind of the event, he'll take care of that part of the arrangements, together with certain contingencies covering my own destiny. So I say to Wally:

"Mrs Fletcher say why she particularly wanted to speak to me?"

Wally shakes his head. I let him go and walk down the stairs and pick up the extension in the hall. The fish is still dribbling away, and the resemblance to Gerald at this moment takes on a particular poignancy.

"Yes?" I say.

"Merry Christmas," Audrey says.

Oh Christ. That's all we need. For her to be pissed up to the gills.

"You're three weeks early," I tell her.

"Yeah, but I couldn't wait to give you your present, seeing as I got it here with me. I mean, what's the point of waiting. It's all gift wrapped, pink bows and black lace edging, know what I mean? And as it's something you never get tired of, doesn't matter when you get it, does it?"

I take a deep breath.

"Listen, you silly fucking cow. You know what you just done, don't you. You only just blown everything – "

"Talking about blowing – "

"For Christ's sake, just leave it out. You're barmy. I mean, you do realize, when I put this phone down, that Wally gets straight back onto it and talks to Gerald and Les? I mean, you do know that?"

"So what?"

"Jesus."

"Let him. It don't matter."

"Well, I tell you what, try telling me that when you got two stripes on your face and your mouth muscles don't work the way they should."

"I told you. It don't matter. They know where I am."

"You what?"

"Gerald and Les. They know I'm here. They know I'm in touch with you. Favourite, isn't it?"

"They know you're here?"

"Yes."

"They know you're in touch with me?"

"That's right."

I feel for my cigarettes and matches but of course that's futile as I'm only wearing my pyjamas.

"So what did you do? Just go to Gerald and say look, I cannot tell a lie, I am not bound for Hamburg pulling birds for the club, I am in fact going to fuck with Jack in Majorca, that all right?"

Audrey laughs.

"All right, all right," she says. "I'll tell you straight. I just enjoyed giving you the shits, that's all."

I don't say anything.

"Look," she says. "They know I'm here, because that's where they asked me to be."

"Now I know it's Christmas."

"Straight. They asked me to come over here." She giggles. "That's not bad. That's exactly what I'll be doing, coming over here."

She begins to build on her giggling so I say to her:

"Are you going to tell me what's going on or aren't you?"

"I'm telling you. They asked me to come. They wanted me to deliver something to you. I'm your actual Holiday Tour Courier."

"Just tell me, Audrey."

"An envelope. They wanted me to deliver an envelope. Maybe it's your Christmas Card."

"Yeah, and it could be my Christmas bonus."

"I'm your Christmas bonus, sweetheart, and you better get down here before I'm affected by the inflationary spiral."

"Look," I tell her. "Just for two minutes. Just start again and tell me what you're doing here."

There's the sound of a glass clinking against the plastic at the other end of the line.

"They told me to leave Hamburg out, as they'd got something important to let you have, and they could only trust me to get it to you. That's a laugh, isn't it?"

"You know what's in the envelope?"

"For once, no. I never asked. All I thought about was getting out here with their blessings, what a giggle that was."

"But you do know what's going on up here?"

"What's going on?"

"About D'Antoni."

"Oh, the yank. Yeah. They told me he'd be staying a few days. Why?"

"That's all they told you?"

"Yeah. Why?"

"Oh, no reason," I tell her. "I mean, them being the straightest people in the world, and all that."

"What's happening, then?"

"Never mind. Where are you?"

"Where do you think I am? At the bleeding hotel. The one I booked into before the Ugly Sisters said I could go to the ball."

"All right," I tell her. "How soon can you get up here?"

"What you talking about? I may have got their blessing, but Wally's going to have something to tell them if I screw with you up there."

"It'll look even more dicey if you don't stay up here."

"Anyway, they told me to give you what I got away from there. In private, like. They want me to give it to you in private."

The harsh giggle crackles down the line again. Audrey, I think to myself, sometimes I wonder. I really do.

"All right," I say to her. "I'll come down. I'll be about an hour."

"Well, don't be any longer. I know you'll hurry. I mean, it's been a few days since you seen any. I hope you been saving it up, and if not, I hope Miss Wrist has been due to your loving thoughts of me."

"I'll be there in an hour."

I put the phone down. The fish keeps on dribbling. I walk back upstairs. Wally's no longer on the landing, but the bedroom door's open. When I go in I'm greeted with a tableau not too dissimilar to the one I was into before the bell tolled. Wally's leaning over the bed, but this time Tina's between the sheets and her legs are drawn up a different way.

"And if you think I'm so fucking stupid not to know what's been going on," Wally's saying, "you got to be out of your tiny mind."

"I just think you're fucking stupid," Tina says, drawing on one of my cigarettes.

"Look, – " Wally begins, but I interrupt him by walking over to the bedside table and picking up my cigarettes and matches.

"My old man thinks you're a dirty old man and that I'm a dirty little bitch," Tina says to me.

"Is that right?" I say, lighting a cigarette. Wally seems to be at a loss for words.

"Yeah," Tina says. "Funny, isn't it?"

I ignore her and say to Wally:

"The Mercedes got plenty of juice in it?"

"Er – yeah, it's nearly full, that is."

"Good."

I go over to the wardrobe and take a shirt and a suit off the hanger.

"Why, you going out?"

"That's right. Down to Palma."

"Well what about him?"

"He's spark out, isn't he?"

"I dunno."

"Course he is. Otherwise he'd have heard the phone and he'd have shot it to bits with his bazooka, wouldn't he?"

"What about us if he wakes up?"

I ignore him and walk into the bathroom and start getting changed. Naturally, Wally follows me in.

"You can't leave us on our own," he says. "Christ knows what he might do. I mean, think of Tina."

"She can look after herself, don't you worry."

I straighten my tie in the mirror and walk back into the bedroom. Tina's no longer in the bed.

"You see?" Wally says.

"Show me the car, Wally."

"Jack – "

"Wally."

Wally shuts his mouth and leads the way out the bedroom. On the way down Wally's tempted to look in the lounge to check on the state of D'Antoni, but my eyes on the back of his neck cause him to think better of it. We cross the entrance hall and Wally opens a door and we go down a short flight of steps that descend into a short corridor that turns at opposite right-angles a couple of times until we're at another door and Wally opens this door and we're in the garage. Wally switches a light and flickering neon finally stabilizes and the white Mercedes is revealed in all it's boring pristine beauty. Wally presses a button and the garage door slides up and a cool wall of air moves into the garage.

"The keys in it?"

"Oh, yeah; the keys," Wally says, and fishes about in his pocket. "Here they are."

I walk round to the driver's side. The door's unlocked. I get in and try not to look as if I'm going to have to get used to the left-hand drive. I light a cigarette and push the key in the ignition. Wally sticks his head in through the rolled down window.

"You ain't going to be long, eh?" he says.

"Tell you what I'll do," I say to him. "If I'm not back by Friday week you can use my aftershave for ever and ever."

I flip on the lights and turn the key and the engine turns over first time. I release the handbrake and the car slides forward and out of the garage. For the next ten minutes I drive at about five miles an hour and when I'm on the mountain road I drive even slower, the hairpin bends and the canyons being what they are. About three quarters of an hour later, when I've negotiated the last bend and I'm on some relative flat, I stop the car and have five minutes to calm my nerves. I never did like driving, and that last three quarters of an hour's just about done me for the rest of my natural. So I sit there and have a smoke and try to imagine what's in the envelope Audrey's brought over. Knowing Gerald and Les, it'll be a letter informing me that there'll be a Mr D'Antoni staying at the villa for a couple of days, and would I afford him every courtesy. Those bastards. I'm really going to enjoy seeing them again, and giving them my opinion of recent events. That will be what I call pleasure.

I flip the cigarette out of the window and a voice behind me says:

"This as far as we're going, then?"

I close my eyes. There's a rustling of soft clothes and when I open them again Tina's finished climbing over the seat and is sitting alongside of me.

"Didn't go very far in the bedroom, did we? So I thought — "

I twist round in my seat and grab her shoulder.

"Bloody hell," she says. "That hurts."

"Listen," I tell her, "I don't give a fuck about that. I'm out on business. Now get out of it and clear off back to the villa."

"You what? I can't walk all that way back up there."

"You should have thought of that."

"Anyway, it's not bleeding safe. I still hurt from what that bastard done you know. It's bleeding painful."

"You should have thought about that, too."

"Oh, piss off."

I light another cigarette.

"Listen, Wally's going to disappear up his own arsehole when he finds you've gone missing, you know that, don't you?"

"So?"

"So that's another reason."

"All right. Take me back, then. Cause that's the only way I'm going back. I mean, you've got to be joking."

I blow out some smoke. She's right. She can't walk back up there. On the other hand, I ought to clout her edds and sling her out and to hell with her. But I've had enough for one day, and the prospect of dealing with Audrey in one of her pissed-up states is already tiring me out.

"I don't even know how long I'm going to be," I tell her. "I may even be all night. What you going to do then?"

"I'll go to the club. No one will mind, will they? They haven't before."

"In that case I should stay there the rest of your holidays if I was you."

"Charming."

"I thought you felt like that," I say to her, switching on the ignition. We drive on for about quarter of an hour without either of us saying anything. Eventually Tina breaks the silence by asking me for a cigarette. I hand her the packet and the matches and when she's lit herself up she gives the packet and the matches back to me by placing them in my lap but the thing is, once she's done that, she doesn't remove her hand, so I say to her: "I told you, I'm on business. You keep on like that you're walking back."

"A twist," she says. "A real twist, that is. The bird walking back because *she* makes the pass."

Chapter Eleven

The front of Palma by night is not as ratty as the back of Palma is by day. But that of course is thanks to the lighting. The lights inside and outside the hotels and the fairy lights along the beaches do the same kind of job that the lights do around Piccadilly Circus, translate tat into magic.

I find the Hotel Los Toros. It's opposite the beach, just over the road from all the thatched parasols. I park the car on the beach side. Tina makes no move to get out.

"The club far from here?" I ask her.

"Ten minutes," she says.

"You've not forgotten where it is?"

"I was only here in August, wasn't I"

"So in that case you won't have any trouble finding it."

"You going over there?" she says, indicating the hotel.

I don't answer her.

"Only I thought I'd have a drink with you before I went to the club," she says.

"You thought that, did you?"

She doesn't answer for a while. Eventually she says:

"All right, I'll go. I'll be at the club when you're ready."

She opens the car door and gets out and begins to walk away. I let her get about ten yards from the Mercedes then I stick my head out of the window.

"Hang on a minute," I say to her.

She turns round and hurries back to the window my head's sticking out of, then she waits for me to say what I've got to say.

"Just supposing I do get through tonight, it might help if I knew the name of the club."

She doesn't quite spit at me.

"Picador," she says.

"Ta very much," I say, and smile at her. She looks at me for a long moment before she turns away.

I wait until she's out of sight before I get out of the Mercedes. Then I walk over to the hotel and walk up the steps. The steps divide a raised narrow frontage that supports four parasolled tables on either side. The tables are deserted all except one. And at that one sits the old dad that was a member of the Dagenham boys' party on the flight over. He's still wearing his Robin Hood hat and his Hammers scarf and his foam-backed overcoat and he's staring out to sea as if he's waiting for his dentures to wash up on the next wave. I pass by him without him being aware of the fact.

I push inward on the plate glass and two things are immediately released into the night air; first, there's that dreadful, female, bathed-and-powdered, after-dinner smell, all antiseptic and expressing the determination to have a good time in spite of the old man. And the other thing is the sound of a Hammond organ fitted with a rhythm attachment. The organist is playing 'South of the Border' and he's so bad and so out of time that if it wasn't for the rhythm box you'd think he was playing free form.

The organ is set up in a small ballroom that opens out from the other end of the bar on my left. There are two middle-aged women dancing together in the centre of the floor and there are various families dotted around in the low seats, thinly spread in the off-season emptiness.

I decide that before I meet Audrey a nice stiff vodka will be in order so I walk into the bar and sit on one of the bar stools and the white-coated drunk of local colour drifts along the bar and raises his eyebrows by way of inviting my order. I ask for a vodka and tonic and I get it poured the way I got it in the café the day before; vodka four-fifths up to the rim, and only enough room for a few bubbles from the tonic bottle. Nevertheless I manage to get some of it down and dilute it a bit more with the tonic. I'm just taking a second sip when one of the Dagenham sons rounds the corner from the ballroom, carrying a tray of empties. As I'm the only one at the bar it doesn't take him long to suss me out as having been on the plane, and as the barman is temporarily missing that's his excuse for a bit of bonhomie.

"They supposed to have waiter service through there," he says, "but it's quicker to do it your bleeding self."

I look at him.

"Don't know what work is, this lot," he says.

I manage not to smile.

"You staying here, are you?" he says.

I shake my head.

"Smart. The cement's not even dry. The hot water only comes on when you don't need it, mid-day. Bleeding manager's a wanker, and the agency girl, she's never here; poking with a fellow what owns a place round the corner. That's all she does all the time."

"So, taking everything by and large, you're having a good time?"

"Oh, we're having a good time, yeah. Just the fucking place."

This time I do allow myself a smile.

"Thing is about this kind of an holiday, you get to meet some right characters, know what I mean?"

Even though I don't, I nod, so that I don't have to say anything.

"I mean tonight. The missuses want to go on this barbecue up in the mountains with about forty thousand other people. Well, me and we can get burnt sausages back home, so it seems reasonable that as they want to go, and we want to stay here, they should go, and we should stay here, right? You're joking. If we're not going, they're not going, and that's that, arms folded, legs crossed, eyes fixed on the pelmets, the flaming lot. We don't go, they don't go. Like kids, they are. So we says to them, all right, as we're staying here, and you're not going, what're you going to do? Not bleeding well staying here with you, that's for sure, they say."

He hits himself on the side of his head.

"Unbelievable, isn't it. We won't go up there with them, so they won't go, they'll martyr themselves, but on the other hand, they'll go somewhere else, so long as it's without us. Beyond me, that is."

The barman reappears.

"Oh yeah," the Dagenham son says. "Two rum and blacks and a vodka tonic. And I'd better have one for dad, I'll have a rum for him, no black. Give him any more beer and he'll be knocking us up all night."

He gives me a wink. The barman dispenses the drinks with all his native warmth.

"Anyhow," the Dagenham son says, "in the end they go off to this club, the mum as well, and leave me and Barry to it down here, which on its own can't be bad. But a bit later on this piece on her own, she comes down and sits at the next table. Maybe she's getting on for forty but you'd never know it. So's my old woman and this one makes her look like a pensioner. Mind you, she's obviously got the bread to coat it." And your old lady can't, I think to myself, you being an impoverished Daghenham worker.

"Anyway, we soon get rapping and it's plain she's had a few and now me and Barry are wondering what we got on our hands as the impression she's showing out is the kind of thing you only read about in Men Only, in fact at one point Barry asks her if her name isn't Fiona, know what I mean?"

I'm beginning to think I do.

"What is her name, by the way?" I ask him.

"What? Oh, turns out to be Audrey as a matter of fact." He picks up his tray of goods. "Don't look like an Audrey, though. A lot classier than that, know what I mean?"

He gives me a wink and an elbow and then he goes off in the direction of outside to deliver the old dad his rum. I get off the stool and stroll down towards the ballroom part. The organist has left off for the time being so I don't have to break step with the rhythm box. There is a step down creating a division between the bar and the ballroom. Once I've taken this step I turn to my right, the direction the Dagenham boy appeared from. And, as they say, my suspicions are confirmed. There, at the table closest to me, is Audrey, couched in conversation with the number two son. Of course, Audrey notices me straight away, but I can tell immediately that she's in the kind of mood where she's going to have as many pounds of flesh as she'd need to open a Wimpy. And in that mood, if I want to find out what happens to be in the envelope before Boxing Day, I'm going to have to play the scene the way she's going to direct it. So I move to the table and stand there until Audrey gives up on this part of the game and deigns to recognize my presence.

"Evening," she says, settling back in her seat. I look at her and the number two son turns round to look up at me and it's not an unfamiliar look, the old askance eyebrows asking the silent question.

"Evening," I say to Audrey.

"Do we know you?" the Daghenham son says.

I shift my attention from Audrey to Barry.

"Course you do," I say, smiling. "I'm the bloke that stands by your table and says 'Evening'."

"I know where I seen you before," Barry says. "You were on 'Who Do You Do' doing an impression of a clever bastard."

"Stand-out, was I?" I ask him

"You are now," he says. "So just push off."

A voice behind me says:

"What's this?"

"A clever bastard," Barry explains.

Benny puts the drinks tray down on the table.

"Oh, yes," he says. "You're right. He's a right clever bastard, he is. Susses out the situation through in the bar and comes round here and starts moving in. Yeah, a right clever bastard."

"Well, just push off," Barry says. "Then maybe we'll forget what a clever bastard you are."

"Oh, I'd hate you to do that," I say to them, sitting down on a seat between Audrey and Barry. The sons look at each other. Then Benny leans over, his face a few inches from mine.

"Listen, my son," he says, "you made your point. You're a brave cavalier. Now if I was you I'd go and try out your technique in one of those Guitar Bars. You're less likely to get hammered in one of those."

I smile at him.

"You don't mean I'm likely to get hammered here, do you?" I ask him. "I mean, what for, and who by?"

The sons look at each other again.

"All right – " Benny begins, but he doesn't finish because Audrey decides it's gone far enough; she probably doesn't want anything spilt down her dress what she bought new in Oxford Street the other day.

"Leave it out," she says, "we're old friends. Let's all be old friends, eh?"

Now even though the Dagenham sons have only been acquainted with Audrey for a short time, they recognize the voice of authority when they hear it. They both look at her.

"One of those mine?" Audrey says, indicating the drinks on the tray.

"Oh, yeah," Benny says. "Here you are."

He hands her her drink. Then he sits down and for a moment there's a silence while the sons practise their hardest looks on me. Eventually I say to Audrey:

"Good flight, was it?"

"Great flight."

"Only I was wondering if you'd landed yet."

Audrey ignores that one and takes a sip of her drink.

"Room nice, is it?" I ask her.

"Nice. Lovely room. I'll draw you a picture, so you'll know what it's like."

"Got somebody to carry your bags up, did you?"

"Yes, I managed that."

"Didn't drop them, did he?"

"Not as far as I know."

"I expect that was a relief."

"Not for me, no."

"No, I could see how it wouldn't be."

"Still, I gave him a tip, just the same."

"That's nice."

"That's what I thought."

In the ensuing silence Barry says:

"You like another drink, Audrey?"

"What do you think?"

Barry puts Audrey's glass on the tray alongside his and his brother's and lifts the tray and begins to get up but before he can straighten himself I lean across the table and plant my glass on the tray with the others.

"Mine's the same as Audrey's."

"Oh, had the operation, then?"

Barry comes to the conclusion that he's not going to give me an argument over my glass so he straightens up and makes off for the bar. Benny offers Audrey a cigarette and lights both of them up. Audrey blows smoke out and says to me:

"Things all right up the road, then?"

"Oh yes, really smashing."

"I told you you'd like it once you got used to it."

"Yes, that's what you told me you know, plenty to do, sparkling company, all that kind of thing."

"I'm glad. I really am."

Just as Audrey's saying that, some of the sparkling company from the villa enters the room, in the form of Tina. She stands in the archway for a minute, then she sees me and gives me a certain kind of smile and starts walking towards our table.

"Oh, fuck me," I say.

"Oh yes," says Audrey. "And who's this?"

"You know who it is," I say to her. "It's Wally's offspring, isn't it?"

"I wouldn't know. Last time I saw her was when she was sitting on Les's knee when she was about eleven."

"She'd like that."

"What's she doing here?"

"Stays with Wally for her holidays, doesn't she?"

"Oh yes? As opposed to a ride in?"

I shrug. Now Tina's reached the table.

"So this is where you hold your business conferences, is it? Well, it's nice and peaceful for it."

She sits down the other side of Audrey.

"Hello, Mrs Fletcher," she says. "On your holidays as well?"

"Remember me, do you?"

"Course. Long time ago, though. These days you're mostly out when I call round to see dad's benefactors."

"Oh, yes? Give you presents, do they?"

Barry returns with the drinks. Benny says to him: "Things get better all the time, don't they?"

Tina looks at him, then says to me: "These on the firm as well, then?"

I give her a look. She smiles sweetly back at me.

"What firm?" Benny says.

"Audrey," I say to her. "Think it's about time we were moving on, don't you?"

"About now, yes," Audrey says, standing up.

"You want to join us, Tina?" I say to her.

"Why? You going somewhere good?"

"Yeah. You'll really enjoy it. Just your scene."

"In that case," she says, and gets up.

The Dagenham boys look as though Storey's just put through his own net. I down my drink and put the glass on the tray.

"Hope the trouble and strifes get back all right," I say to them.

I turn away from them and let Audrey and Tina get out from behind the table and when they've done that I begin to follow them in the direction of the bar. Barry says:

"That's what I really like. A geezer what pays his corner."

I turn round and walk back to the table.

"Well, I agree with you," I say to him. "So when I go through the bar I intend getting a grip of the barman and sending you through a couple of Snowballs, all right?"

I turn away again and catch up with Audrey and Tina and when I've done that I herd the stupid cows over to the bar and sit them down; I mean, if Audrey hadn't been trying to stir my pudding with Tweedledum and Tweedledee then Tina wouldn't have had the opportunity to drop bollocks the way she did. And if Tina hadn't crept back then Audrey wouldn't have the aroma up her nostrils she now has.

I stand between the two of them and get a grip of Tina's upper arm.

"Now listen," I say to Tina, "Audrey and me's got some business to do, and I mean business. So just bugger off to where you were going and stay away from those two fairies, all right?"

"Why should I?"

"I'll tell you why; because if you don't your old man'll end up behind a whelk stall without a pension and there'll be no more duty free holidays and no more art school fees and no more of the gear, but what there will be will be having Wally breathing down your neck until you meet your chartered accountant and go and live in Bromley."

The barman appears and I order a drink for myself.

"Well," Tina says. "You got a point."

"So clear off and let us get on with it."

She puts her hand on my knee and gives me her sweetest smile.

"Seeing as you're such a little charmer," she says.

She slides off the stool but her hand stays where it is.

"Going to pick me up later, then?" she says. "After you've finished your business?"

"It might take a long time," I tell her.

"Well, you know where it is, when you're ready to get me."

The hand finally leaves the knee and Tina floats off towards the foyer. I stop watching her progress when I hear the sound of Audrey's fingers snapping at the barman.

"I'll have another one as well if you don't mind."

"You don't think we ought to go to the bedroom?" I say to her.

"I want a drink."

"You don't mean to tell me you haven't got any up there?"

"Listen, I want one down here. Or do you want me to go into the glasses routine?"

I order her a drink.

"Boring up at the villa, then, is it?" she says.

"You know Wally."

"Yeah, I know Wally. Now I know his daughter, don't I?"

"You met her before."

"Not when she was wearing stockings and a suspender belt."

"I beg your pardon?"

"Stockings and a suspender belt. You could see them through the cheese-cloth. Don't tell me you didn't notice."

"No, I didn't notice."

"No, you probably got first hand knowledge."

I don't answer her.

"Well?"

I still don't answer.

"You been poking her, haven't you?"

I shake my head, in all sincerity, secure that I'm telling the truth.

"Pull the other one," she says.

I shrug.

"I'll rip that suspender belt off her and strangle her with it."

"Listen," I tell her, "if you thought I'd had her off she'd have been hanging from the chandeliers by now, so leave it out, eh? I'm waiting to get the message it was so important for you to get over here."

She switches moods again.

"Oh yes," she says. "I was forgetting about that. Meeting new people, and all that."

"Where is it?"

"In my room. Where do you think it is?"

"Well for fuck's sake let's get up there."

"You want to get up there, do you?"

I close my eyes.

"Are we going or aren't we?"

"It's up to you. I've been waiting since I got off the plane."

"Yeah, well you'll have to wait a bit longer," I say to her. "I've got one or two things to tell you before we get down to any of that."

"Feel like getting down, do you?"

There's no talking to her so I guide her off the stool and walk her into the foyer where the lifts are and press a button.

"You do know which floor you're on," I ask her.

She gets into the lift and it's her turn to press a button. The door slides to and Audrey folds her arms and leans back against the panelling, eyes closed, a dreamy expression on her face.

"If I thought you had had her," she says, "you know what I'd do to you, don't you?"

I've got a pretty good idea, but I don't tell her I have.

The lift stops and the door slides open and all we have to do is cross the hall and Audrey's taking her room key out of her handbag. She unlocks the door, pushes it open and stands back for me to go in first.

Compared to the rooms at the villa this one's a matchbox. There's just enough room for a couple of single beds and a fitted wardrobe. There's a bathroom off to the left and between the single beds there's a bedside table and on it there's an ice-bucket with champagne sticking out of it. It has the atmosphere of the inside of a suitcase. Audrey follows me in and closes the door and locks it and puts the key back in her handbag. Then she goes over to the bed and sits down on the edge and leans across it and with a bit of a struggle pours two glasses of champagne and manages to manhandle mine over to me without spilling too much of it, but that's immaterial as far as I'm concerned because I say to her:

"You got anything else?"

She looks at me.

"You what?"

"Anything other than that. To drink."

"What's the matter with you then?"

"I'm sick of the sight of it. I've seen enough this twenty-four hours to send me back to large browns.

"Oh yes?"

"Yes. Now where's the bleeding envelope?"

Eventually Audrey tears her gaze away from me and puts the glasses down on the floor and reaches her handbag and opens it and takes out a long brown envelope and hands it to me. I tear the top off and slide out a small sheet of paper typewritten on both sides. I begin to read.

Dear Jack,

By now you will have met Joseph D'Antoni, the associate of our associates in the States, and also by now he'll have told you his story. We left that to him rather than tell you ourselves for various reasons, one being that we wasn't sure he'd make it there and if he didn't well what was the point of spoiling your well deserved holiday, eh, Jack? Didn't want you fretting did we? Anyway, as it transpires, he did make it, so now you know the story, what he's told you. Only you don't, as it happens and neither did we until today, so don't think yourself a cunt for not sussing it because we didn't either. You know we're pushovers for a hard luck story. It seems Joseph didn't tell us everything and that what he did tell us was cobblers anyway and the real story is he took some liberties and our associates don't know exactly how much he already said but if he says anymore not only them but us as well will be in dead lumber concerning a certain side of our operation, because if the lot over the water go down the pan we not only lose considerable readies we might go down it with them, if you get our meaning. So our friends get in touch with us today and it comes up that you're over there and them being not a little bit pissed off with us it's their suggestion that we do something about it, it being convenient that you and he are both out there, so to speak. We know that you will get our meaning and we don't have to tell you what sort of bonuses will be in order regarding this one. Any removal work that might come in necessary Wally will put you right on and we know you can take care of things without disrupting your well earned holiday too much.

Gerald and Les

P.S. let us know how things go when the phone comes back on again.

When I've finished reading the letter I hold my thoughts in a kind of deepfreeze while I pick up the two glasses that Audrey's set down on the floor and drink them dry, one after the other.

Now I've worked for the Fletchers for nearly twelve years, and many events have occurred over those years, many strokes have been pulled by the two of them, some of them so bizarre that they wouldn't bear chronicling. But over the years I've grown accustomed to those kind of strokes, because I've been put in so many times. I mean, there was once a time they sent me out to fit up Jimmy Madison by pulling a job that had all the hallmarks while Gerald and Les were treating him to lunch at the Club, the idea being that when the law came to Jimmy's doorstep he'd think he had it cast-iron with Gerald and Les, only what they said they intended saying when Old Bill checked up, what that not only had they not had lunch with him, they'd never even heard of him, not even his old mum what bore him gloriously into the world, and that denial, together with the testimonies of various handpicked witnesses, would put Jimmy away and out of competition for at least until Millwall won the European Cup. Anyway that was the story I was told, but what was really on was that a member of Old Bill who was on the wages sheet had been indiscreet about how he spent his money; and so to scotch any impending investigation he'd been set to pull a few names out of the hat, Jimmy and the Fletchers being among them. So they'd got together and worked out that if the member of Old Bill was put on to the job, was tipped off about Jimmy, named him, then due to Jimmy's alibi was made to look a right berk, the impending investigation would be speeded up by the vigour of the press. Which was all fair enough except that nobody put me in it, and as it happened a smart copper broke down a witness and I got put in it via a different route. I didn't go down, because our brief was too good, but the point was, I could have done, and I wouldn't have put myself in that position if I'd known all about the double shuffles the Fletchers were playing at with Jimmy.

Now I know life's cheap, and when you're in my line of business you have a lot come your way you have to chew on hard and swallow but you do, as often as possible, like a chance to choose what's coming at you, and on more than one occasion the Fletchers have put me in things where if I went down, not only would they lose the best Number One in the business, but — and this is what riles me — is they either don't care they've got the best Number One in the business or they don't know they've got the best Number One. Either way, they don't care if they lose the best Number One, the geezer that's kept them out the centre court more times than they'll even know about. And it hasn't exactly been unknown for me, as a matter of policy as far as the firm's concerned, to see to transgressors from members of the opposition on a more or less permanent basis, the more or less depending on the degree to which your religious belief extends. Now obviously, unless warm emotion enters into those events, as it sometimes does, one would rather be watching the Spurs giving the Arsenal a pasting, but in those cases stoicism is always a comfort for both parties, as it were, but an even greater comfort at times like those is the knowledge that there but for the grace of God goes me; it's not just the Fletchers' necks I'm saving.

But this, this is something else. Apart from what those bastards want sorted, what is stoking me up to the valve of ten is the way they've gone about it; not only that, they think I'm the kind of cunt that'd believe the crap in the letter. Oh yes, I'm supposed to say to myself, I can see as how it would be, very unfortunate, Gerald and Les being put in lumber like that, and them only thinking as how they was doing somebody a favour, the way they often do. Naturally, under the circumstances, as I work for them, I'll be pleased to do the honours then finish the holidays that they've been good enough to provide for me out of the kindness of their hearts.

I walk between the two beds to where the champagne is and stock up my glass again.

"What is it?" Audrey says.

I sit down on the edge of the opposite bed and look at her.

"You read this?" I ask her.

"Course I haven't read it."

"Don't flannel me. You read everything of theirs whether they know it or they don't."

"Well, this time I haven't, all right."

I light a cigarette.

"And you don't know what's happening at the villa."

"Only that one of the yanks is staying there, yeah, I know that."

"Well, I'll tell you why he's supposed to be staying there, then I'll tell you why he's actually staying there. It's better than Andy Pandy, because although it's on the same intellectual level, there's more twists to the plot."

Audrey looks at me as if I'm a drunken husband telling her nobody loves him at two in the morning when he should have been home for his fish supper at half past seven. So I wipe the look off her face by first telling her the events starting with my arrival at the villa, leaving out the bits concerning Tina. Then I avail her of the contents of the letter which she has just delivered unto me. When I've finished doing that I pour two more glassfulls of champagne and hand one of them to her. She takes it from me, and like me, after I'd read the letter, she downs it in one. After she's done that she thrusts her glass in my direction and I fill her up again and when she's drained that one she launches into a descriptive monologue concerning the latest strokes of Gerald and Les, putting into words the thoughts I've been having, only some of the words Audrey's selecting do far more justice to the eggs than the rather mundane similes I've come up with in my own mind, but then the profession Audrey was in before she took up with Gerald afforded her a much greater command of the English language than I'll ever have. When she's exhausted everything she knows and also once again the champagne glass, she stretches out her arm and I fill the glass for her. For a while after I've done that the room itself is full of silence, but outside in the darkness there's the sound of a pneumatic drill going to work on the next hotel to be finished by the start of the season.

It's Audrey who eventually breaks the bedroom's silence.

"So what you going to do then?"

"What do you mean?"

"What I say. What you going to do?"

"What do you think I'm going to do?"

There's another silence. Again it's Audrey that breaks it.

"We've got a lot to come out of the firm," she says. "When we make our move, I mean."

I don't answer her because I don't consider the question worth answering.

"You know what I'm talking about," she says. "When we upset the applecart we're going to be set for life. I don't have to tell you that. When we make our move, we're not just worth a fortune. We're worth a fortune each."

"I do know that."

"That's good," she says.

"I'm glad you think that. So what you leading up to."

"Nothing. Except to remind you we're not ready to move yet."

"That's right. I am aware of that."

Audrey nods.

"So?" I say to her.

"So we can't make that move unless you're still working for them, can we?"

It's my turn to nod in agreement.

"You're right about that, too," I tell her.

She stretches her arm out for her glass to be re-filled again. I lift the bottle and when I've poured she takes a sip and lies back on her bed.

"Well," she says. "There you are."

I pour myself some more champagne.

"Where am I, would you say?" I ask her.

She closes her eyes and snuggles the back of her head into the pillow.

"Well, it won't be any sweat, will it?"

I don't say anything.

"All right, they're cunts," she says. "That we know. They gone about things in their usual way, which is a piss-off. It makes me boil up, it really does. You know that. But on the other hand, we're in business for ourselves. We can't afford to move yet, the time's not right. We can't do anything now which gets in the way of what we've planned since we ever set eyes on each other."

"Which means?"

"I know how you feel. I feel the same. I can't stand it when I think those two think they got the nous to put anything over on you or me. You know how I feel about that."

"Yes, I know how you feel about that."

"At the same time, there's something that ultimately makes me feel better, and that is the knowledge that they're not; they're not smarter. Ultimately it's us that's screwing them, and what will be delightful is their contemplation of that fact when they're where they're going to be when we're where we're going to be. That's going to be half the fun, that knowledge, the knowledge of their knowledge."

"Yes, that's true as well."

"Well, then, looking at it sensibly, what's the odds? Some months from now, we'll be laughing. I mean, it's not as if you're coming new to this kind of thing. For instance, I remember the night you had to go out and top Tony Bridges because of the liberty he took and that amount of money what was missing from what happened in Wembley that time. Before you went to report back to Gerald and Les you stopped off on the way and gave me a right seeing too, and after you'd done that you had five minutes kip and then had a shower and went off to tell the bastards how things had gone."

"Yes, I remember that."

"Wasn't any sweat, was it?"

"Tony took a big liberty."

"I know, and so did this one by the sound of it."

"It's not personal, like with Tony."

"So fucking what? You won't lose any sleep. And there'll be no danger. Nobody knows he's on the island. It's better than Epping Forest up there for getting rid. Never find anything in a million years."

"Well, that's all right, then."

"Course it is. It's worth wearing, just this once."

She stretches her arm out for another refill. She's still flat on her back, her eyes are still closed. I pour her champagne and she takes a sip and then waves her arm about until she's located the bedside table. Then she puts the glass down and puts her hands to the waistband of her skirt and unzips the zip and raises her bum and wriggles out of her skirt. After she's done that she unbuttons her blouse and eases that off her and she's left lying there in this silk slip with lace trimmings that she often wears when we're getting at it. Then she draws her knees up and the sound of her tights is like static electricity.

"So now we've settled that," she says, "why don't we settle the other business what we're supposed to be meeting about."

There's more static as her knees part, revealing the black underwear beyond the lace edging of the slip, and whatever I've said or thought about Audrey in the past, one thing has always been constant, that being that the prospect of sinking one with her is never better than the actual act, and the familiarity of that act has never bred contempt, rather it has re-enforced the memory of how good it's going to be when its got down to, which, in my experience, is a rare experience. And no one knows this better than Audrey. Audrey, in fact, would get along extremely well without any of the considerable brains she has in her head, just on the strength of what she could achieve in the wide world by the use of her body. But for once, and only once, she's going to be surprised and disappointed. I reach for the phone on the bedside table and pick up the receiver. The sound makes Audrey open her eyes.

"What are you doing?" she says.

Nothing happens at the other end of the phone.

"Eh?" she says.

"I thought I'd just phone Gerald and Les and tell them how much I'm enjoying my holidays and thank them for the arrangements they've made for me."

Audrey sits up on the bed.

"You what?"

I put the phone down and pick it up again. Still nothing.

"I said what you doing?" Audrey says.

"I know. And I told you."

"You're joking."

I don't answer her. She reaches over and tries to grab the phone off me but I push her away and she bangs her head on the wall at the top of the bed.

"Christ," she yelps, but I'm not interested in any of that, all I'm interested in is getting through to those eggs in London and telling them all the things I'm really looking forward to telling them. But of course the crack on the head makes Audrey come back strong and it's only a matter of seconds before we're thrashing about on the bed like a couple of kids fighting over who has the teddy bear. Now normally this kind of behaviour would be good warm-up stuff for things to come but not now, because I'm so stoked up everything that is not the phone call is superfluous, so I try and stop the proceedings by fetching Audrey one round the ear-hole but the effect that has is only to intensify her activity; at the moment she is concentrating on trying to do irreparable damage with her knee to that part of my body which she loves best. I give her another one but only to similar effect so I take hold of both her wrists and straddle her and pin her down that way and wait for her to come to terms with the fact that there's no way she's going to be able to do anything about the situation. So for a while I stare down at her and she stares up at me and nowhere in her expression can be found a trace of the memory of eight happy years. After a while she says:

"I always thought Gerald was the most stupid bastard I ever met. Which was why I married him, his stupidity being an asset as far as what I intended doing. Then I met you, and it became what *we* intended doing, me thinking you were smart, as it were. But now it looks like I was wrong. I did Gerald an injustice. He's not even as stupid as I am, thinking how smart you were."

"Listen," I say to her, "I've eaten their shit for long enough. Of all the strokes they pulled on me, this is the biggest. And this time I don't swallow. If they want D'Antoni seeing to, they can get their fucking rowing boat out and come over and see to him themselves. By which time I won't be here. I'll be paddling at Cleethorpes with a hankie on my head.

Audrey shakes her head.

"You berk," she says. "You bleeding berk."

I let go of her wrists and cock my leg and swing off the bed and pick the phone up again and still there's nothing but a stem reply so I smash the receiver down and pour myself some more champagne.

"I mean," Audrey says, "not only are you prepared to fuck up the whole of our remaining lives, you're going to do it by speaking your piece via the hotel switchboard. Jesus. I must have been mad, that's what I must have been."

"You want some more?" I ask her.

She sits up and places her feet on the floor and bends forward and picks up her handbag and takes out her cigarettes and lights up.

"I said, do you want some more?" I say to her.

She lifts her legs back onto the bed and leans her back against the wall and stares at the wall opposite. Outside, the drill is still pumping away reminding me of what I would have been doing if the Fletchers hadn't dropped me in all this bother. I have another listen to the receiver but whoever's supposed to be on the switchboard must be out picking up a little bit extra on the building site opposite because there's still nothing. So I forget about that for the time being and drain my glass and button up my jacket. This last activity engages Audrey's attention.

"What you doing now?" she says.

"I'm going up to the villa and collecting my gear and my readies and then I'm clearing out of this karsi," I tell her. "Oh yes, and before I do that I'm going to make the phone call from up there to express my long-held beliefs about your old man and his brother."

"You're really going to do that?"

"I've told you what I'm not doing."

"And what about me?"

"That's up to you."

"You know what'll happen if you go."

"No. I don't know what'll happen. You tell me."

"If you finish yourself with Gerald and Les, you finish yourself with me."

"Oh yes?"

"Yes. I've planned things for too long. And I suppose it's never occurred to you I could go on my own. It doesn't necessarily have to be with you?"

"Really. You could get somebody else to do the shopping without you getting shopped yourself?"

"I don't think that'd be a problem, no."

"Well, that's all right, then. That's fine. That's sorted. We know exactly where we stand."

"Too right we do."

There's a short silence.

"In that case, have a nice holiday."

"Too right I will."

"Good. Don't forget, if all else fails, there's always room service."

"Fuck off, pig."

"In Spanish, there's no answer to that."

I walk over to the door and open it and manage not to slam it hard enough for all the plasterwork to disintegrate, not to mention the unfinished hotel next door.

Before I leave the hotel and get into the Mercedes I go into the bar and order myself a large vodka. The bar is as empty as before and while I'm drinking my drink I consider the scene in Audrey's bedroom and what she put on me about our well-laid schemes and there's no contesting that her facts are right; it could well be that my refusal to give D'Antoni a seeing to could bring to an end a less than beautiful friendship and the prospect of an eventually beautiful retirement. I mean, Gerald and Les, cunts that they are, could very easily have me put down, not that face to face I'd be easy to put down even by a team fielding eleven Norman Hunters, but they could arrange it in their normal roundabout kind of way, like dynamiting my Karsi seat or putting piranha fish in my water bed. But, in spite of these considerations, the way I'm feeling right now, it'd be more of a likelihood that I'd get to them before they got to me, and it wouldn't be indirectly; I've always partaken my pleasures directly of the flesh. And for that matter the ironic thing would be that being as I am so pissed off with the fact that D'Antoni ever took the trouble to get himself born and into my life in the manner in which he has done, I might easily drive back up to the villa and snuff him just on a personal basis.

I order another quick one before I go, and while it's coming the organist starts up his water torture again; this time it's "Tie a Yellow Ribbon". I down my drink and try hard not to draw an analogy.

Chapter Twelve

Well, sod her, I think to myself. She can do what she bleeding well likes. She can come the old brass bed as much as she wants, I've heard it all before, and in circumstances more salubrious than a Mediterranean shoe-box. I done all right on my own so far; if I retired tomorrow on a bachelor basis, I'd still never run the risk of getting chalker's cough or batterer's elbow as a result of having to earn a living. And at least I don't have to contemplate the end of my days shifting Gerald's dentures round the back of the alarm clock. Jesus, she must think I still draw the curtains to watch television.

Going back, up the hairpins, is still as difficult, if not more so, as it was coming down; with the automatic transmission you can't rely on the gears as a hedge against deflation; you just have to keep pushing forward and hoping the clutch is all the master race cracks it up to be. The journey also takes twice as long and is twice as aggravating but that aggravation is in keeping with my general state of mind, adding fuel to the flame that Gerald and Les have lit deep inside me.

I finally reach the gap that opens into the dirt-track that leads to the villa and after the slow switchback I rock over the last hill and glide down towards the villa. The black-out's still in force; there isn't a crack of light to be seen. Wally would have got on with Vera Lynn. I stop the Mercedes in front of the glass frontage instead of bothering to put it back in the garage; charades time is over. Except, of course, for Wally, who has locked up the glasswork. So instead of giving the glasswork a kicking I walk into the garage and try the door that obtains into the house. (After all, although it garages a Mercedes, there's still room for an Austin.) The plasterwork corridors are as silent as I expect them to be, and when I get to the hall, the dribbling fish is still the main source of action, but it's only an aural sensation, visually everything being pitch black. I try and get my bearings so as I can find the lights and while I'm doing that something whistles to the floor about four inches from my left ear and makes a fucking great crash on the floor beside me. The sound shakes the plate glass and when the shuddering dies down there's the patter of tiny feet up on the landing, coming to a finale with the slamming of a bedroom door. I restrain myself from ripping the fish off it's pedestal and carrying it upstairs and ramming it down Wally's throat, because that can wait until I've called up Gerald and Les. What I do do, though, is to call up to Wally:

"It's me, you stupid bastard."

That should give him enough to macaroni about until I've made the phone call.

I finally find the lights, and when the hall's illuminated, so's the source of the crash; Wally's heaved a Spanish plant pot down from off the balcony and I smile, not because I've nearly ended up wearing my brains on the outside, but because on its way down the pot has clipped an even bigger lump out of the fish's top lip and it provides me with a piece of wish-fulfilment that urges me to get to the phone. I flip the lounge lights on. The lounge is empty. No D'Antoni catching midges. That's fine with me. I hate being inhibited.

I pick up the phone and go through about twenty minutes of jokes with International exchange until I finally get through to the club and it's Maurice who picks up the phone.

"Hello, Maurice," I say to him. "It's Jack."

"Jack? I thought you was on your holidays?"

"That's what I thought."

"What happened? You get rained off?"

"Something like that. Listen, Gerald and Les about?"

"Yeah, I think so. Why, you want to talk to them?"

No, you cunt, I think. I just want to know if they're tucked up in bed safely.

"Yes, Maurice. I'd like to talk to them."

"Hang on. I'll put you through."

There's a silence, then Gerald's voice comes on the line, full of its usual trust and openness.

"Yes?"

"Hello, Gerald."

Of course, he knows immediately who it is, but to give himself time he says:

"Who's that?"

"It's Jack, Gerald."

"Jack? Where you calling from, then?"

In the background I can hear Les asking Gerald what's going on and Gerald clamps his hand over the mouthpiece and relays something back to Les. I take no notice of that and say:

"I'm calling from the villa, aren't I."

"Oh. Yeah. How's things, then?"

"Fine. Things are just fine."

"That's fine."

I leave it to him to take it from there.

"You seen Audrey?" he says.

"Yes, I've seen her."

"She give you that letter?"

"That's right."

In the background I can hear Les still asking what's going on and Gerald clamps his hand over the receiver and this time I can make out the gist of what he's saying, which is that he thinks I'm going to be a bit difficult.

"You read it, then?" he comes back to me.

"That's right."

Gerald decides on a change of tone for his next delivery.

"Well, that's great," he says. "Look, we're sorry things worked out the way they done, but we been dropped on ourselves good and proper this time, as you can see, and we got no alternative, had we? I mean, if we'd known, we'd have put you in, wouldn't we, but there was no time, was there? You know the way things happen."

"I certainly do, Gerald."

"Yeah," he says. Les says something in the background and I can hear Gerald tell him to piss off for a moment.

"Well," Gerald says to me, "how is the geezer?"

"He's fine."

"He's still there, then?"

"Oh yes, as far as I know he is."

"As far as you know?"

"Yes. I just got in from seeing Audrey, didn't I?"

"Oh, yes."

"So I thought I'd just phone first, like."

Gerald's tone changes slightly.

"Why did you think that, Jack?" he says.

"Because I just thought I'd tell you and Les to go and fuck each other before I packed my bags and made for the airport."

"You what?"

"Listen, you cunt, you heard what I said."

There's a short silence.

"Yes, I heard."

There's more from Les in the background, to the effect that he's finally got the gist of what's going on and that he would like to have the receiver to himself for a moment so that he can tell the cunt on the other end of the phone what he thinks about things in general. But Gerald, for the time being, prevails, and it's his voice that stays on the line.

"Now look, Jack," he says, "I realise this comes hard to you, but it comes hard to us as well. We was dropped on, and as a result, you was dropped on, seeing as how you are in our employ. See what I mean? And like I say, all things being equal, you *are* in our employ, and what affects us, affects you, so to speak."

"Listen, Gerald," I say to him, "let me tell you this. Nobody's been dropped on in this one except me and not only once but twice. So don't add bleeding insult to injury. I know you bastards of old. This little lot's been done and done since the last time Billy Bremner shook hands when he was on the losing side. You, neither of you, never had the bottle to put it to me straight but having said that, you think to yourselves that when I get over here *I* won't have the bottle not to refuse, that's what really gets up my nose. Well, you pulled this kind of thing once too often, and the news is this, there is no news. I'm zipping up my flight bag, and the geezer, as far as I'm concerned, he can stay here and take over from Wally when and if Wally should ever happen to snuff it.

Gerald says: "Now look, Jack — "

"Don't you give me that. You look. I cleared up enough karsis for you for the last years and I'm not starting clearing up Continental ones."

Gerald starts to say something but at the other end of the line there's a clatter and Les comes on the line.

"Listen, you cunt," he says, "you work for us so you fucking well do as you're told."

"And you know why I work for you, don't you?"

"Why's that?"

"Because if I didn't you wouldn't be in a position to employ anybody. You'd both be in Durham paying the tame screws to serve you champagne so's you'd look bigger than the other stiffs. Without me you couldn't employ anybody to run the three card trick in Oxford Street."

"You thinking of coming back, Jack?" Les asks me.

"That's right," I tell him. "Quick sharp."

"Only when you do, don't smile too often, otherwise your ears might fall off."

"Well, who you going to get to do it for you, Les? You think I'm going to put the razor to myself? Or maybe you're going to make a virtue of expediency and do it yourself. That'd be a novelty, wouldn't it?"

There's a silence from Les. Then he says:

"Where's Audrey?"

"Now?" I say to him. "By now I should think she's well set up with the Dagenham Boy Pipers."

Before he's got a chance to answer I put the phone down. Then I go upstairs to my bedroom. It's in darkness so I switch the light on and at that precise moment downstairs the phone begins to ring. I ignore it and Wally, wherever he's hiding, ignores it too. I begin to pack my gear and the phone carries on ringing. Eventually, outside on the landing, there's the sound of D'Antoni calling Wally's name which once again puts Wally in his cleft stick. The phone keeps ringing and D'Antoni keeps on calling and I keep on packing. Eventually the phone stops and I put the last pair of socks in my case and D'Antoni comes into the bedroom, looking the way he always does between drinks.

"The phone," he says. "You hear that?"

I turn to look at him.

"No," I say to him. "I thought I was imagining things."

"Why'd it ring?"

I don't say anything.

"Who'd be calling here, at this time?"

"Well, I may as well confess. This whole thing was a great ploy cooked up by *This is Your Life*. The phone was just a signal. You're this week's subject. The cameras are on their way up now."

D'Antoni takes a few steps forward.

"Listen," he says. "The phone's supposed to be off."

"Yeah, the rains, and that."

"So now it's ringing."

I shrug.

"Who'd be calling?" he says.

"Maybe Wally's old mum to see if he's eating proper."

"And maybe it's the guys, the fellows."

"They always phone up to see if you're in before they pay a call, do they?"

"Look, it could just be them, see if anyone's here to pick up the phone."

"Like on the movies."

D'Antoni's about to say something but he goes pale and says something else.

"I gotta go to the bathroom."

And that is where he makes for, via the adjoining door in my bedroom, but when he gets to the door he finds it locked, so gulping back the imminent vomit he rushes out onto the landing and attempts to effect his entrance by way of his own bedroom but from what I hear I gather that that door is locked too because D'Antoni rattles the door and fucks and blinds and then there's the sound of him throwing up and it certainly doesn't come from inside the bathroom. Then the reason becomes apparent because the bathroom door on my side is opened and out steps Wally; only the minute he sees me standing there he steps back again and slams the door and there's the sound of the key being turned and straight away there's some more battering on the other side of D'Antoni's door.

I cross the bedroom and call through the door to Wally.

"Wally, I want to talk to you."

No answer.

"Wally, come out of the karsi."

"Not bleeding likely. You think I'm barmy or something?"

"Wally, come out. Or do you want me to come in?"

"I didn't know it was you, Jack. I thought it was them other geezers we been expecting."

"Come out, Wally."

There's a short silence then the key turns again and the bathroom door swings inwards and after a while Wally appears in the doorway and we look at each other.

"Honest," Wally says, poised to scuttle back behind the door at the slightest movement on my part.

"Wally, come out. Come and sit on the bed. I got something to tell you."

I turn away from him and walk over to the bed and sit down so that I'm facing him again. He doesn't move so I crook my finger and eventually Wally begins to make it across the room and as he gets close to the bed he notices the open suitcase containing all my nice neat packing but in the circumstances he forbears mentioning it. Instead he sits down on the bed as if it's just been used by two sailors in a Cardiff brothel.

"There won't be any geezers," I say to him.

Wally looks at me.

"What do you mean?"

"No geezers. There'll be no geezers coming to see off nobody."

"How do you know that?"

"I just do. Now get on the blower and fix me up on a flight out."

"You're just saying that; it's just you don't want me feeling bad."

I give him a long look.

"All right," Wally says at last. "But how'd you know? I mean, who put you in it?"

"Wally, you've never been one for asking questions. Don't start changing the habits of a life time. So just get on the blower will you, before I start remembering about that plant pot."

Wally begins to rise, but before he's halfway up I grab his collar and sit him down again.

"And Wally," I say to him, "not a whisper to D'Antoni. Nothing. Understand that? Nothing."

Wally knows better than to ask why, so in return for his silence I let him go and he gets up and he begins to walk towards the door only to find D'Antoni's appeared framed in the doorway. Wally stops walking and D'Antoni starts and when he reaches Wally it's D'Antoni's turn to get a grip.

"The phone rang," he says. "Who was it?"

"How do I know?"

"Why didn't you answer it?"

"I was in the Karsi, wasn't I?"

"The phone's supposed to be off."

"They must have fixed up the lines."

"And what else must they have fixed up?"

"What?"

D'Antoni slaps Wally's face for him.

"It stinks. You know that?"

I get up off the bed.

"Leave him alone," I say wearily. "It was probably the Fletchers phoning up to see if you've still got the top of your head on."

D'Antoni releases Wally who nips round the back of him and out onto the landing.

"I want my guns," he says. "Give them back."

"Can I be in your gang if I do?"

"Listen — "

"Oh, for Christ's sake. Leave it out, will you?"

"I need them."

"What for? So's you can put the fear of God up Wally? Find some other way of passing the time."

I walk out of the bedroom and along the landing and down the stairs and into the lounge. Wally's already on the phone, getting through to the airport, obviously listening while someone else on the other end is giving him the rabbit. I walk over to the drinks and pour myself a vodka and Wally never takes his eyes off me; it's like being watched by a shit-house rat, and it gets on my nerves, so I draw the curtains and slide open the window and walk out onto the patio. The swimming pool is a lighter shade of pale against the rest of the blackness. I walk over to its edge and contemplate its stillness but I'm not allowed to get my thoughts into any kind of orderly flow because from the balcony on the first floor comes the sound of D'Antoni's voice asking me, in his own inimitable way, what I think I'm doing. I turn round and look up at the balcony but the light from the window below doesn't illuminate D'Antoni's figure. He's probably lying on his stomach with a continental quilt over his head. When I don't answer D'Antoni begins all over again, so to leave myself out of that one I go back inside and close the window and draw the curtains. Wally is in the act of putting down the phone and he even manages to make that look as though he's been caught with his hand in the till.

"There's one non-charter tomorrow," he says, his tone already apologetic.

"And the good news?"

"It's not till the afternoon."

Before I have time to comment, D'Antoni is in the room.

"What were you doing?" he says to me.

I ignore him and sit down and close my eyes.

"Out there," he says. "You want to get yourself blown away too?"

I continue ignoring him.

"Or maybe you won't," D'Antoni says, making for the drinks, waving a revolting finger at me. "Maybe you won't. Maybe you're in on the deal. Maybe you just get the phone call and fifteen minutes later you slide open the windows to let them know they can come in now, it's safe."

"That's right," I tell him. "You finally twigged. While you were on your back catching flies I drove down into Palma and discussed the deal with them. They'll be here any minute."

D'Antoni stops pouring the drink he's started pouring.

"You don't believe me?" I ask him.

D'Antoni remains in the same position.

"Ask Wally. And if you don't believe him, take a look out the front. The car's out, and it's pointing this way."

D'Antoni looks at Wally.

"Don't take no notice of Jack, Mr D'Antoni," he says. "Jack's just having a little joke, aren't you Jack?"

"Did he go out?"

Wally looks to me for help but he's never going to get any so he says:

"Well, yeah, he went out, so to speak, but it ain't like what he said. All he did was go out for a bevy, like. That's all."

D'Antoni rushes past Wally and into the dripping darkness of the entrance hall and peers out through the night-black glass. When he's finally distinguished the shape of the Mercedes from his own contorted expression he comes back into the lounge as if he's just taken one round the earhole from Ali.

"You were telling the truth," he says.

"I was a good scout," I tell him. "Dib dib, dob dob."

D'Antoni puts his drink away, then hurries over to the cabinet so that it's not too long a time between drinks. When he's put the second one away he starts making himself a third and while he's doing that he says: "I was right. Why should I trust anybody, just because they're with the Fletchers? Bread is bread."

He downs the third one but the drink only gets far enough to clash with a short sharp laugh that's risen up as far as his throat. While he's gargling with laughter, Wally takes the opportunity to slide off out of it, and myself, I can't help considering the irony of the situation, if only D'Antoni knew how close he is to the truth, and how easy it would be for me to flesh out his fantasy. So I decide to tell him something to stop his wailing that is as close to the truth as he'll ever get.

"Listen, mate," I tell him. "I'm not here to knock you over. You're forgetting when I arrived I didn't even know you were here."

"An act. It could have been an act."

"So why are you still walking about? I didn't even have to announce myself. And supposing it was a con, I could have laid you low any time I felt like it. So could Wally, come to that."

D'Antoni clears his throat and pours himself another drink and although he doesn't like to acknowledge it he sees the apparent sense in what I've just said, if not the four-fifths that remain submerged. So what he does is to take his drink and wander around the room with the grace of a bear covered with bees, voiceless for the time being. Eventually he homes in on a wicker chair and sits down and proceeds to stare across the room at me.

"You in the war?" he says.

"Oh, yes," I tell him. "I was in the war. Only I fought it on the home front, seeing as I was three when it broke out."

"Yeah, well neither was I," he says. "Only, my brother was. He died a couple of years back. Big C. But one story he told me, when he was in the Ardennes slugging it out with Von Runstedt, he was called in before his top brass and given a very peculiar assignment, that being to take a few guys out at night and ambush some guys, wipe them out, and return to base. Only the peculiar thing was the guys they were ambushing were our own guys, and my brother was ordered to make the whole deal look as though the Krauts did the job."

I sip my drink and say nothing.

"Naturally, my brother did the job. He did his work. Why shouldn't he? He got his orders, and the people he got them from out-ranked the people he had to go to work on. So he did his job. Never did find out why it was done. He just did it."

"Interesting," I say to him.

"Yeah. That's what I thought."

I get up and pour another drink.

"Why'd you go?" he says.

"What?"

"Out."

"Like Wally said. I went out for a bevy. A drink."

"Where'd you go?"

"Palma."

"All that way. With all this on the premises."

"I like drinking in company."

"What kind of company?"

I turn round and face him.

"Company that doesn't concern you. I mean, I was supposed to be coming here on my holidays. I could have made contingency arrangements."

"Ass?"

"Whatever you like to call it."

"You got that here too?"

"Have I?"

"What you mean?"

156

I spread my hands.

"Where?"

When it's sunk in D'Antoni slowly lifts himself up out of his chair, then begins to move in the direction of the hall, the motion accelerating like a broken film being fed back into the projector. I drink my drink and listen to his progress round the villa, calling, at turns, Tina and Wally, and being answered by silence. Another drink later and D'Antoni reappears.

"Where is she?" he asks.

"Could be anywhere," I tell him. "As long as it's got drinks and fellers."

"She's out?"

"By now, that's very likely."

"She went out?"

"She stowed away when I went into Palma. In the back of the car."

"And she didn't come back?"

I shake my head.

"You left her there?"

"That's right."

"Jesus Christ."

"She can take care of herself," I say innocently. "I thought you knew that?"

"You bastard, you know what I mean."

I shrug.

"Anything could happen," D'Antoni says. "Supposing she gets smashed out of her mind and the cops pick her up and bring her home; maybe the guys've gotten in with the cops, maybe – "

"Yeah, and supposing Wally poisons you with his fried squid." I get up and make for the drinks. "For Christ's sake."

"Listen, it's not your ass. Maybe if it was you'd need three pairs of pants with your suit."

I ignore him and make my drink.

"Yeah," he says. "I can see it, if you were on the line. Under the covers, sucking on your security blanket."

I start to walk across the room.

"Which reminds me," I say to him, "I must go and check if Wally's filled my hot water bottle."

I walk out into the hall and start up the stairs. D'Antoni follows after me.

"You're nothing, you know that," he shouts after me.

I turn round. D'Antoni has one foot on the bottom step.
"If I'm nothing, why aren't you waving your shooters about?"
D'Antoni doesn't answer.
I look at him for a minute before turning away.

Chapter Thirteen

In the dark, lying on my bed, smoking, I consider what to do when I get back to London, whether to do it to Gerald and Les first or wait and see if they've got the sense to forgive and forget, and if they haven't, wondering in what manner they'll choose to remember. If, of course, after all these years of my allowing them to lie fallow they're still up to moving for themselves. On the other hand, there's probably one or two self-lovers who imagine that flaking me could take them to the top of their profession. On the other hand again, if I were to do unto Gerald and Les as they would do unto me, the tame law that they employ might remain unconvinced that the readies that play such an important part in their decision-making processes might not be so cast-iron and regularly forthcoming if the Old Firm was disbanded. Old Bill might even feel the need to put on a show trial, just to keep the paper readers happy, and I'd be number one down the steps. A number of possibilities, I think to myself. And all because I've lost my rag about being asked to top a wop whose shuffling off would be basically a matter of sublime fucking indifference to myself. I stub my cigarette out and reflect on how much good my holidays have done me. Even Cleethorpes had nothing on this.

From downstairs there is no sound whatsoever. D'Antoni is probably embarking on route for his third hangover of the day, whereas Wally is probably maintaining a low profile in the karsi belonging to the next villa which is approximately four miles down the road. Again, in the quiet, I try and work out which alternative I'm going to take, but the quiet is too quiet, it's not like the night-buzz background back in Soho, and my mind goes as blank as the Spanish silence. But the silence doesn't stay blank for very long. In through the windows drifts the far-off sound of a car gasping up the mountain road, a noise like a very small bronchial gnat. The sound drones on and on, never seeming to get any closer. Then, abruptly, it stops. For a minute or so, inside and out, everything is quiet again. Then the silence is broken by the sound of D'Antoni flip-flopping up the stairs, the noise of his beach-shod feet sounding like tripe being thrown on a monger's slab.

Inevitably, he appears in the bedroom doorway.

"You hear that?" he says.

I don't answer him

"It's stopped now."

"Then I can't hear it, can I?"

"It stopped out there on the road."

"The noise?"

"An automobile. It stopped on the road."

"It's a steep road."

"There's only one reason to stop out there and that's to call here because there ain't nowhere else."

"Maybe they ran out of petrol."

"And maybe it's Mickey and Donald and Goofy out having a midnight picnic."

I don't say anything.

"Where are the guns?"

"I forgot."

"I want them."

"No."

"You really want me knocked over don't you?"

I don't answer him.

"I mean, you like the idea so much, why'n't you just go ahead and fix up the job yourself?"

There's no answer to that either.

"So what are you going to do?" D'Antoni asks.

"You mean about knocking you over?"

"Listen, you bastard, the hills could be crawling with pistols."

"Or, like you say, maybe it's Mickey and Donald and Goofy on a midnight picnic."

D'Antoni stands there for a minute or two, then he turns around and disappears into the darkness, pad-padding as far as the top of the stairs. Then there is silence again. Silence, that is, until the darkness is reversed by the illuminating of the hall and the landing from down below.

"What the Christ," shrieks D'Antoni.

There is no immediate reply to that.

"Turn 'em off, you mother," D'Antoni continues.

The lights go off, sharp.

After a little time has elapsed, Wally's voice drifts up from the well of the hall.

"What's the bleedin' game, then?"

My earlier remarks have allowed a little brave petulance to act as a splint for his tonsils. D'Antoni tells him to shut up and keep quiet. I light another cigarette. Time passes and the silence gets heavier.

Eventually Wally says: "What's going on?"

D'Antoni shuts him up again.

More time, more silence, and a couple more cigarettes. D'Antoni and Wally remain frozen in the black aspic. Then something happens.

It happens outside. The surface of the silence is rippling with the sound of footsteps on the gravelled part of the villa's approach. For a little while this is all that happens. Then D'Antoni's Disney croak floats into the bedroom.

"Now you hear," he says.

I don't answer him, neither do I move.

"They're here," he says. "They came for me."

The footsteps get closer. Then they stop. I can hear D'Antoni crawling along the landing back in the direction of my bedroom, and while he's on his way back, he makes another request to have his shooters back, but he's cut short in the middle of his appeal by the sound of tinkling laughter from beyond the plate glass, or at least that's the way Audrey would describe it. To me, it's the sound of the well-pissed brass, and immediately I begin to feel a little more at home. Then the laughter is augmented by more of the same, in a slightly higher key.

"Broads," D'Antoni says.

The laughter dies down, then wells up again.

"There's broads outside," D'Antoni says.

"They got Women's Lib in the Mafia yet?" I ask him.

"What?"

I get off the bed.

"Forget it."

I switch on the light. D'Antoni is on all fours, half-in and half-out of the bedroom doorway. He looks up at me like a cat caught in headlights.

"Get up," I tell him. "You got nothing to worry about. It's only Wally's skin and your philanthropist's old lady."

"What?"

"Gerald's missus."

D'Antoni looks back at me, his mouth hanging open.

"Mrs Fletcher," I tell him. "You mean to tell me you never met Mrs Fletcher?"

"Why?"

"Why what?"

"Why's she here?"

"Well, seeing as how for one reason or another the villa's in her name, why shouldn't she be?"

"You know why she's here?"

I let him off the hook.

"She probably came on account of Gerald and Les. See if you was all right, and that."

"You know she was coming?"

"Not until tonight. I saw her in Palma. She's staying there."

Something I said seems to make sense to D'Antoni.

"She's staying there, hey? That's not bad."

"What?"

"Her on the look-out in Palma." He gets to his feet. "That's not bad. They said they'd look after me real good."

And they meant it, I think to myself.

The footsteps clatter across the flagstones and then there's the noise of plate glass shuddering as one or the other of them try to slide the door open. It doesn't. And from the language when it doesn't I gather it's Audrey as tried the sliding. I walk past D'Antoni and out onto the landing. By now Audrey is giving the plate glass a right seeing to, the shuddering glass accompanied by more of the language. I reach the balustrade and call down to Wally to put the lights on, but Wally is no longer there, which is no small surprise if he's recognized the voice of Audrey. So I go downstairs and find the light switch and flick it on and Audrey and Tina are illuminated against the deep blackness like twin Cinderellas. I look at them and they look at me. It doesn't need a breathaliser to rate their condition. In the hard light from the hall they look like two moths drunk with neon. Tina is grinning at everything in the whole world whereas Audrey is at the stage of drunkenness where the amount of things that she finds amusing is rapidly diminishing. We continue to look at each other. Audrey is fucked if she's going to indicate in any way at all that she wants to be let in. I smile at her for a minute to two, letting her bask in the sweetness of my smile, then I walk across the hall and unbolt the panel and slide it open.

"Enjoy that, did you?" Audrey says.

"I always enjoy seeing you, Audrey," I tell her. "You coming in?"

She's about to give me an answer to that one when I notice a movement behind her shoulder and she sees that I've noticed and that the movement has nothing to do with Tina and therefore instead of giving me the answer her expression changes into a mirror-image of the one I was giving her beyond the plate-glass, and the movement which in fact has drawn my attention is the parting of some bushes on the perimeter of the block of light and the emergence of the Dagenham boys, flicking the dewdrops off their prick-ends, grinning into the bright plate glass as though they're seeing Blackpool Illuminations for the first time.

"What the fuck's this?" I say to Audrey. "You gone into the mystery tour business?"

"There's no mystery about this, darlin'," Audrey says, walking past me into the hall. Tina begins to sway in after her, like a reed caught in the slipstream of a powerboat.

"Wally!" Audrey shouts. "The above have arrived. Start mixing the drinks."

Behind me, the lounge lights come on, and Wally emerges from round the corner and gives her the big glad.

"Hello, Mrs Fletcher," he says. "This is great. It's really great to see you."

"I know it is," Audrey says.

Wally starts back-pedalling into the lounge.

"Yeah, it's great. A real treat. Unexpected, like," he says.

There's a marked change in the tone of Wally's voice. He now sounds like a snide kid whose mother's arrived on the scene to put everybody who's in the right in the wrong. Audrey, followed by Tina, follows Wally into the lounge. Meanwhile, the Dagenham boys have filtered into the hall, the assertory movements of their necks making them look like geese. I turn to face them and give them the look. Son number one looks back but from the state he's in it's difficult to tell whether anything as specific as my expression is registering. Number two son says:

"This is favourite. Better than Pontinental."

"Too bleedin' right," says Benny.

They start to move in the general direction of Audrey and Tina, sniffing like mongrels on heat. And I never did like dogs.

"You going in then?" I ask them.

Number two son snaps up.

"You what, sunshine?" he says.

"I said, you going in?"

"Yeah, that's where we're going. In."

"Only I thought you might be supplementing the rate of exchange by running a taxi service."

The sarcasm doesn't reach as far as Benny who says: "We hired one of them runabouts for the fortnight. Jesus, it's even worse than one of our Friday afternoon cars, ain't it — ?"

Barry ignores him and musters himself to make a reply to me, and it's sort of like him trying not to be sick in reverse, all sweat and swallow.

"Here," he says, putting his hand in his racing jacket and pulling out some pesetas. "You done your job smashing. Have a drink on me, my old son, and don't tap me again on the way out."

I'm just about to do more than tap him when Audrey reappears in the hall and says:

"I thought you two was dying for a flamin' drink?"

"We are," says Barry. "We was waiting for the butler here to fetch it."

"He'll fetch you something else if you carry on like that."

The boys grin at what they imagine to be Audrey's very funny joke and shuffle off through into the lounge as if they're entering a Chinese chippy on a Saturday night.

I watch them go through and I'm considering following them and serving them their drinks in my own inimitable way but I don't get to do that because I'm distracted by a noise up above my head, something that sounds like a foal breaking wind. I look up and I can see D'Antoni's head at floor level on the balcony, peering down from the top of the stairs, his lips pursed and responsible for the farting sound.

"What's going on?"

His voice is a cross between a whisper and a shout.

"It's party time," I tell him.

"Who is it?"

"It's a delegation from the T.G.W.U."

"What?"

"It's all right. It's not the Boston branch of the Mafia."

"Listen — "

"You want to find out, come down and join the party."

D'Antoni's disembodied head begins to wobble and the veins on his forehead stand out like a printed circuit.

"Listen — "

I walk into the lounge, where I don't have to listen, at least to him. The scene in there is very cosy. Everybody has got their drinks, due to the speed Wally has used to demonstrate his eagerness to please. The two Dagenham boys are still looking round like they're in St Paul's Cathedral. Tina is sitting on the floor, and Audrey is sprawled out on one of the leather sofas, her legs splayed out in front of her, feet shoeless, her drink clutched to her bosom. She raises a leg and plants it on the table in front of her. Benny distracted from his appraisal of the villa's architecture.

"Christ, — " he says. "Stockin's."

Audrey looks me in the eye and says:

"Yeah. I used to wear them for a friend of mine what I used to have."

Barry says:

"My old lady wears stockings."

"Yeah?" says Benny.

"Yeah. Surgical. A right turn-on, they are."

They both laugh fit to bust their anoraks.

"And winceyette drawers. And then she wonders why I'm out pulling every night."

More laughter.

I go over to the drinks and make myself one and when I've done that I go and sit down opposite Audrey. Audrey ignores that fact and says to Wally: "Bring some music, Wal, will you?"

"Yeah, sure. Anything in particular?"

"No, I'm not particular. Something with a bit of balls. Make a change round here, that would."

"So would being particular," I say to her.

Audrey looks at me and smiles her sweet and sour and cocks another leg up onto the table. Barry is slightly to my left, swaying a bit, not believing his luck at being able to see right up to the maker's name.

"If you're not careful," I say to Audrey, "we'll be able to see all the way up to the top of your clouts."

"Clouts," Audrey says, snorting with laughter. "Bleeding clouts. Tell where you was brung up, can't you."

"You can tell that," I tell her. "Also, you can tell where you weren't."

Audrey gives out with her fishwife cackle, to prove how coarse and drunk she is, but she's not being as clever as she thinks she is, because I've seen this act before, that act being appearing more drunk than you actually are, to give yourself an opportunity to bluff the opposition into a false sense of security, but what as yet I'm unable to suss out is who the performance is aimed at, and for why.

While these thoughts are coursing through my mind, Wally has sorted a cassette and bunged it into the machine which is custom-built into the wall adjacent to the back of my head. He's chosen a Shirley Bassey, which in the circumstances is a complement to the act Audrey is putting on for the benefit of the assembled company. And, after all, Big Spender is the number Audrey always uses when she's auditioning hopefuls at the club. And while she's listening to the music, now, she allows her features to relax into the kind of expression she normally reserves for the more successful of successful applicants, the ones who occasionally have to go through the rigours of an extra audition, that audition not necessarily being anything to do with the act they'll be presenting on the club stage, in public. So in the event, my gaze strays over to the closed-eyed figure of Tina, chin-on-knee on the floor, swaying very slightly to the beat of the number, and I consider whether or not Audrey is boiled up enough to have her revenge on me in that direction.

Barry manages to break the rabbit/ferret syndrome of his gaze and moves to get a little closer to the object of his fascination, sitting down on the leather next to Audrey. He strikes a pose not unlike a down-and-out character out of Film Fun, presented with the just rewards of a job well done, those being a fat cigar, bangers and mash, and a bottle of pop.

"Well," he says, "this is better than feeding rum and blacks to the old lady."

"Yeah," says Benny. "All it does is give them headaches."

More Tweedledum and Tweedledee laughter.

"Here, darlin'," Barry says to Audrey. "Rum and blacks give you headaches?"

"I don't get headaches," Audrey says.

"No, I didn't think you would."

More of the same from the sons.

"What about you, darlin'?" Benny says, nudging Tina in the back with his knee, "I bet you don't get headaches either, do you?"

Tina carries on swaying and not opening her eyes.

"I'm very happy," she says. "Very, very happy."

At which remark, Wally decides to make his presence felt.

"Tina," he says, "ain't it about time you was climbing up the wooden hills?"

With the same contented expression on her face, Tina says: "Piss off."

The sons go into their chorus again.

"Yeah, piss off," says Benny.

"Yeah," says Barry, "either that or fix us up another drink."

"Now look here," Wally begins, but Audrey cuts him off short.

"Turn it in, Wally," she says to him. "She ain't only grown up to be your daughter."

"Well, I mean to say," says Wally.

"You don't mean to say anything," Audrey says. "You never did. Your stock-in-trade is saying fuck all. It always was. That's why you're here. So. If you got nothing to say, stop pretending you have, and pour the drinks again."

Wally allows himself the luxury of shooting a glance at Tina, but apart from that he goes to work on the job that Audrey's suggested. I notice though, that he misses out Tina and serves my drink last. Just a passing observation. And while I'm observing that, I also observe that I'm getting the fish-eye from Barry.

"Well then, squire," he says, when he realizes I'm returning the compliment, "you the owner of this little pile, are you?"

The accompanying smirk I'm getting from him is a real stoker, but until I've sorted what Audrey's playing at I'm prepared to swallow and go along with the panel game.

"Not all of it," I tell him. "Just a couple of air bricks in the west wing."

"Put them in yourself, did you?"

"That's right. After I'd dug out the foundations."

Benny suddenly gets the idea we're having a serious conversation. "What you mean, foundations? They don't have foundations out here. Too much trouble, that is. Bleedin' wops start at the top, judging from our hotel."

"Not like the workmanship that comes off your production line," I say to him.

"What you mean?"

"I once had one of your heaps," I tell him. "Until then I didn't appreciate the true meaning of panel-beating."

"You're taking a bleedin' liberty," he says.

I shrug. Barry says: "You a liberty taker, are you?"

"It has been known."

"Taking one now, are you?"

"I dunno. You tell me."

Barry leans forward.

"All right," he says, "I'll tell you. I'll – "

"Oh for Christ's sake," Audrey says. "Can't you think of any better ways of proving you're butch?"

Barry looks at her.

"Any time, darlin'. Do you mind having an audience?"

Audrey, of course, wouldn't care if it was the middle of Wembley stadium on Cup Final Day, providing that I wasn't in the crowd, knowing, as she does, what the consequences would be if she ever pulled that kind of performance on me; it's different with birds at the club. That I'll wear, because she's no ulterior motives directed against me. So, in the event, as a reply to the Dagenham son she stands up and gets in time with the music and sways over to where the drinks are. I get up too and join her as she's pouring the second half of her drink.

"What's the bleeding game, then?" I ask her.

Audrey takes a sip of her drink.

"Any game that's going, sweetheart," she says, hiding behind the fifty per cent falseness of her boozy act. "Any game at all, and any number can play."

"Brought this lot to make the numbers up, did you?"

"They *are* the numbers. From tonight you're not included in anything."

I pick up a bottle and hold it poised over my glass.

"Stop playing the silly buggers. It's Jack Carter you're talking to, not your old man. I'm not exactly your Wilton or your Axminster. Just cut out the cobblers and tell me what you're really about."

Still she persists.

"You've had your chance to find out what I'm about ducky," she says. "Now it's time somebody else had a turn."

She turns away and begins to make it back to the sunken area. I pour my drink and drink half of it and then top it up again. I look at the group in the sunken area. They're like figures in an empty swimming pool and Wally hovers round the edge playing the role of lifeguard, as well he might, because Benny is now sitting on the floor right next to Tina, in a mirror position, the only part of him not reflected being his right hand which is somewhere underneath the edge of Tina's cheese-cloth, although Wally, as yet, has not sussed this development, not being precisely adjacent to the proceedings.

"The beauty of this situation," says Barry to nobody in particular, "is that if we tell our old ladies about it, there is no way they're going to believe it, so we're in the bleedin' clear, aren't we?"

"Makes no difference," says Benny. "I never tell the old cow nothing. She can like it or bleedin' lump it and if she lumps it she knows where she can bleedin' go looking for herself."

"Too right," says Barry.

As he's endorsing his brother's views on the essence of matrimony, the light in the hall is switched off. Barry flicks his head in the direction of the blackness.

"What's that then?" he says. "Is it remote control, or has the bulb gone?"

I walk over to the edge of the sunken area.

"It's the resident ghost," I tell him. "All castles in Spain have one."

"Oh yeah?" he says. "What is it? A Spanish plasterer what got too close to his work?"

"No," I tell him. "It's the spirit of the last bloke Audrey had up here and ate for breakfast. Last thing he ever did was switch the light out, that was."

"Not quite the last," Audrey says, sitting down next to Barry again and again giving the assembled company a treat. Even I can see right up to the top and I'm standing on the upper level.

"What is the name of this gaff, anyway?" asks Barry. "The Casa Nova, is it? Get it? Casa Nova. Casanova?"

More laughter.

"The Karsi Nova," Benny says.

And more.

While that's going on I saunter over in the direction of the blackness and as I approach I can make out the shape of D'Antoni's head peering round the corner of the wall, like some voyeur who by rights should be on the other side of the plate glass. I'm far enough away from the assembled throng for anything I say to go unheard so I say to D'Antoni: "Looks like a late night chat show, don't it?"

"Who are they?"

He still sounds as though Henry Cooper's fetched him one in the gut.

"Pick-ups," I tell him. "A bit of rough trade for the lady of the house."

"Is she crazy? Jesus. Doesn't anybody care what all this is about?"

I don't answer him.

"She could blow everything, what she's doing?"

Mentally I agree with his words, but I give them a coarser interpretation. Especially, looking back at the group, now that I can see that Audrey's sitting on the floor with her back to the settee, her head not all that far away from the vicinity of Barry's crutch.

"Don't worry about it. They're smashed. In the morning they'll think they dreamt it."

"How'd they get up here?"

"They're in the Seat, parked out on the road? Forget it. Nothing's going to happen."

"Look – "

"Calm down. Come and join the party. That's the only thing'll kill you round here."

I walk back to the centre of the room. I don't have to look back to know that D'Antoni has declined to step out of the shadows; however, Wally moves instead, intercepting me before I reach the edge of the sunken area, and judging from the expression on his face he's had a different aspect of the sub-cheese-cloth activities of Benny. Under cover of the noise of the music he says to me:

"Here, Jack, I mean to say, is this going to be a bit strong?"

"Changed your tune a bit, haven't you? Where's all the open arms bit gone to?"

"It's not the open arms I'm worried about."

"Well, take it up with the lady of the house," I tell him. "She's in charge."

As if to underline my statement, Audrey's voice climbs above the level of the music.

"Here, Wal, you got the new batch in?"

Wally turns away from me and shows Audrey his other face.

"Beg pardon, Mrs Fletcher?"

"The new batch. They get here all right?"

"Oh, them. Yeah, thanks Mrs Fletcher. Smooth, like as usual."

"Checked them out, have you?"

"Oh, yes. Mint condition, they are. Course, I didn't check them all yet, seeing as they only just come in, like."

"I bet."

"Well, been seeing to our guests like, ain't I?"

"Yeah, well, see to our guests now, then."

"Eh?"

"They need livening up. Don't want them nodding off, do we?"

"No."

"So wheel the projector out. Let's have some real holiday movies."

Barry says: "What's all this, then?"

"Thought you might like to watch some home movies."

"Blues, are they?" Barry says, thinking she's joking.

"Course they bleedin' are," Audrey says.

"You what?"

"What did you think they was: this is Aunt Edna paddling and that's those nice people from Watford in the background what was on the same table as us on the barbecue?"

Barry clasps his hands and rubs them together. "Christ," he says, "it gets better. It's Christmas all over again."

Wally has not yet moved so Audrey says to him:

"Come on, then, Wal. Get your skates on. We're only here for a fortnight."

"You want me to get the projector now?" he says.

"Yeah, that's right, Wal," Audrey says. "And a couple or three films as well, eh, or there won't be no point in getting the projector, will there?"

"I'll have to go down to the basement to get it," Wally says.

"That's right," Audrey says. "Handy, that is, because that's where the films are as well. Save you a journey, won't it?"

"Yes," Wally says. He turns away and begins to walk towards the blackness of the hall.

"And make sure they're different ones you get," Audrey calls after him. "Not all the same, eh, Wal?"

Wal disappears into the blackness and I listen to his footsteps disappearing in the direction of the basement door: either D'Antoni's doing an impression of the fish's reflection or he's cleaned off out of it because the sound of Wally's footsteps disappears naturally into the darkness. Audrey, in the event of Wally's departure, makes a production of struggling up from the floor and over to the drinks for a refill. I walk over and join her.

"You're taking lots of chances tonight," I tell her.

"Oh yes?"

"I mean, for all you know D'Antoni could have been on sentry duty with his magnum."

"Could have been, couldn't he?"

"On the other hand, how could you be so sure I wouldn't open the door and smack your teeth down the back of your throat?"

"Perhaps you would have done at one time, sweetheart. But now you've lost your balls, I reckoned I was in no danger of that happening."

I come to the decision that it's been too long since I fetched Audrey one so I decide to remedy that state of affairs when Barry arrives in the vicinity of my right shoulder, to which part of my anatomy he applies his bear-like hand, not pushing, exactly, but resting there with a certain force which would need application from myself in order to move forward against his outstretched arm.

"You getting bother from him, darlin?" he asks Audrey.

"Bother?" she says. "From him? You must be joking."

Now, naturally, the Dagenham son poses me no problems whatsoever, except perhaps one, that being leaving off before I actually put him out of this life forever. And I have to confess, that whereas I seldom indulge in that kind of business except in a strictly professional capacity, at this moment I would enjoy taking a Busman's Holiday and seeing him off in the way it should be done, a way that he would be both unlikely and unlucky if he were to ever encounter it again. On the other hand, I would probably get more satisfaction out of giving Audrey one or two, it being her that is getting farther up my nose than anybody else in the assembled company. But I never get round to choosing between the two alternatives because Wally has returned with the jollies and he announces his presence by dropping the films and putting down the projector and jumping in, as it were, at the deep end of the sunken area, his actions inspired by the fact that it's not now just a matter of Benny having his hand up Tina's cheese-cloth; events have progressed, and Tina's giving Benny a massage, albeit on the outside of his trousers. But before Wally has time to drag Tina up off the floor to the safety of his bosom, Benny has sussed what's about to happen and he's surprisingly neat at getting up and getting a grip on Wally, and quite an effective grip at that, because he's grasped Wally by the balls, and Wally's only course of action is to flail his limbs about like a monkey on a stick.

"What's your fucking story, then, Grandad?" Benny says. "What's your story all about when it boils down to it?"

"Jesus Christ," Wally screeches. "Let go for fuck's sake."

"Yeah, let go," Audrey says. "He's got to operate the machine."

She uses the diversion as an excuse to walk back to the centre of the room, and at the same time Barry drops his hand as he turns away to watch the curtain raiser to the forthcoming entertainments. I restrain myself from giving him one in the back of the neck and limit my arm movements to putting some more alcohol into my glass. So Benny then lets Wally go and Wally sits down on the leather for a minute or two until the tears have shed themselves from his eyes. Then, when he can see again, he sets the projector up on a low stool outside of the sunken area and breaks open one of the boxes and begins to thread the celluloid through the machine. When he's done that, he flicks on the projector for a second or two to see that it's taken properly, then he goes over to the wall and switches off the lights. Now the whole villa is in darkness. Wally walks back to the machine and trains it on the white wall and switches on again. Blank leader flickers on the whiteness. Then the title appears, out of focus. Wally adjusts the lens and the title is as sharp as one of Les's suits.

RANDY THREESOME, the title reads.

"Here," Barry says to his brother, "remember when Sammy Spencer used to run the Blues in the paint shop at twenty pence a time?"

"Yeah. Favourite, that was. Then that bleedin' shop steward had to put his spoke in."

"Never got re-elected, though, did he."

On the wall, the action begins.

It starts the way they all do. The bird is sitting on the inevitable sofa, leafing through a magazine. Close-up of her looking bored. Back to the initial shot. She closes the magazine, lies down on the settee, then begins giving herself a seeing to. That goes on for five minutes or so then there's another shot, outside this time, and guess what, it's the man to come and see about the waste-pipe under the sink. The girl pulls her drawers up and lets the man about the waste pipe in and from then on there's about ten minutes of action centring around the kitchen table and of course it's got sod all to do with unbunging the plumbing.

Then drama rears it's ugly head in the shape of the returning husband, by which time I'm over by the window and parting the curtains and looking out at the comparitive excitement of the movement of the sky at night. Still, judging by the remarks, the rest of the audience is appreciating the action.

"Bet your old lady wouldn't mind getting one like that up her regular," Barry says to his brother.

"How'd you know she don't?"

"Cause she told me, last time I gave her one."

Laughter.

"Jesus, look at him. Makes the other fellow look like our old dad before he's had his mild."

"After, you mean."

The projector whirls on. I turn round to look at the group, illuminated as they are in the stream of white light from the projector. So far as I can see nothing is as yet happening between Audrey and Barry, although at the other end of the settee Tina still has her eyes half closed and Benny is close enough to be up the cheesecloth again.

"You seen this one, Wal?" Audrey says.

"Yeah, this is one of the ones I seen."

"In that case why did you run it?"

"Eh?"

"Think it's good, do you?"

"Well, not bad, yeah."

"It's bleedin' terrible. No bleedin' idea. Jack, who done this one?"

She must be bleeding barmy, shouting the odds in front of the sons, but there's no real point in me having that thought because she is, and always has been bleeding barmy; the only time she's not is when she's running the business with me on behalf of the Brothers Grimm, and I consider that all things being equal, I'm lucky to have survived as long as I have; maybe the parting of the ways will be no bad thing and I'll maybe be able to pick up my old age pension in my old age.

"This one one of Terry's, is it?"

"I wouldn't know."

"Course you do. It's one of Terry's. Written all over it. Apart from the fact he's using his puffy mate again. Look, he's getting him to do his thing again."

And indeed Terry has, because his mate is going down on the other bloke while the girl is going down on him.

"Fuck me," Barry says, "the dirty bastards. Yeech."

"Makes you want to fetch up," Benny says. "People doing something like that. Fucking lettuce leaves."

I smile to myself. He should have been present at some of the gatherings Gerald and Les have laid on in the past and witnessed some of the heavies with a couple or three topping jobs to their credit behaving exactly as the so-called lettuce leaf in the movie is behaving.

On the wall the activities come to an end with the concerted sparting from the two male leads, then the square becomes blank white again.

"Christ, he only bleedin' swallowed it," Barry says.

"You can learn to swallow anything in time, can't you, Jack?" Audrey says, snuggling a bit close to Barry.

I don't answer her, taking the view that everything comes to him who waits.

Wally removes the spools off the projector.

"Are you bothering with another one?" he asks.

"They can't be as piss poor as that," Audrey says. "Try one of the others."

Wally loads the projector and the shaft of light begins to flicker again. This time the title says : CLASSROOM RAPE.

The title fades. We're presented with a different scene, but from the immediate evidence it's not going to be a lot different from the first one. This time the bird's in schoolgirl gear, and instead of sitting on a sofa leafing through a magazine she's sitting at a desk leafing through a magazine. We're shown a close-up of the magazine which is full of the unlovely faces of the almost current batch of pop stars and it's not long before the inevitable happens and she's got her hand in her drawers and she's having a go at herself. Ho-hum. The shot changes and it's of another girl sticking her head round a door and reacting to what's going on out of shot, hand to shocked mouth, all the usual palaver. The thing that lends interest to this pantomime, though, is that underneath the false blonde pigtail wig, the face is somewhat familiar, but before memory has arranged the features into place the film cuts and we're back with the self-absorbtion of the girl at the desk, only this time the camera is set a bit farther back and the background is sharper, and although I hadn't really considered it before, the setting isn't the usual curtained living room, it's a much bigger area than any council flat or any semi and the furniture and ornamentation are of a different variety, consisting of a variety of easels and casts of various pieces of classical sculpture. I've just about taken that in when the film cuts again to the familiarity of the girl at the door who now is pantomiming to a person or persons unknown, and as it happens it turns out to be persons, because a trio of young yobbos appear behind her in the doorway, all done up fifties style, in leather jackets and drapes, but the thing giving the lie to their assumed period is the hairstyles. Also, they don't have the feel of the genuine article, the real patina of thickness, they look much too self-aware in a different kind of way. But it isn't these fine fellows that have my interest at all. It's the girl beneath the blonde plaits who is holding my attention because I've just realized who she is. I look across at Wally who is squatting on his haunches by the projector. He's paying more attention to what he's plucking out of his nose than what's happening up on the wall so as yet he hasn't twigged who's a part of the action, which has by now developed to the part where our starlet in the blonde plaits is urging the job trio into spread-eagling the magazine reader across the desk as a prelude to doing their worst. But Wally doesn't have long to wait to be put in it because of course it's Barry who is the next to suss it out.

"Here, hang about," he says. "Hold on."

"That's — that's — "

"Yeah, all right," I tell him, standing on the raised part of the floor so that the back of his head is level with the toe of my moccasin. He takes no notice and leans forward, still pointing.

"It's her. It's the bird."

He reaches across Audrey and shakes his brother by the shoulder and his brother takes his tongue out of Tina's ear and turns round to see what Barry is on about.

"Look at the bleedin' film," Barry urges. "Look at it, you wanker."

Benny looks at the screen and while he's doing that Audrey fights her way up from the back of the settee and pushes between the Dagenham sons and has a look for herself. At this time, on the screen, the girl in the blonde plaits is taking off the drawers of the first girl who is still being spread-eagled across the desk. Then the film cuts to a close up of the girl in the blonde plaits who is grinning at the camera as a result of her latest accomplishment and if there was ever any doubt, there's none now.

I look at Wally again. He's still got an index finger up his left nostril but now his eyes are focussed on the images playing on the plaster.

"Fuck me," Benny says, "it's her. It's the bird."

Tina turns her head slightly and half-opens her eyes and she looks at the wall too.

"S'me," she says. She giggles and then she closes her eyes again.

Wally remains frozen on his haunches, his finger still up his nose.

"I don't believe it," Audrey says. "I really don't believe it."

"It's right," Barry says. "It's her. Look at it."

It is then that Wally moves. I'm prepared for this but he doesn't do as I expected and take the shortest distance between two points so there's nothing I can do to impede his progress, because what he does is to walk down the steps into the sunken area and very carefully pick his way through the outstretched legs until he's got to the part of the settee where Tina is. When he reaches her, he stands in front of her for a moment or two, looking down at her, before he stretches out an arm and grabs her by her hair and yanks her up off the settee. Then several things happen all at once. Tina starts screaming and flailing at her old man and Benny stands up to intercede on Tina's behalf, but Wally, with his free hand, lands a lucky punch for the first time in his life and he's even lucker that Audrey's legs are at the back of Benny's knees, making the punch look even more effective. Benny sprawls across Audrey and finishes up with his head in his brother's lap. Audrey immediately starts shrieking about her drink and his drink which she's had spilled on her dress, and at the same time Wally starts smacking his offspring round the head, while on the wall his offspring is going down on her pinioned co-star.

"You bleedin', fucking, bastard, whoring tart," Wally tells Tina, each word accompanied and underlined by a blow. "No wonder you was slung out."

He begins to go through his description of her again, blow by blow, and I'm getting to the point where I'm thinking Tina's had enough strap when Benny struggles himself up off the heap on the settee and grabs hold of Wally and sends him flying to the far end of the sunken area. Benny begins to go after him but Tina is already in front of him, leaning over her old man and taking her turn at shouting the odds. Benny pushes her to one side and starts to give Wally a right old kicking, and now it's really time, so I put down my drink very carefully on the edge of the sunken area and wade in.

The kicking Wally's getting hasn't prevented Tina from carrying on with her shouting and so Wally's getting it both physically and verbally. But not for too long because I get behind Benny and spin him round and give him a little trio of mine that's come in very handy ever since my bouncing days. First of all I hit him very hard in the gut. Then, as he's doubling up, I accelerate the process by grabbing hold of his hair and pushing downwards so that with some speed his face happens to coincide with my up-coming knee, which is also moving at some speed. And that is all there is to it. Never been known to fail. Minimum effort, maximum effect. Benny goes to the floor like he's made of marble.

I turn round again to face the inevitable rise of Barry. He's half way up off the settee when I ask him if he wants any of what his brother's just got. It appears he thinks he does, because he puts his glass down on the low table and exchanges it for a bottle which he smashes on the table's edge and point in my direction.

"All right," he says. "That was a good one. Now let's see you do it again, under these circumstances."

He starts to grin but before the grin can get very broad I put my foot to the edge of the table and shove it as hard as I can so that the far edge drives into Barry's shin just a couple of inches below his knee-cap. He bellows out and drops the bottle and his hands go to his injury. I walk round the table and give him a couple similar to what I gave his brother and as a consequence there's not going to be much heard from him for the next five minutes or so.

I turn back to Wally. Tina by now has shut up and straightened up and looks completely sober. Wally is still sitting on the floor, nursing his ribs.

"You all right, Wal?" I ask him.

"Not too bad. He was wearing beach shoes."

"I wish they'd been climbing boots," Tina says.

"You," I say to her. "Upstairs."

"You what?"

"Upstairs."

"Look, you – "

"I told you. Upstairs. Or if you like, I'll take you."

She looks at me.

"Right," I say. "Now fuck off out of it."

She looks at me for a little bit longer.

"Well, at least you proved *one* thing today," she says.

Then she begins to walk out of the lounge.

"What's that supposed to mean?" Audrey says, taking her eyes off her dabbing for a moment to look up at me.

"Fuck all," I tell her.

There is a silence. The film is still beating against the plasterwork. All three of us look at it for a while. The plot has been dispensed with. The first girl is no longer acting the victim. The proceedings have developed into the usual free for all. I walk over to the machine and switch it off. The room is pitch black again. I go over to the wall and find the light switch and when the room is relatively bright again the first thing I see is that D'Antoni is standing inside of the lounge area, hands in pockets, grinning all over his face.

"Well," he says. "Well, well, well."

All three of us look at him. He crosses the room to where the drinks are. All three of us are still looking at him. He starts to pour himself a drink and while he's pouring he says:

"That was some movie."

None of us say anything.

"It really was. One hell of a movie."

He puts the bottle down and takes a drink from his glass. Then he laughs.

"A Star is Born," he says.

He laughs again.

"Cute. A real Shirley Temple."

He sings the first line of "On the Good Ship Lollipop". When he gets to the word "Lollipop" he makes a sucking noise, which makes him laugh even louder.

"You met Mr D'Antoni, Audrey?" I ask her.

"I have now," she says.

D'Antoni comes down into the sunken area and sits down on the matching settee opposite Audrey.

"So you're Mrs Fletcher," he says. "No wonder I didn't get to meet you last time I got over."

"Shame, wasn't it?" Audrey says.

"That it was."

There is a silence.

"Hey, Wally," D'Antoni says, "how about running the movies again. I didn't catch all of it."

Wally doesn't answer.

"Come on. She looked a great little performer."

Wally begins to get up but he'd never be a match for D'Antoni, so I say to him: "Go and make some coffee, Wal."

Wally stands where he is for a moment.

"All right," he says eventually, and makes for the hallway.

D'Antoni shakes his head.

"Jesus Christ," he says. "Wait till I tell them this one."

"Tell who?" I ask him.

D'Antoni looks at me. "You're funny, you know that?"

"Yes, I'm almost as funny as you."

D'Antoni shakes his head again.

On the floor, Barry begins to stir. I squat down and grab him by his collar and prop him up against the settee. Although his eyes are open it's quite some time before he sees me.

"You with us, squire?" I say to him.

His mouth moves but no sound comes out.

"You want some more before you go home to your old lady?"

His mouth moves again, to the same effect. I lift him to his feet and point to the floor.

"See that?" I ask him. "That's your brother. You're going to take him home, all right?"

I let go of him and he manages to stay on his feet. Then I bend down and pick his brother up off the floor and drape his arms round my shoulders. Then I take Barry's arm and begin to walk out of the sunken area. The movement starts to revive Benny who heaves right from the bottom of his stomach, the suddering effect causing one of his teeth to finally dislodge itself and rattle very faintly on the parquet floor.

We make it up the steps and across the rest of the room and out into the hallway. When we get to the plate glass, Barry has survived sufficiently to support himself so I slide back the opening and indicate the black night air.

"There you go," I tell them. "It's somewhere out there where you want to be."

I guide them through the opening and outside.

"If you wake up tomorrow and think of playing evens, don't bother," I tell them. "Come back here and I'll fucking crucify you. Either that or I'll put your old ladies in what you been up to."

Benny puts his hand to his face and only just manages not to sink to his knees.

"Right. Enjoy the rest of your holidays."

I slide the plate glass shut and watch the sons of Dagenham stagger down the steps and off across the flagstones in the direction of the track. When I've made sure they're properly on their way I cross the hall and go down the corridor to the kitchen. Wally is standing by the sink, examining the plughole, or something that's just gone down it. I light a cigarette. The sound the flame makes Wally turn away from the sink.

"Won't be long," Wally says.

"That's all right, Wal."

The silence is long and strained. Eventually I break it by saying: "I shouldn't worry too much about it."

Wally snorts, very softly, very bitterly.

"She's a fucking tart, that's what she is."

I shrug.

"Maybe," I say. "On the other hand, you do enjoy that kind of thing yourself, Wal."

"She's my own flesh and blood."

"Yeah."

"Well, I mean."

"Could be something in that."

"What?"

"Being your own flesh and blood. In the family, and that."

"What are you getting at?"

I shrug.

"You mean like heredity?" Wally says.

"Something like that."

Wally looks at me. The percolator begins to bubble. Wally turns away to see it.

"Anyway," I say, and walk out of the kitchen.

Back in the lounge D'Antoni and Audrey are still sitting in the same positions but since I went away the ice seems to have been broken somewhat.

"Well, I appreciate that, I really do," D'Antoni is saying as I re-enter the lounge.

"They just thought it might be a good idea, what with the business contacts over here."

"Yeah. I can see that."

"I was just telling Mr D'Antoni, Jack, how Gerald and Les thought it'd be a good idea if I came over and sussed out some of the places we know what might be likely to be ports of call for anybody who might be looking for somebody."

"Oh, yes?"

"Yes. And as you're up, you can get me another drink."

I wonder to myself why, after the words we had earlier in the evening, she still imagines she can push me the way, for appearance's sake, she sometimes does in front of Gerald and Les, and live so long without me hauling her off the final definitive punch. But I swallow again because I wouldn't like to put her out of this world without finding out the real reason for her coming up to the villa. So I say to her:

"I just been into the kitchen. Wally's fetching the coffee in a minute."

"Mr D'Antoni's right," she says. "You are funny."

I smile at her.

"It's been a funny evening," I say.

"I can't believe that film," Audrey says. "Her being in it, and that."

"You didn't recruit her yourself, did you?"

"Course I didn't. I don't have anything to do with that side of things no more. You know that."

"Funny. Tonight was just like old times really. Reminded me of picking up the rough trade and getting them drunk and persuading them to perform. Really took me back. I'd almost forgotten how good you were at that part. You know, the scrubber, smashed out of her mind."

"Yeah, well I should start getting used to forgetting things," Audrey says. "Know what I mean?"

Wally enters with the tray of coffee. While he's putting it down on the low table, Audrey says to him:

"I may as well stay here tonight, Wally. You didn't put Jack in the master bedroom, did you?"

"No, I didn't do that."

"You can get that ready for me then. Sweep the scorpions out the bed. I'd hate to get stung on me first night."

"You almost did," I tell her, putting my drink down and picking up my coffee. "Anyway, if you don't mind, I'm taking my Horlicks up to bed with me. I've got last week's Beano to catch up on."

I walk out of the lounge and make my way upstairs to my bedroom. The room is empty of Tina. My bed is turned down exactly as I left it. The cot is unruffled. The sheer physical relief is beautiful. No more sparring matches of any description. Just the crisp sheets. I put my coffee down on the bedside table and crawl into the bed and it feels exactly like it did an hour ago; I'm beginning to think of it the way I think of the one I've got at home after a hard day looking after Gerald and Les. I close my eyes and start to drift away to blackness for as long as I can before Audrey's inevitable arrival.

Chapter Fourteen

The dream is very clear, very sharp. Gerald and Les are the spitting images of themselves. And that's more or less what they're doing in the dream, because they're in the dock at the Old Bailey, and I'm on the stand, giving evidence against them. I'm not exactly saying anything, but I know that's what I'm doing. And I know what the result of what I'm doing is going to be. So when the judge reaches for the old black cap, I'm not exactly surprised. He doesn't say anything but then he doesn't have to. Gerald and Les look at him, bow, then they turn in my direction and take their shooters out and point them at me but they don't fire straight away. Instead, between me and them, in enormous close-up, is the face of Audrey, smiling at me. Then the shooters sound off and although Audrey is still smiling the same smile, blood begins to dribble out from between her teeth, vying for brilliance with her lipstick.

Then I wake up, and I realise that the perfume of the dream is a reality, because Audrey is crawling into bed next to me, and she doesn't stop when she's beside me, she keeps going until she's on top of me, squashing her mouth and the rest of her against me, her stocking'd legs slithering up and down like pistons. A hand slides down to my waist and undoes my pyjama cord. Then Audrey's head goes under the sheets and she starts travelling south, a direction I'm normally more than partial to, but tonight I don't want her being bad-mannered when she's talking to me so I grab hold of some of her hair and arrest her progress. Audrey's voice muffles up through the bedclothes.

"Jesus Christ!"

Her head re-appears, an inch or so away from mine.

"What's the bleedin' game, then?"

"Finding out yours, that's what."

Audrey rolls over onto her back.

"I mean," I say to her. "Considering we reached the end of the road a few hours ago, this is a bit sudden, isn't it?"

There's a long pause before Audrey answers.

"You really are a berk, aren't you?"

I don't say anything.

"I come to tell you something to your advantage, as they say."

"Why should you do a thing like that?"

"You really are a berk, aren't you?"

It's my turn not to say anything for a while.

"All right," I say eventually. "So why the circus? Why not just use the phone if you've got something to tell me?"

Audrey sighs.

"Because, sweetheart, you're not easy to convince of anything face to face, let alone over the phone."

"Not to mention via Her Majesty's Mails."

"Yeah, well that's what I want to talk to you about."

"Come to apologise for the spelling mistakes, have you?"

"Listen, you stupid bastard, I've had a phone call since you left the hotel."

"I thought you might have."

"Yes. Well."

I reach out and pluck my cigarettes off the bedside table. I light two up and hand one to Audrey. After I've inhaled I say: "So what did they have to say?"

"You mean after they got through describing their feelings about you?"

"I can imagine all that. It's the other part I'm interested in."

"You should be. You'll find it fascinating."

She doesn't go on to tell me how fascinating I'll find it. What she wants me to do is to ask her to tell me. Which, of course, I do, seeing as Audrey is prepared to wait until Stanley Bowles tells the referee it wasn't a penalty, he just fell over himself. I say to her:

"All right. So tell me what I'll find fascinating."

"Well, what it all boils down to, they decided to take contingency measures, haven't they? They decided to pass the brief elsewhere."

"And that's fascinating, is it?"

"You don't think so?"

"What else could they do? They painted themselves into a corner and for once Jack the Lad isn't lifting them out of it. So they're still in the corner. They got to do something, haven't they."

"That's right. And they got to do something about you, haven't they? I mean, since you've resigned, they don't want you starting up in competition, do they?"

I stretch out my arm and stub out my cigarette.

"I'll worry about that when I get back off my holidays."

184

"You will."

"That's right."

Audrey doesn't say anything for a while. Eventually I say to her:

"So what are they?"

"What?"

"The alternative arrangements?"

"Oh, them. Nothing really."

"You what?"

"Forget it. You're on your holidays, aren't you?"

"Listen, you came up here to tell me something I'll find fascinating. You came all the way from Palma to tell it to me. And now you're not telling me."

"That's because you don't really want to know."

"I see."

"It's right."

I don't say anything. After a while she says:

"You're not going to change your mind, are you?"

"You what?".

"About D'Antoni. You're not going to change your mind."

"You know I'm not."

"And you're still prepared to screw up everything we been working for?"

I don't answer her.

Then she suddenly sits up and gets out of the bed, taking most of the top sheet with her.

"Then you deserve everything you get," she says, and walks out of the bedroom.

I don't attempt to pull the sheet back on the bed. In fact I don't move at all. I just lie there and stare up into the blackness until my eyes gradually close and I succumb to the deeper blackness of sleep.

For the second time that night I awake to the scent of perfume. Only this time it's not Audrey's.

"Wakey, wakey," Tina says.

She takes it in her hand and waves it to and fro like a rubber metronome. I take hold of her wrist and pull her hand away.

"No fun," she says. "Like I always say, you're no fun."

"Piss off."

"I got nowhere else to go, have I?"

"You got the camp bed."

"Yes, I know," she says. "Only it seemed a shame that we had to be the couple that dropped out of the game."

"You what?"

"Us. Not like the other two."

"What like the other two?"

"Mrs Fletcher and the spaghetti-eater."

"What about them?"

"Christ. What do you think?"

I think various thoughts and then I say:

"Where are they?"

"Last time I saw them was when I went back into the lounge for me fags. They was on the settee. Only they wasn't sitting, know what I mean? And her only with her stockings on. I mean to say."

I sit up and swing my legs over the side of the bed.

"You're too late if you think you'll get there just in the nick of time."

I sit on the edge of the bed, thinking. I come to a decision but before I can get off the bed the sound of Audrey and D'Antoni giggling their way up the stairs drifts in through the open door. Then there's a slight pause and after that the clink of a bottle and the opening and closing of a bedroom door. Followed by the turning of a key.

"I told you, didn't I?" Tina says.

I don't bother getting up off the bed. Instead of kicking in doors, I decide to expend my energy in a different way. I turn and look down at the pale indistinct shape of Tina and remember how distinct it had been on the wall downstairs.

"All right," I say to her. "Since you been asking for it." I lift my legs back on the bed and go down on her and for once in her life she doesn't come up with a pertinent comment on the action. Not one that sounds like any word that has yet been invented, that is.

Comes the dawn.

I open my eyes and not for the first time since I came to the villa it takes me a minute or two to bring my senses to bear on where I actually am. Then, when I've established that, I turn my head to my right and my eyes pull focus on the open-mouthed, closed-eyes face of Tina. She's snoring very, very softly, looking more like one of the plaster madonnas in the background of the Life Room than the character she played out in foreground. I look at her for a moment or two, then I reach out for cigarettes and while I'm doing that Wally appears carrying a tray which supports the morning pot of tea. His reaction on seeing the *tableau vivant* on the bed is not to drop the tray, all he does is to hesitate slightly on his course to the bedside table, and when he reaches it he places the tray on the table top with the dignity of a goalkeeper who's picking the fifteenth ball out of the back of the net. I light my cigarette. Wally turns away and begins to walk out of the bedroom.

"Well it's not as though you didn't have no idea what she was like," I say to him.

Wally keeps on moving.

"Wally."

He stops.

"Turn round when I'm talking to you."

Wally turns round.

"Don't come it with me, mate," I tell him. "All right?"

Wally doesn't say anything. I take a draw on my cigarette.

"I'll have the lot for breakfast." I tell him. "O.K.?" Wally nods briefly, then turns away and goes out of the bedroom.

I smoke some more of my cigarette. Tina opens her eyes.

"Was that the silly old fart?" she says.

"Shut your mouth," I tell her, and get out of bed.

Chapter Fifteen

I sit alone in the kitchen, mopping up the dip from my empty plate with the remaining slice of bread, when in comes Audrey, wrapped in the negligée I'm more than just somewhat familiar with. She approaches the table and takes one of my cigarettes from the packet and lights up and then goes and props herself up against one of the work surfaces. I light myself up and the two of us look at each other.

"Have a good night, did you?" I ask her.

She doesn't answer.

"All right, was it?"

"You going to knock me about, are you?"

I smile at her, but in fact to give her several round the earhole is what I would dearly like to be doing right now. But I swallow because it would only give her more satisfaction than she's already getting at the moment.

"Why should I do that?" I ask her.

"Why shouldn't you? Don't tell me you undergone a complete character change."

"Maybe I have," I say to her. "Maybe the holiday done the trick like Gerald and Les said it would. Made a new man of me, it has. Completely changed my life. Given me a completely new perspective. Just like the travel brochures said."

"Did they say to stay out of the sun as well?"

"You what?"

"To avoid going bleedin' barmy."

"Well, I wonder about that. About what's barmy. I mean, you're going back to the pair of them. You got Gerald's halitosis to look forward to till you're eligible for your pension."

"At least I'll live to see that day."

I smile at her and shake my head.

"Depends what you call living."

Audrey shrugs.

"Well, for starters, the last four or five hours could qualify as a definition," she says.

I don't say anything. Audrey alters her stance and adopts a

woman to woman pose, confident and risqué.

"Honestly, I was surprised. Well, I mean, you know me. I can usually keep going the longest, know what I mean? But not last night. Not with him. He was still going strong well into injury time."

"Pity you won't be able to have him as a partner."

"Yeah, that's what I was thinking. He could certainly add experience to the board of directors, as it stands, so to speak."

I pick up my cup and drain down the last of the tea and instead of throwing the cup at her I help myself to some more tea. While I'm doing that, out of the corner of my eye, I notice that Audrey is looking at her watch.

"I wouldn't have thought that came in very handy last night."

She looks at me.

"I'd have thought a stop-watch would have been more use."

Audrey keeps looking at me for a minute or two before she says: "What time you say you were leaving?"

"Ten past three."

"Isn't there anything earlier?"

"If there was, I'd be getting it."

"So you'll be staying most of the morning."

"Yeah, pity about that one."

She looks at her watch again and she seems about to say something else when in walks D'Antoni looking spruce and shiny as sandalwood like he's just spent a couple of hours in a high-class massage and sauna, which is a fair simile, considering that he's recently been getting the treatment from Audrey. He walks over to Audrey and puts one of his hands on one of her tits and says:

"So you're an early riser."

"I could say the same about you."

If I was to ever seriously reconsider my decision about D'Antoni, now would seem to be as good a time as any.

"When you get back," D'Antoni says to Audrey, "I want you to do something for me. I want you to say thank you to Gerald and Les for looking after me so well. And when you tell them that, I want you to look them straight in the eye and smile at them and for you to really mean it." D'Antoni looks round at me and laughs. "That's funny, hey?" he says.

I don't say anything.

"And if you do tell them, it won't matter," he says. "Because by that time, I'll be long gone."

He laughs again. Audrey disengages her left tit and moves from between D'Antoni and the work surface.

"Anyway," she says. "My bath'll be ready by now."

"Yeah," D'Antoni says. "I turned it off."

"Thanks," Audrey says, and goes out of the kitchen.

D'Antoni looks at the kitchen table.

"That all there is, tea?"

I don't provide him with an answer.

"Well, this morning, it don't matter," he says.

He opens a cabinet and gets himself a cup and sits down opposite me and pours himself some tea. He takes a drink and pulls a face and takes another sip and says: "Jesus." He shakes his head. "Jesus," he says again.

I put my cigarette out and light up another one.

"You wouldn't believe last night," D'Antoni says.

I don't say anything.

"Christ. I known some in my time. I seen all the tricks. But that was all of them rolled up into one, you know that?"

There is more silence from myself.

"If you wouldn't get your balls cut off, because of your situation, I would recommend that with no reservations whatsoever."

"You would."

"No reservations whatsoever. I had some heads, I never yet had one like the one I had last night."

"You haven't."

"Never."

I'm just about to see him off when the phone rings, but only a couple of times. D'Antoni leaps up in the air and knocks his tea all over the table.

"The phone," he says.

Then he rushes out of the kitchen in the direction of the phone, even though the sound is no more. I hear him shouting for Wally, as if that's going to provide him with some kind of answer. I take my cigarette packet out of the spreading lake of tea and walk out of the kitchen and across the now sunbright hall and into the still-curtained lounge. D'Antoni is standing in the middle of it like somebody who's turned up at Wembley on the wrong day.

"The phone rang," he says.

I walk past him on my way to the drinks and manage to restrain myself from putting him right through the plate glass beyond the curtains.

"You heard it," he says. "It could have been a signal."

"Oh, fuck off," I tell him, pouring my drink.

D'Antoni walks over to me and stands behind me inches away. He stabs a finger dead centre between my two shoulder blades, causing me to pour some of my drink over my fingers. "Listen, less crap from you, hey?"

Now I have the perfect excuse for smashing D'Antoni into the ground; before, he may have sussed the reason why I felt like planting him, and I would under no circumstances give a character such as D'Antoni the satisfaction of knowing something like that. But this response is fraught with no such barriers. I turn round and draw back and the phone rings again, just twice, then stops. D'Antoni whirls round and his movement puts him out of my range so I'm left standing there like a hammer-thrower who's let it go in the wrong direction.

"You see," D'Antoni says, striding towards the phone and pointing at it. "It's got to be. It's got to be a signal." I'm beginning to have the same opinion, but not for the same reasons as D'Antoni. I turn back to the drinks and pour myself a large one and down it and turn round again and begin to walk out of the lounge.

"Ain't I right?" D'Antoni says. "A signal. It's got to be."

I keep going and turn the corner and start towards the stairs. The sound of bathwater being turned on greets me as I begin to climb.

Behind me D'Antoni says:

"You got to give me back my – "

I turn round and grab him by the collar of his robe and push him up against the nearest plasterwork.

"Listen, you cunt," I tell him, "you're lucky to have reached half past nine this morning. You're lucky I didn't cop for you before I cleaned my teeth. So if you want to stay lucky, stay away from me, or I'll solve everybody's problem for them."

I turn away and go up the stairs and open the door to Audrey's bedroom and my first impression is that it's even bigger than mine, and it's decorated differently too, showing evidence of Gerald as interior decorator; there is a mirror along all of one wall behind the bed, and the whole ceiling is mirrored. On one wall, there are a dozen beautifully framed pornographic photographs. I look into the mirror behind the bed and it becomes a movie screen, reflecting my imagination of the scenes it was fed the night before. Then my concentration is broken by the running water being turned off. I look towards the closed door of the adjoining bathroom. There is the sound of rippling water. I walk over to the door and open it without making a sound. Audrey is just lowering herself into the bathwater, her back towards me. I wait until her little bum is touching the surface of the water and then I say to her:

"Now then."

She shrieks as if the water's scalded her cheeks and rises up and twists round to face me. I don't say anything else. I just look at her.

"Jack," she says to me. "Now look, Jack. You said you wasn't going to knock me about, right? You told me that, didn't you?"

"Yeah, I told you that."

"You did, didn't you. You told me."

I begin to walk towards her.

"Jack, you did, didn't you?"

"Yes, that's true, relating to previous events. That's what I told you. But if I knock you about now, it'll be to do with a completely different set of events."

Audrey pushes herself up against the rose pink tiling.

"Jack!"

I get to her and give her one, just to make her shut up. When she's done that, I sit down on the edge of the bath and light a cigarette.

"You hear the phone just now?"

Audrey looks at me and a different fear comes into her face.

"The phone?"

"Yeah. Rang a couple of times. Two rings each time."

She doesn't say anything to that.

"Well, it did. Two rings each time."

"I had the bathwater running, didn't I?"

"So you did."

There is a silence.

"Come on, Audrey," I say to her. "Let's be having it."

It's a little while before she answers.

"I'm going to say it again, Jack. Stop being a pighead and cop for him."

I give her the look and from the expression I get back I know for certain she's never going to ask that one again.

"Right," I say to her. "So I'll say it again. Tell me the things that you know, Audrey."

Audrey slides down the tiles and perches on the couple of inches of the bath on her side.

"Got a fag?"

I pass the packet to her, and she begins to take one out but what happens is in the process she accidentally shakes half a dozen out and they land on top of the mound of bubbles that's snap crackle and popping on the surface of the water. I light up the cigarette she manages to get into her mouth and after she's inhaled and exhaled she says:

"I come up here to tell you, didn't I? But you didn't want to know, did you? You couldn't see why I'd come."

She inhales some more and I wait for her to go on.

"I didn't hear the phone just now. Straight up. But I was expecting it to ring like that. Only not this morning. Late this afternoon or tonight. But not this morning. Because you were going on an afternoon flight, I wasn't too worried. See, if it rang twice like that, and I wasn't by the phone a second time to pick it up first ring, then the fact that I *didn't* answer meant that an hour from it ringing I'd be in my bedroom keeping D'Antoni occupied so's it be easy for them to walk in and get it over with."

"And me?"

"Well, just because you'd turned it down, there'd be no reason for you to interfere with two old mates going about their business would there?"

"Two old mates?"

"Con McCarty and Peter the Dutchman."

I don't say anything for a minute or two.

"So," I say eventually. "That's what you intended to tell me. When they've done for him it's down to them to see to me."

"That's what Gerald and Les've told them, yes. But I knew you'd be gone before they got here, so after the barneys and that I thought, stuff it, why should I?"

"Oh yeah?"

"That's what I thought."

There's another silence between us. Audrey breaks it by saying:

"That's why I humped with D'Antoni last night. So's it wouldn't seem too previous, like, if I came on strong after the phone calls."

"Oh yeah."

"Why should I tell you if it wasn't?"

"I wonder."

I throw my cigarette in the bathwater.

"Funny, isn't it?" I say. "Con and Peter. The favours I done for them."

"They just work for the firm."

"Yeah, I suppose they do. I mean, Peter I can understand. He's been looking for this one for years. But Con, though." I shake my head.

"Well, I suppose, as they say, that's life."

I stand up.

"So what you going to do? Clear off out of it?"

I bend over and scoop up a handful of bubbles out of the bath and look at them.

"You put Wally in on what's going off?"

"You're joking. He only gets to know when they're coming down the drive."

I turn my palm downwards and shake the bubbles back into the bath.

"So what you going to do?" Audrey asks again.

"I'm going to wait and have a chat with me old mates, aren't I? I mean, must be all of three days since I set eyes on them."

"You're barmy. You could be well out of it."

I lean over the bath again only this time it isn't bubbles I pluck out of it, it's Audrey. I sit her down on the edge of the bath that I've been sitting on and I tell her: "Listen, you thick bitch, for years and fucking years I kept those two wankers upright, and by default, yourself. It's because of me you got interested in how the firm was run, and consequently got a taste for running it, and consequent to that you got stacked away what you got stacked away in our joint and non-native bank accounts. And now you, the three of you, you all think if I'm not seen to jump for once in my life then I'm eligible for the drop and I'm not even accorded the honour of facing it out on my own patch, they can't wait five fucking minutes to switch me off, and I've been responsible for every thread in their mohairs. So that being the case, I intend enjoying the last day of my holidays, and instead of sending Gerald and Les a card to tell them what a good time I've had I'll express my enjoyment and gratitude in a different way, in a manner which will also challenge their cloud seven assumptions about themselves and about myself. All right?"

Audrey pushes my hands from her shoulders and digs up a bit of bottle from somewhere. "Listen, you cunt, you don't have to come on like this. All you have to do is walk downstairs and screw down D'Antoni and it's like the magic wand, everything is back the way it should be, Midas isn't sticking to his gelt any more. Jesus, I only came on strong about D'Antoni this morning in the hopes you'd spring to your feet and do him there and then."

"Oh, yes," I say to her. "About that."

I give her one across the face and as she's ensured that I no longer have a grip on her shoulders she falls backwards into the bath and bunches of bubbles fly up and stick to the tiles like an explosion of disturbed ameoba. Audrey splashes around in an attempt to resurface, spitting the suds from her mouth as though she's just taken one in the mouth for the first time. I bend over and grasp her slippery arms and pull her up out of the water.

"So," I say to her. "Now we've got that out of the way, the plan stays the same."

Audrey spits out the last of the bubbles.

"You what?"

"The plan. What everybody's fixed up between themselves. Remember that?"

"What, you want me to keep D'Antoni busy like I did last night?"

I wipe a dribble of bubble from the corner of her mouth and support it on the end of my little finger.

"Exactly like you did last night," I say to her, transferring the bubbles to the centre of her lips.

She brushes the bubbles away and says:

"Why should I? I've got myself to look after now. Why should I do that, now I know what you're up to?"

"For the reason, my love, that you told me what you told me. Even though you did leave it a bit late."

I take a grip on her jaw with my thumb and forefinger and shake her head a little bit.

"You were going to do it anyway. Now you can really enjoy it, seeing as you got my blessing." I let go of her. After a little while she says:

"You're never going to row yourself out of this one. You know that, don't you? Even if you get off this island."

"Listen, loved one, I'm going to get off this island, because I want to see the faces of Gerald and Les when I turn up in the role of my surrogate postcard. So have your bath and be downstairs in fifteen minutes because that's the time I've got you down to start performing."

I turn away and begin to walk towards the bathroom door.

"What happens," Audrey says, "if everything goes your way? I mean, just supposing, like, you get out of here; you see to Gerald and Les and the tame law and everybody else, just supposing all that comes off. What happens to me?"

I stop walking and turn to face her.

"What do you mean, what happens to you?"

"We still partners, are we?"

"I thought we dissolved that in a hotel room in Palma."

"Did you really?"

I don't say anything.

"There's still a simpler way," she says.

"I'll see you downstairs in fifteen minutes," I tell her, and turn away again.

Chapter Sixteen

Downstairs in the lounge, D'Antoni is peering out through the still-drawn curtains, poised shiftily like Grigsby in *The Lady from Shanghai*.

"Has the milk been delivered yet?" I say to him.

D'Antoni whirls round and almost fetches the curtains with him.

"What's happening?" he says. "Where'd you go?"

"Nothing's happening, and you know where I went. I went upstairs, didn't I?"

"What for?"

"I went to the karsi, didn't I?"

"There's one down here."

"Is there really? Silly of me."

I walk over to the button that operates the curtains and they swish apart. D'Antoni retreats from the light with the madness of a moth in reverse.

"Bang, bang," I say.

"Listen," he says. "You'd be the same. You don't know the score. You're from nowhere. You don't know what kind of guys these are."

I smile to myself and open the windows and walk back to the drinks and pour myself another one.

"For Christ's sake pour yourself a drink and calm down," I tell him. "You got nothing to worry about."

I walk past him and out onto the patio. The pool is as flat as formica and the day's heat is already building up. By the pool there's a lounger with the back raised, under the shade of a parasol. I walk over and get on the lounger and stretch out my legs and prop my back up and survey the mountains. They're still the same colour and they're still as boring. I take a sip of my drink. D'Antoni's voice drifts across from the open windows.

"Get back in here."

I take a sip of my drink.

"Those calls," he says. "I know what they were."

"Don't be silly. Who would they be intended for?"

D'Antoni doesn't answer.

"Well, there you are then."

"It smells, that's all I know," D'Antoni says.

From further back in the lounge comes another voice.

"What smells?"

"Nothing."

There's a clink of glasses and Audrey says: "I thought the drains might be acting up again."

D'Antoni goes back into the lounge and for a while there's the sound of the two of them talking together and from the tone of their voices Audrey's swinging the conversation the way she's supposed to. I sip my drink and continue to watch the mountains. Nothing happens to them but inside the villa the talking eventually stops. I give it another five minutes and then I get off the lounger and walk back into the villa. The lounge is empty except for the aroma of Audrey's perfume. I cross the lounge and walk upstairs. The door to Audrey's room is closed. I keep going until I get to my room. This time Tina is lying on her stomach, but although the position is different, the snoring is the same. Without waking her, I dig out D'Antoni's shooters from their hiding place and then I go back downstairs and look for Wally. I try all the usual places but I finally find him in the garage, sitting on a petrol can and staring out at the brilliant square of white sunlight beyond the open garage door.

"What you doing sitting in here on your tod, Wal?" I ask him.

"As a rule, nobody comes in here, that's why," he says.

"Yeah," I say, perching my backside on the edge of tyre. "It must be a piss-off, you having the run of the place all year round and then suddenly everywhere you turn there's characters in every room."

Wally doesn't answer. I look out into the sunlight.

"That Merc's going to get warmish if you leave it out there much longer," I say.

"Fuck the Merc," Wally says.

I take out my cigarettes and light up.

"Anyway," I say, "there'll be a couple more for you to fall over shortly."

Wally looks at me.

"What?" he says.

"A couple more. Coming up the villa."

"Who?"

"Con McCarty and Peter the Dutchman."

Even in the garage gloom, Wally's change of colour is noticeable.

"Con and Peter?" he says.

I nod my head. Wally gets up off the petrol can and walks over to me.

"Jack," he says, "what the fuck's going on, eh?"

"Nothing you need worry about," I tell him. "Only when they get here, if you're around when they first arrive, don't get the megaphone out, will you? Just let them come in and do what they want and keep your mouth shut, eh?"

"Jack, listen — "

"Don't worry about it. I've told you. There's nothing to worry about."

I get off the tyre and walk out into the sunlight and go over to the Merc. I put my hand on the bonnet and it's like touching a kitchen range.

Compared to the rest of the day, stretched out under the bushes, it's relatively cool, but that is only relatively. From time to time I make myself feel better by looking between the leaves at the path that leads to the road, and imagining what it would be like lying out on that hot earth. I look at my watch. Any time now, they should be here.

An hour later, and I'm still looking at my watch, and there's still nothing. I swear to myself. The only way they can get to the villa is along this path. But even if there was another way, there's been no sound of a motor up on the road, and even if they'd parked miles away, I'd still have heard it, up in this silence. I swear again and get to my feet. I look towards the road. Nothing. The path's just the same as when I came down it the other night, only sunlit. I turn and look towards the villa. That's still the same too. Except from beyond it, from the side where the swimming pool is, black smoke is billowing up into the clear blue sky.

I make my way out of the bushes and start hurrying back down to the villa. I round the corner of the building. The pool is still as flat as before. There's nobody on the patio, but there is an oil drum, and the oil drum is where the smoke is gushing from, and a few feet away from the oil drum is, if I'm not mistaken, the petrol can that Wally was sitting on when he was in the garage.

I walk a little closer to the oil drum and while I'm doing that Wally emerges from the lounge windows carrying a stack of boxed films, which he starts throwing, one by one, into the drum.

"What the Christ are you playing at?" I ask him.

Wally continues throwing the films into the fire.

"They already got Geronimo, you know. It's too late to warn him now."

Wally throws the last box into the drum.

I'm getting rid of that lot, aren't I?"

"What lot?"

"Those ones. You know the ones I mean."

He looks at the smoke for a moment, then he goes back inside the villa. A few minutes later, Audrey appears framed in the sliding glass.

"What the fuck's going on?" she asks.

"Wally's getting rid of the family album."

Audrey looks at the smoke.

"The films?"

I nod.

"They'll dock that lot out of his wages," she says, then she goes back inside and pours a drink and re-appears.

"They're late," she says.

"Course they're fucking late."

"So what am I supposed to do?"

"Keep following instructions. That shouldn't be no hardship."

"He just sent me down for some more booze. He hasn't even started yet."

"Like I say, shouldn't be no hardship. In fact, I thought the smoke was coming out the bedroom window."

"Piss off."

"What's he doing now, chalking on the wall? Must be like the old days, waiting for the Saturday nighters."

This time Audrey waits a minute or two before saying anything.

"If you climbed the wooden hill right now, we could be getting the champagne iced up ready for Peter and Con's arrival."

I just look at her. She shrugs.

"Suit yourself."

She plucks a bottle off the drinks cabinet and turns away, swishing off in a slipstream of perfume.

" 'I did it my way'," she sings, as she rounds the corner.

I grit my teeth and pour myself another drink and while I'm doing that Wally re-appears with another batch of boxes and walks past me out onto the patio. I follow him out and I'm in time to see the flames shoot up and the smoke billow out and it reminds me of the time I witnessed the last of William Dugdale's mortal remains prior to the scattering of his ashes in Epping Forest. Wally watches the smoke for a while. Then he picks up his cigarettes and matches that are lying on the stonework and lights himself up and at the moment he's setting fire to the end of his cigarette he catches the petrol can with his left foot and topples it over on the edge of the pool so that the can see-saws on the edge and shug-a-lugs petrol onto the surface of the water. Wally shakes the match out and bends over and rights the can but his movement is so quick that petrol spills upwards out of the mouth of the can and lands on his forearm and on his slacks and Wally begins to fuck and blind but the fucking and blinding is shortlived because immediately the noise Wally is making becomes different, a scream, because the match he threw away didn't go out, and the splashing petrol is adding fuel to its flame, rippling across the stonework to the bottom of Wally's slacks which start to take light, causing him to start leaping about like Mick Jagger, again knocking over the petrol can. More petrol spills out and the flames join the fresh lot and race across the stonework to the oil drum to augment the celluloid heat. Wally engages himself in a battle with the belt that's holding up his trousers, but he's never going to finish first. So I walk over to him and give him a shoulder which sends him flying off the stonework and out into the pool. The splash Wally makes is like a small explosion, throwing water up to sizzle onto the lighted petrol. Wally surfaces and spits out water as if he's in competition with Gerald's fish.

"One of these days, Wally," I tell him, "you'll do something without doing it arse about face."

Wally continues splashing about in the water.

"Jack," he says, between mouthfulls.

"I expect you never learnt to swim before you learnt to set fire to yourself."

"Jack - "

"You really are a prize cunt, Wal," I tell him. "No wonder they put you out here, all on your own."

"Jack — "

I shake my head and I'm just about to turn away when I notice a curious thing. Instead of just the large billowing shadow of the smoke reflecting in the pool, there are two new reflections, gliding softly into view like a couple of watersnakes striking out from a canal bank.

"Jack — " Wally says again.

"It's all right, Wally," I say, turning round. "I realize what you were trying to spit out."

It's funny, looking at Con McCarty and Peter the Dutchman in the Spanish sunshine. They don't look real. They look like something out of Madame Tussaud's except the wax is beginning to melt. Con is wearing his eternal leather hat and his leather coat, but Peter, of course, is wearing something more appropriate to the climate, the latest in Mediterranean casual wear, offset by the purple tints of his sunglasses and his bleached hair that's roughly the same colour as the sunshine. He looks like a bent barman trying to pull them in Piccadilly. The one thing they do have in common, though, are the shooters they're carrying in their hands.

"Well, well," Peter says. "You shouldn't have bothered."

Wally splashes towards the edge of the pool and I don't say anything so Peter continues.

"I mean," he says, "the *Son et lumière* display. Wally doing his Esther Williams bit. All it needs is Busby Berkeley wielding his megaphone."

Con looks at the mountains.

"Leave it out, Peter," he says. "It's too fucking warm."

"Is it just the heat, or do you feel embarrassed?" I ask him.

"You not going to give us any trouble, are you Jack?" Peter says.

"Course not. I'm on my holidays, aren't I?"

"In that case," Peter says, "you won't need what you got stuffed up your shirt, will you?"

Peter walks over to me and holds his hand out. I give him D'Antoni's automatic. Behind me the fire is still sending heatwaves up and down my back.

Wally gets to the edge of the pool.

"Give us a hand, Jack," he says.

"What, after the one you just gave me? Fuck off."

Peter grins.

"Poor old Wally," he says. "Never could make it on his own."

"Come on," Con says to Peter. "Let's be getting on with it."

"Just enjoying the sunshine a minute, sweetheart," Peter says, taking a folded piece of paper out of his shirt pocket.

"We enjoyed the bleeding sunshine all the way up the bleeding road, when the taxi blew out, didn't we?" Con says.

"Philistines," Peter says. "All I get is Philistines to work with."

"You should start walking a different way then, shouldn't you?" Con says.

Peter ignores him and unfolds the piece of paper, studies it, then looks at the villa. In the meantime Wally makes it out of the pool and sits on the pool's edge, coughing and heaving as if he's just done a lap round White City.

"Yes," Peter says, agreeing with whatever he's been turning over in his mind. "Right."

"You're sure?" Con asks him.

"There's no need for you to come," Peter says.

"What you talking about?"

Peter gives him a look and the look doesn't have to take me in for Con to get his meaning.

'Well, all right," Con says.

"That's right," Peter says.

Peter keeps the look on Con for a minute longer then he turns away and walks towards the sliding windows, leaving Con looking even more embarrassed than before.

"You'll get over it," I tell him.

"You what?"

I grin at him.

"Never mind. Come and have a drink."

I start to walk towards the villa.

"Hang about, Jack," Con says.

I stop walking and face him again.

"Leave it out, Con. You're not going to do it that way. You'll probably leave it to Peter, anyway."

"Jack, this ain't my idea, you know."

"Yeah, I know. So come and have a drink."

I turn away and start walking again and apart from dropping me there and then Con has no choice but to follow on the principle that he can't risk letting me out of his sight. He's right with me when I reach the plate glass and he's still by my side when I reach the drinks. Peter, by that time, has traversed the lounge and is now, I imagine, half way up the stairs.

"What you like, Con?"

"Some kind of beer," Con says. "Lager, if you got any."

I bend down and open the refrigerated cabinet and while I'm doing that Con takes a moment out to look round the room and inwardly digest its splendours and so it's no problem for me to take D'Antoni's other shooter from behind the lagers where I stacked it earlier, and stand up and put the snub barrel against Con's lips and get a grip on his own shooter. Con goes rigid. I press the barrel tighter against his mouth and shake my head and Con stays rigid.

Then, after a little while, Con relaxes and smiles and with his free hand pushes my shooter away from his face.

"Christ, I don't mind," he says. "So you overpowered me. Not a lot Gerald and Les can do about that, is there?" We look at each other and then I smile back at him.

"You got lager in there, or just shooters?" Con says.

"Help yourself," I tell him. "I got something to do. Only, I will take your shooter, just in case the lager goes to your head."

Con shrugs and hands me his shooter and is about to turn his attention to the refrigerated cabinet when from upstairs comes the sound of a shot. Fuck it, I think to myself, Peter moved quicker than I thought he would. I run across the lounge and then there's two more shots and I'm in the hall and I'm more than somewhat surprised to see that Peter has only made it as far as the top of the steps and it's for sure that he hasn't fired his one because he's standing there like a rabbit at the arrival of a ferret. I begin to run up the stairs and Peter whirls round and sees the two shooters I'm carrying and hauls a couple off at me but luckily they're wild because while he's hauling them off he's also throwing himself to the landing floor which affects his aim more than a little bit. But at the same time they're not wild enough to make me feel inclined to continue to the top of the steps so I about-face and scamper to the bottom of the steps and round the corner of the lounge, colliding with Con in the process. At the same time a door upstairs slams and Peter hauls off another shot in the direction of the slamming door and the next thing I hear is Audrey screaming meaningless odds along the passage, and Peter, more intelligible, shouting:

"You fucking bitch, you and your ponce, you set us up."

It's my turn to shout now so I stick my head round the lounge corner.

"Peter, you bleedin' egg, it ain't a set up. Leave it out and get Audrey out of it. He ain't supposed to have a shooter."

"I know he bleedin' ain't, don't I? Oh, yes, I know that."

Audrey's screeching stops and farther down the landing there's the sound of a different door slamming and I guess that Audrey's made it to my room, where Tina's still laying her lonely locks.

"I shouldn't stay there if I was you," I call to Peter. "He knows you're there now."

I must admit I enjoyed that one.

"Yeah, and so do you, don't you?"

"Suit yourself," I call back.

204

"What's going on, for Christ's sake?" Con says.

"I've no fucking idea. I'd copped for both the bastard's shooters."

"So what's happening?"

"I've told you. I've no fucking idea."

As I'm saying that there's a blur of movement out in the hall and I swing round just in time to see Peter legging it from the bottom of the stairs to the other side of the ornamental fish. He crouches down and rests his gun arm on the fish's tail. Con and I retreat fully round the corner.

"Leave it out, Peter," Con calls to him. "Jack's in the bleedin' dark like we are."

"Oh, yeah?"

"Yeah, so stop buggering about."

I leave them to their little argument and walk over to the plate glass and out onto the patio. The flames are much lower now, and Wally is no longer sitting on the edge of the pool, which is not an altogether surprising fact. I look up at the balcony that runs along the face of the villa. Then I pick up one of the recliners and walk over to the wall. I turn the recliner arse about face and prop it up longways against the wall and use the tubular steel cross pieces as a ladder until I can get a handhold on the balcony's wrought iron work and pull myself up. When I've done that I swing my leg over and walk over to the plate glass of my window. The curtains are still drawn but the window is open. So in I go.

Audrey is crouched by the door, listening. She is naked except for my jacket which she's draped round her shoulders. Tina is sitting on the bed, and she, of course, is just plain naked. Neither of them notice me slide through the curtains.

"I done the downstairs windows," I say. "Shall I do these ones now?"

They both swing round like you've never seen and Audrey's like the colour of heart failure. Her movement causes her to sit on the floor and I wouldn't lay odds on her ever getting up again.

"Jesus," she says. "Jesus Christ."

"What's happening?" Tina says.

I ignore her and say to Audrey:

"What you been playing at, then?"

Audrey doesn't answer. She just stays where she is on the floor, propping her back up against the door. So I put the shooters on the bed, walk over to her and lift her up and give her a couple and ask her again. She shakes free and starts screaming the odds again.

"I was trying to row you out of your bother, wasn't I? Seeing as you lost your bottle I was stopping you from being topped, wasn't I?"

"What do you mean? What was all the shooting?"

"Some of it was me and some of it was him."

"Audrey – "

"Listen, you berk. In the bedroom, in the dressing table drawer, Gerald always keeps a little shooter, don't he? So when it turns out that Con and Peter's late, I reckon that if when they arrive D'Antoni's already topped, you're not going to get topped yourself, especially if I say *you* done the topping. Then everything's the same as it was, ain't it?"

I look at her and overcome the temptation of telling her how little I appreciate people taking a hand in my destiny. Instead I say:

"So what happened?"

"After the last session, I go to the bathroom, don't I, and on my way back I sit down at the dressing table like I'm going to fix myself up and I open the drawer where the shooter is, only I don't exactly have any way where on my person I can hide it, if you get my meaning. So I look in the mirror and weigh up the odds of managing it from the dressing table but because of the way he is on the bed he's only going to get one up his arse. That being the case, I ask him to fetch me a drink and he swings his legs over the side of the bed and starts busying himself at the bedside table. So while he's thus occupied I take the shooter out of the drawer but I'm snookered by Gerald's Hall of Mirrors set-up, via which D'Antoni susses out what I'm up to. I've not even got the safety catch off before he's up off the edge of the bed, and coming at me throwing bottles and God knows what in my direction. Anyway somehow the shooter goes off before he gets to me and although I'm not aiming I get him in the top of the leg and although he screams like a tart it doesn't stop him throwing himself at me and the two of us finish up on the floor. What with him slowed down a bit I manage to get away from him but not before he's collared the shooter and hauled a couple off that are not too wide of the mark, I can tell you, and I'm pleased to get out the door, at least, until Peter starts hauling them off in all directions."

"So he's still in there now."

"That's right."

"And he's all tooled up."

"I just told you."

I shake my head.

"You done well, Audrey. It's almost as good as how well you done that time in Wembley when your helpful efforts meant a lot of talking to the Filth before everything was back to normal again."

Audrey throws one at me but I've seen that one coming a mile off, but that doesn't prevent her launching into a jawbone solo.

"You ponce, I could be topped by now on your account."

"Not on my account, darlin'. Anything you get in this life's down to you."

"Yeah, like Con and Peter seeing to you when they done D'Antoni."

"Yeah, about that," I say to her. "You done very well in that department. Now you've made sure D'Antoni's fixed up with a shooter that makes it nice for everybody, doesn't it?"

"I thought you liked things the hard way."

I grab hold of her again.

"Listen, you and Wally between you really fucked things up."

Tina says:

"I know I'm only here on me holidays, but what's happening? What's all the shooters going off for?"

I don't have to tell her to shut up because another voice does that for me and that voice belongs to D'Antoni.

Of course I don't move until he tells me to, and when he does it's for me to turn round with my arms raised. Which, of course, I do.

D'Antoni's leaning against the jamb of the open bathroom door. Apart from the shooter he's pointing at me, he's naked except for Audrey's negligee, which he's wearing round his thigh like a tourniquet, the blood making the pale pink purple. So there we all are, a trio of nudes and me, only because the way D'Antoni's looking at me I'm feeling more naked than the lot of them put together.

"You bastard," D'Antoni says to me. "I knew it all the time. It stank all along. You came here to set me up, you mother."

"Er, well," I say. "About that. It's not really what you think."

"Don't try," D'Antoni says. "It'll make no difference. You know that."

I shrug my shoulders in agreement and consider the irony of the situation. I feel rather like Bobby Charlton would if the ref accused him of diving in the area.

"But I want to watch you wait for it," he says. "That's going to be some fun."

He slips a little on his injured leg and while that's happening I flick a glance at the bed ostensibly to check if it's possible for D'Antoni to see beyond Tina and suss out the shooters, but what in fact I do see is Tina's hand, out of sight of D'Antoni's vision, very slowly and cooly working its way towards the nearest of the pair, set off so elegantly as they are against the silk of the sheets. I try to catch Tina's eye so's to tell her not to, but she has her gaze, quite rightly in the event of what she's doing, fixed on D'Antoni.

"There is this," I say to D'Antoni, "and whatever you think, you ought to hear me out; those characters down there, they want me too. So if you choose to believe me, I could do you a favour while doing myself one, I mean, help you get out."

"He's right," Audrey says. "Jack's right. He really is."

D'Antoni smiles at us.

"Sure – " he begins, but Tina interrupts him.

She interrupts him by calling my name and snatching up the shooter from the bed and attempting to throw the shooter in my direction but there's no point in my attempting to catch it because D'Antoni, as I knew he would, has fired automatically in the direction of the disturbance, and he's good, because the bullet enters Tina's flesh at her throat, causing a very neat thin arc of blood to surge out onto the parquet flooring, and not such a neat sound to rattle around in the bubbles on the inside of her throat. The shooter she was holding echoes the rattle in her throat as it hits the floor, then Tina falls slowly sideways and snuggles down against the silk sheets, her body covering the second shooter, the jet of blood still pouring out of her with a perfect regularity, like the water from the mouth of Gerald's fish.

I, myself, don't bother to move because, of course, D'Antoni's shooter is now back covering me. The sound in Tina's throat begins to die down and from downstairs there is nothing but silence. After a while D'Antoni speaks.

"All right," he says. "O.K. Now you, Audrey, you walk across to the bed and you kick the shooter towards me."

Audrey, who has been as stone as the downstairs sculpture ever since the bullet hit Tina, does as she's told, but in the process Audrey slips in Tina's blood and goes arse over elbow between me and D'Antoni and I use this distraction to simply open the door and nick out and close it with a little help from a couple of shots in the woodwork from D'Antoni; my departure is also orchestrated by a few descriptive screams from Audrey, something to do with me leaving her in it, but I reflect that it's time for her to be a little more philosophical regarding the ways of the world. I mean, how am I to get her out of it if I'm still in there with her?

I leg it down the landing and take temporary cover in the doorway of Audrey's room, but it's like I thought, D'Antoni doesn't come blasting down the hall after me. I wait a minute or two and then call downstairs.

"Peter, it's me. You going to play silly buggers or are you going to let me down?"

"What's going on up there?"

"You could always come up and see?"

"You didn't top him, then?"

I don't answer that one.

"Only Wally's down here and he's getting a bit concerned about the state of his offspring."

Wally's voice drifts up from the stairwell.

"Yeah, Jack, what's going off?"

"Nothing."

"Where's Tina?"

"She's on the bed."

"D'Antoni in there with her?"

"Yeah. And Audrey."

"What they doing?"

"I wouldn't know, would I? They're in there and I'm out here."

There's silence from downstairs.

"Am I coming down or aren't I?" I call down again.

"Yeah, all right," Peter says.

I leave the doorway and go to the balcony and look down. Peter's still by the fish but now he's no longer crouching, he's leaning against the fish as though he's waiting for a beach photographer to take a snap of him. Con's standing by the lounge corner, a drink in his hand, still with his leather hat on. The odd man out is Wally, who is halfway up the stairs and still climbing.

"Where you going, Wal?" I ask him.

"Something's up," he says.

Now he's at the top of the steps.

"Nothing's up, Wal."

He keeps on walking. I put a hand against his chest.

"Where you going?"

"I got to see what's going off."

"You go in there and you'll get topped."

Wally's about to give me an answer to that when from down the corridor there's the faint sound of a door handle being turned and with the instincts of a stoat Wally darts into Audrey's bedroom, out of sight. Myself, I'm a little slower, and for the second time today I find myself looking at D'Antoni and his shooter, only this time it's pointing into Audrey's neck. Audrey is still naked but D'Antoni has got himself into his sports shirt and slacks, and he says to me: "I don't have to explain the situation to you."

I express my understanding by not moving. D'Antoni jabs the shooter further into Audrey's neck and she starts moving down the corridor. They progress a little way and then from downstairs comes Peter's voice.

"You coming down or what?"

D'Antoni and Audrey stop. D'Antoni says:

"How many of them?"

"Two."

"Tell them I'm coming down and tell them how I'm coming."

I clear my throat.

"Peter, he's coming down, only with Mrs Fletcher, if you get my meaning, so don't boil it over, all right?"

Silence.

"You heard me?"

"Yeah, he heard you," says Con. "Didn't you, Peter?"

Eventually Peter says: "Yeah, I heard."

"Tell him you're going down first," D'Antoni says.

"I'm coming down first," I tell Peter.

There's no answer.

"Peter!"

"Right."

I hope various thoughts apropos of Peter's brief aren't going through his mind in terms of capitalising on the present situation, but I don't, at the moment, have a great many alternatives to hand. I look at D'Antoni and Audrey and Audrey looks back at me and says: "You couldn't just do as you were told, could you?"

I don't answer her. D'Antoni says: "All right. Move."

I turn round and start to move to the top of the steps. Down in the hall, the tableau is as before, except that by the fish Peter is a little less relaxed.

"Start down," D'Antoni says.

I turn back to D'Antoni.

"Where do I go when I get to the bottom?"

"Just start down," D'Antoni says, and while he's saying that, beyond his shoulder I see Wally nick silently out of Audrey's room and start off down the corridor towards the bedroom where Tina is. Christ, I think to myself, that's all we need to elevate the balloon. But, like I say, I've no choice; at present I have to do what D'Antoni tells me to, so I start down the stairs, not quickly at all. I'm half-way down before I sense that D'Antoni and Audrey are standing at the top of the staircase, watching my progress.

"Stop there," D'Antoni says.

I do as I'm told.

"You by the fountain. Throw your piece as far as you can throw it."

"Fuck off," Peter says.

"You better tell him that isn't the way to talk, Mrs Fletcher," D'Antoni says to Audrey.

"Do it, Peter," Audrey says to him.

Peter doesn't answer and also he doesn't look as if he's inclined to follow D'Antoni's instructions.

"Peter," I say to him. "Don't be a cunt. Gerald won't thank you for getting Audrey topped."

Peter looks disgusted, as if Madeley's just put through his own goal.

"Oh, fuck it," Peter says, and throws the shooter listlessly in the direction of the bottom of the stairs.

"That's fine," D'Antoni says. "Now the other guy."

Con spreads his hands.

"You came too late," he says. "I already had mine cleaned out."

D'Antoni weighs that up for a moment.

"Just move over to your partner," he says.

Con downs his drink and puts his glass on the floor and straightens up and walks over to the fish and stands next to it and clasps his hands in front of him like he's on an I.D. parade.

"Fine," D'Antoni says. "That's fine."

Which leaves me, standing on the steps, like an employee of the Grand Old Duke of York.

"Now," D'Antoni says. "I been waiting for this. I figure this is a good time as any to pay you off for the good job you done on looking after me. It's bonus time, Carter."

For the moment, I don't move.

"You not going to beg?" D'Antoni says. "You not going to ask for help from your dear old mother who's been dead all these past years?"

I don't say anything.

"Pity," D'Antoni says. "I would've liked that."

If, I'm thinking to myself, I dive now, off the stairs, I'll probably break my fucking neck, but at the same time, there's no percentage in staying on the stairs, so I get myself mentally set up for the move, but before I can make it the stair well is as full of sound as the noise of a shooter rattles round the plate glass and the plasterwork. But the odd thing is, I don't feel any pain, and the scream isn't mine, so I twist round and look in the direction of the noise and it's not come from D'Antoni's shooter at all because his shooter is spinning away from him, closely followed by a piece of shoulder, and he's clawing at where it used to be. At the same time, Audrey is augmenting the noise D'Antoni's making, but unlike D'Antoni, she's no longer upright, she's thrown herself to the balcony floor, and because of her position I can see the top half of Wally, holding the shooter that Tina buried beneath her, holding it two-handed, all set to let D'Antoni have another one, which of course D'Antoni is more than aware of, but being without his shooter, there's not a lot he can do about it, and by now he's beyond rational thought and so he starts moving towards Wally, as if that will help, like a goalkeeper trying to narrow the angle. I also notice that Peter, always the opportunist, has raced across to where his shooter lies, and Con, he's placed himself in a position to get better cover from the fish, adjusting his leather hat as he does that thing.

At the same time, Wally lets go two more shots.

They're both wild, naturally. But at Wally's range, it doesn't matter. The first one doesn't make an awful lot of difference to D'Antoni's present condition, it hits him in the left wrist, causing a minor explosion of flesh and bone to shatter down over the edge of the balcony. Normally, of couse, the effect would have D'Antoni on his knees, screaming the way he wanted me to scream, but the situation being what it is, a matter of life and death, it doesn't even slow D'Antoni down, he keeps going forward, and it's the second shot that counts, because that one catches him in the stomach, dead centre. The power of the shot flips him round, like a dealer flipping over a card, so that he's facing the opposite way to where he was going, and as he's still moving, that means he's going towards the top of the stairs, but between him and that destination is Audrey's quivering body, which he's no longer aware of, because he trips over it, sending him headlong to the top of the steps — but he prevents his ultimate demise by hanging on to the end of the balustrade; he tries to pull himself to his feet, but a great internal shudder causes him to slip a little bit, cough, and expel a great gout of blood in the general curving direction of myself. And that, basically, is the last conscious act his body performs, because three, sharp, sweetly measured shots ring out from the floor below and form a three-leaf clover around D'Antoni's heart and then D'Antoni very slowly lets go of his grip on the balustrade and comes to rest with his torso lying head first down the first three steps, his legs still on the balcony.

Down below, Peter cries out in triumph.

"How about that?" he says. "Who wins the glass ash-tray, then?"

But his self-congratulation is short lived because Wally appears at the balustrade and, still two handed, points the shooter in the direction of Peter's voice; and if D'Antoni had lost his grip on rational thought, Wally's present state of mind makes D'Antoni seem as lucid as Norman Vincent Peale. He looks like Karloff's stand-in as he hangs over the balustrade, homing in on Peter.

"You cunts," Wally screams. "Look what you done."

"Leave it out, Wally," Peter says. "What you on about?"

Wally answers by pulling the trigger. The bullet screams off the floor and up over Peter's head. Peter dances backwards like Jagger in reverse. From behind the fish, Con says to Peter:

"Dodge out of it in a different direction, will you?"

Peter ignores Con and joins him behind the tail fin.

"Fuck off," Con says. "There ain't enough room."

"All of you," Wally screams. "You all done it, you cunts."

Wally hauls three or four off in the direction of the fish. Shrapnel-like scales ripple off the plate glass.

"For fuck's sake, Peter," Con says, holding down his hat.

"All of you," Wally screams, twisting round in my direction. "All of you."

He lets one go at me, but again, I've seen it coming, and by the time the bullet's in the plaster, I've made it to the bottom of the stairs and am well on my way to joining Peter and Con where they are, which is approximately half way up the fish's arse. This must be the perfect end to a perfect holiday.

"Here," Con says. "Find your own fucking hole."

Wally steps over Audrey, negotiates D'Antoni's body, and starts down the stairs, his steps as measured as Gloria Swanson's in *Sunset Boulevard* only he doesn't have Von Stroheim to tell him what to do. The only thing that's straight about Wally is the direction of his shooter, which is pointing directly at the fish. He hauls off another shot, and more fish scatters to the four corners of the hall.

"Peter," Con says. "For fuck's sake. You got the shooter."

"You what?" Peter says, like he's a mesmerised gay at Garlands Palladium performance.

"You," Wally screams. "All of you. All of my life."

Another shot. More shrapnel. Peter rises up from behind the fin.

"Wally," he says. "You got to leave this out."

Wally says: "You, you fucking poof. Yeah, you first."

Wally takes aim, but Peter, looking more sorrowful than angry, fires his shooter twice. One in the neck, one in the eye. For a second or two, Wally remains upright, then he just crumbles, like a demolished chimney.

For a while after that, the hall is silent, the whole villa is silent, except for the dribbling of the ornamental fish.

Chapter Seventeen

I hand the final drink to Peter. He takes it out onto the patio, to join Con and Audrey. Audrey is still naked, but at this stage of the game her state of nakedness is not exactly the highest item of interest on the agenda.

I follow Peter out into the sunshine. Con is sitting on the lounger, his bulk giving him the appearance of a squatting frog. Audrey is standing by the pool, staring at the mountains. Peter lights a cheroot from the last match in a book of matches and slings the empty book into the still-billowing incinerator.

After a while Con says: "Well, there you go then."

Nobody answers that one.

"Yes, I agree," Con says. He raises his glass. "Cheers, Con."

Audrey turns round from contemplating the mountains and begins to contemplate me instead.

"Well," she says eventually, "you done it good and proper this time."

"Oh, yes," I tell her. "Oh, yes. That one's all down to me, that one is. I done all those, lying in there. Personal. Only I must be slipping, as I now see I left three other characters out of it what I should not really have overlooked."

"You done the one you was told to do in the first place then none of this lot would have happened, would it?"

I look at her and shake my head.

"Course, it wouldn't have anything at all to do with those eggs in London who at present are probably sitting behind their desks writing out their Christmas-card lists, would it?"

"Yeah, well they'll be crossing a few names off it this year, won't they?"

"Yeah, about that," I say. "Nobody in the present company intending fulfilling their brief to the letter, would they?" I look at Peter and he looks back and puffs on his cheroot. "Peter?"

He shrugs.

"I done my ones," he says, looking at Con. "Anything else is down to the other half of the act."

"Piss off," Con says.

"Don't make any difference to me," Peter says. "It's you as got to go back and tell them what you didn't do."

"Piss off," Con says.

"Ah, well," says Peter, and wanders inside to get himself another drink.

"Yeah," Audrey says to me. "About going back. You still planning on doing that?"

I don't consider that one worth an answer. Audrey folds her arms and adopts an over-the-garden-wall stance, except that with her being naked and that her tits flop over her forearms like she's a kid holding an armful of party balloons.

"Well, in that case," she says, "I'll just make sure I'm not about when you get back."

"Since when you been frightened of a bit of wind and piss?"

She doesn't answer.

"Because that's all there'll be. As you well know."

Peter appears in the window's opening, clinking the ice in his drink.

"Apart from all these speculations about the future," he says, "there's one thing that has a certain immediacy about it, not to say piquancy."

"What's that?" Audrey says.

"Well," Peter says, "it's normal to have the bouquets with the funeral, but the weather being like it is out here, we're going to have a different kind of bouquet, if you get my meaning."

Audrey looks at me.

"Well?" she says.

"Oh, that's down to me as well, is it?" I ask her. "Seeing of course, as how I had nothing to do with the topping of them."

"Precisely," she says. "Gets back to what you should have done, don't it?"

A long silence follows, drifting over the swimming pool like the smoke from the incinerator.

Eventually Con says:

"They many more of the Blues downstairs?"

Audrey says:

"Racks of them. Why?"

"Just wondering."

"Why?" I ask him.

Con shrugs.

"Just wondering. I mean pretty big, that incinerator, ain't it? I

216

mean, sort of family size, know what I mean?"

All of us, we all look at Con, who blandly avoids the concerted gaze and unhurriedly carries on pecking at his drink.

After a while, Audrey says:

"You know, I've got to say this, I really have, seeing as how it's not often I get to experience something what turns my world upside down, so this is why I'm saying what I'm going to say. Which is that, in the way you always align yourself with whatever policy Jack takes, on the firm, I always used to think you were a bit of a wank, thinking round things, rather than through them. But on the evidence of what you just said, I take all that back. I can see now you been influenced by the wrong people, nothing more. I mean, merely a question of sociology, nothing more nor less. I would like you to know, I take it all back."

"Bingo," Peter says. "The lady in the flanellette draws wins the Wincyette sheets."

"Fuck off," Con says, and continues his glass animal routine with his drink.

For a while nothing happens.

Then Peter looks up at the sky, then down at his watch. "Getting on," he says. "Eighty in the shade, I shouldn't wonder, in about half an hour's time."

A burst of black smoke issues from the incinerator, gushing upwards into the previous mild greyness, like the cough of a smoker who's smoked one pack too many.

Con gets up off the lounger, stretches, like he's ready for a dip, but at the same time doesn't care that the last one in's a fairy.

"Well," he says. "I don't know what you think, but that's what I think. Further than that I cannot go."

"Con," I say to him, "personally, I find that no small relief to hear that. I would hate to think, from my point of view, that there were other boundaries left to be pushed back, even farther, if you were to set your mind to it."

Peter drains his glass and shrugs off his jacket.

"Fuck the philosophy," he says. "Do we start now or don't we?"

Epilogue

The club smells exactly the way it always does; a cross between the inside of a plastic wallet and the inside of a disposable Hoover bag. I press the button to the Penthouse lift and the perfume is intensified in spades. I am delivered of my destination and cross the windowless hall which is occupied only by Terry Malloy. Seated in the reproduction Hepplewhite, he speaks, but does not rise, which would of course be asking too much.

"They're in," he says.

I nod, not caring to put too fine a point on it.

"Go through," says Terry. "They're in there."

I nod again, and press the button to Aladdin's cave. The scene before me is as a thousand times before. Breakfast trays littering the Swedish surfaces, Gerald looking scruffy in his two-hundred-quid's-worth, Les looking immaculate in his.

I don't have to wait long to judge the tenor of the interview.

"Well, Jack," says Gerald, "you done well, then, didn't you? You really done well for us this time."

"Thanks," I say to him.

"I mean, don't matter we can't never go back there again. That don't matter, do it? Eighty thousand irretrievable quids' worth of property, that's fuck all, is it Jack?"

I don't say anything.

"No," says Les, "not compared to the squaring money both to their filth and ours."

"Of course," I say to him, "no squaring money due to me, of course."

"You what?" Gerald says.

"Did I hear right?" asks Les.

"Yes," I tell him. "You heard very right."

Gerald and Les look at each other. Gerald is smiling. Les is not.

"Come on," says Gerald. "You're joking, aren't you?"

Les shakes his head.

"No, he's not joking," he says. "The cunt is serious."

I nod my head.

"That's right," I say. "For once I agree with you, Les. Too right

I'm serious. You dropped me in it and I'd no idea, and you wouldn't even do that to Sammy the doorman without even discussing the possible outcome."

"You're paid," Gerald says. "You want Sammy's wages and piece of mind, or do you want what you're getting for what you're doing?"

"What I don't like," I tell them, "is the manner it was done. You don't have a pair of bollocks between you, so you drop me in the Balearics and leave it to the minor characters to fill me in."

"I wish we had," says Les. "I really wish we had."

"Well," I say to him, "chance would be a fine thing. The upshot is, come what may, I am as of this moment, freelance. In other words, available for weddings and funerals, open to offers, say, like from the Colmans, as for an instance."

"Only if you can get as far as the nearest phone," Les tells me.

"Hang on," says Gerald, "hang about."

He lights up the remaining inch of one of his disgusting cigars, then addresses himself to me.

"You serious, Jack?" he asks.

I don't say anything. And neither do they. The silence continues until, behind me, the door of the Penthouse opens, revealing Audrey, looking for all the world as if she's had a nice quiet few days in Ibiza.

"Hello," she says. "Everybody all right, are they?"

There is another long silence, which is broken by Les about to speak, which is cut short by Gerald jumping in before Les can get the words out.

"Well now," says Gerald. "This is nice. All girls together once again."

He stands up and walks over to where the drinks are.

"Nice," he says. "I'll get us all a drink and we can all discuss 'What we did in the Holidays'. I'm sure it'll be interesting, but not interesting enough to affect a tried and trusted business partnership, eh, Les?"

Les remains silent.

"That's what I thought," says Gerald, poised by the drinks. "Jack, what you going to have? The usual?"

ALLISON & BUSBY CRIME

Jo Bannister
A Bleeding of Innocents

Denise Danks
Frame Grabber

John Dunning
Booked to Die

Chester Himes
All Shot Up
The Big Gold Dream
Cotton Comes to Harlem
The Heat's On
A Rage in Harlem

H.R.F. Keating
A Remarkable Case of Burglary

Ted Lewis
Get Carter
GBH
Jack Carter's Law

Ross MacDonald
Barbarous Coast
The Blue Hammer
The Far Side of the Dollar
Find a Victim
The Galton Case
The Goodbye Look
The Ivory Grin
Meet Me at the Morgue
The Moving Target
The Way Some People Die
The Wycherly Woman
The Zebra-Striped Hearse
The Lew Archer Omnibus Volume 1

Margaret Millar
Ask For Me Tomorrow
Mermaid
The Murder of Miranda

Richard Stark
Deadly Edge
The Green Eagle Score
The Handle
Point Blank
The Rare Coin Score
Slayground
The Sour Lemon Score

Donald Thomas
Dancing in the Dark

Donald Westlake
Sacred Monster
The Mercenaries